The Sword of Orley

Also by Stewart Farrar

THE SNAKE ON 99
ZERO IN THE GATE
DEATH IN THE WRONG BED
WHAT WITCHES DO (non-fiction)
THE TWELVE MAIDENS
THE SERPENT OF LILITH

The Sword of Orley

STEWART FARRAR

ST. MARTIN'S PRESS
NEW YORK

For
Nefertari and Horemheb
in the womb of time

CHAPTER I

The dream had always been the same – until this time. Always the slow-motion horror of the Black Mass, with herself as the naked altar; yet not herself, for herself stood to one side and watched, paralysed. Her one self could feel the smooth limestone beneath her back (the desecrated stone which had once been God's altar), feel the foot of the chalice between her breasts where her hands held it upright, and the trickle of its overspill on to her hollowed belly, feel *his* chill fingers slide the defiled Host into her vagina while her body quivered and her mind screamed.

Her other self was aware of the flagged floor under her feet, of the weaving candle-flames in their dim ecclesiastical setting, of the insidious incense, of the two robed male figures that leaned over the pale flesh – the older one gaunt and purposeful, the younger afraid but spellbound. Aware, too, of the sweat on her palm as she gripped the useless sword-hilt – useless because her arm could not move.

She had dreamed it so many times that she knew the awful ritual by heart; knew every sonorous phrase (some English, some reversed Latin) obscenely parodying the Mass; knew every gesture and its meaning; anticipated each tremor of the supine body striving to control its abhorrence; knew instinctively, even, that for the gaunt celebrant, the woman's abhorrence was itself a savoured ingredient of the magic – and knowing, gripped the hilt all the harder.

Yet it was only at the start, each time as the dream began to take shape from the fog of sleep, that she became aware of having dreamed it before. No detail of it had ever broken through to her waking consciousness – only a dim sense of

7

recurrent horror that faded with the light of day. Recognition only came with sleep when, once or twice a year perhaps, the horror was reborn.

This time it had been as always, phrase by phrase and gesture by gesture – up to the very last moment. The dream always ended at the same point, the insertion of the Host; as though the aftermath of that blasphemous invasion were too much for even a dream to bear. In her supine self, she felt the humiliation of preparation; for while her body could be compelled to feign submission, it could in no way be forced to provide its own natural ointment of welcome. The gaunt one knew this, and there was always a glint of mockery in his cowled face as he anointed her in readiness, and the bittersweet perfume of musk and jasmine oil arose from her loins. She knew she could not close her eyes, so she pressed her head back against the stone, staring upwards at the oaken angel in the roof from whom no help came. Then the moment of despair as the traitorous oil unlocked the gate, and the desecrated wafer was within her.

The naked glare of damnation was intolerable to face; the only escape was oblivion.

But *this* time there was an instant more – a flicker of time between the horror and the forgetfulness, in which she was her other self, looking down on the outraged human altar. And in that instant she knew that at last – after all these helpless years – her sword-hand had begun to move.

Jane sat bolt upright in bed, in a sweat of brief panic. Where the hell was she?

Reason and wakefulness took charge, and she shook her head, making herself breathe deeply. Of course; the Green Man Hotel at Orley. The team had arrived last night; Bruce and Ted were in the next room, sensibly asleep, doubtless; they would all three be here for the next three weeks; the investigating of Orley Grange promised to be more interesting than most holidays were; and everything was all right. Take hold of yourself, Jane Blair. At twenty-six,

8

history teacher, B.A. (Hons.), you're too old to be scared silly by waking up in a strange bedroom.

As she lit a cigarette and poured herself a glass of water, she suddenly realised: I've had the Dream again.

She realised it with a mixture of relief and frustration. Relief because that, and not the strange room, explained her sudden awakening; and frustration because, again as always, she had no idea what the dream was about. Only a featureless certainty that it was recurrent, and unpleasant. The nearest she could get to it was a vague feeling that it was a dream of rape; and yet even that, while she knew it was somewhere near the mark, was not quite convincing.

Jane was a normal, well-educated child of the century whose outlook had been shaped by Freud, so she was undisturbed by the thought that her subconscious might dream about rape. *Id est quod Id est*; disreputable fantasy had its essential place in mental health. But a healthy person ought to be able to take it out, look at it, and recognise it for what it was, undismayed. It worried her slightly that recall seemed impossible; because if the Dream *was* recurrent (and she knew in her gut that it was) it presumably had something to say to her, and she felt she ought to know what it was.

Sitting on the edge of the bed sipping her water, she had another sudden thought; only a momentary flash of thought really – a fugitive hint that *this* time something had been different, and that in the difference there was a flavour of . . . Of what? Hope? Exultation? . . . Whatever it was, it had gone. She tried the old trick of diverting her attention to something else (counting the ribs on the glass tumbler, this time) in the hope of jumping back on the thought and catching it unawares . . . No good.

Oh, well.

She stubbed out her cigarette and got back into bed. By now, experience told her, the backwash of the Dream would normally have vanished, smoothed out by the stronger signals of the real world. It seemed to be taking rather longer to disperse this time . . . It *must* be the strange room. Familiar reality always banished fantasy quicker than unfamiliar.

As she was drifting back to sleep, a cock crowed. The eerie sound made her shudder, and she wondered mistily if she would dream the Dream again.

But she didn't. Not tonight.

CHAPTER II

The Curator was going to be a problem, Jane decided. Nothing you could put your finger on, exactly; he had been courteous and correct from the start. After all, they had the permission of Orley Rural District Council; Orley Grange was the Council's property; and the Curator was the Council's meticulous servant. So the team had a right to be here and to expect his cooperation. But he did not have to like them, or to approve of what they were doing, and he did not; so his cooperation was going to be within the strict limits of his written instructions. The chill of his correctness made that quite clear.

Right now his eyes were saying it, too. Jane, Ted and Bruce (having settled into the Green Man and stowed their equipment in a room which had been allotted to them in the private wing of the Grange) had asked if they could accompany the next of the guided tours which started punctually every hour, on the hour, from ten until four on open days from the Tudor front door. (Please purchase your tickets on entering; 20p adults, 10p children under 14; illustrated booklet 40p. No dogs. No smoking. No camera tripods. Refreshments, souvenirs, and postcards on sale in stable yard shop. Grange and shop closed all day Thursdays. Orley R.D.C.)

The Curator had said 'Of course', brusquely. Jane had offered to buy tickets, hoping to thaw his hostility, but she had been waved aside. Free access to the whole of the Grange (except the Curator's own flat) was part of his written instructions, his rigid profile conveyed.

So the three of them hovered on the edge of the small

11

crowd of visitors – the holiday-making families, the child who would not be quiet, the umistakable note-taking schoolmaster, the young couple who seemed to have paid their forty pence just to gaze at each other. As he delivered his rote-learned commentary, the Curator flicked an occasional glance of resentment towards the team, though his voice did not alter. Bruce was clearly aware of it, and winked at Jane when the Curator's back was turned. Ted, of course, noticed nothing; strange that anyone so kindly could be so insensitive.

'The Great Hall in which you stand, ladies and gentlemen, is the oldest part of the Grange, dating back to 1362. The Manor of Orley, with four others, was granted to the Montgris family by William the Conqueror, but they lived elsewhere till the fourteenth century, when Sir John Montgris decided to make Orley his home. He built this Great Hall, with a courtyard and a gateway on the south side which were demolished in Henry the Eighth's reign, when Sir Richard built the south wing and added the first floor. The Grange was occupied continuously by the Montgris family until the last baronet, Sir Christopher Montgris, died childless in 1867. It was inherited by a cousin, Mrs Elspeth Kolinsky, who had married an American banker. It remained unoccupied until 1904, when Mrs Kolinsky's grandson, Mr Hiram J. Kolinsky of Boston, Massachusetts, presented it to Orley Rural District Council for the enjoyment of the public.'

Jane had to smile; the vulgar apostasy of Elspeth (the Curator seemed to imply) had been more or less atoned for by the generosity of Hiram; a curtain could be drawn over the whole regrettable period, and back to business.

'You will note the ten columns of oak, five on each side of the Hall, shaped with an adze and secured by wooden pegs. The spaces between these uprights were filled in with wattle and daub . . .'

Jane stopped listening for a while. She had done her homework before she came; the Curator was telling her

12

nothing new, and his little jokes (one or two to each room) were too laboured to enliven what she had already learned. Although this was her first visit, she knew the surprisingly well-written official booklet almost by heart, and had studied every reference she could lay her hands on; being a history teacher, she was no stranger to sources.

So she let the monotonous voice, and the restless or awestruck visitors, fade into the background of her awareness, and enjoyed herself using her eyes and her feeling for atmosphere. She replied to Bruce's shrewd remarks, and to Ted's banal ones, but offered none of her own. She was too silently busy to want conversation.

Orley Grange certainly lived up to all Bruce had told them about it; one of the finest and best preserved half-timbered manor houses in England, set in hilly parkland, within and above the bend of a tree-escorted river. Growing and maturing stage by stage from the fourteenth century to the seventeenth, it must have been blessed with gifted builders and craftsmen; for while each part was a model of its period, the whole had preserved a satisfying unity – and no eighteenth-century neo-classicist nor Victorian romantic had, thank God, been moved to upset that balance. Great Hall, Lesser Hall, Elizabethan Ballroom, Priest's Room, Plaster Room, Dame Angela's Room – 'all members one of another', Jane found herself thinking.

'I wonder if we'll find anything?' Bruce said as the party straggled ahead of them into the Withdrawing Room.

'Don't know,' Jane answered, and was surprised to realise she had almost forgotten their purpose here. Oh, well – three whole weeks to think about that.

Bruce seemed about to pursue the subject, but was distracted by the Grange cat rubbing itself against his legs. He bent and stroked it. It obviously was the Grange cat, because it had accompanied the tour the whole way; a big placid-looking tom with black body and white legs.

Jane, too, bent to fondle it. To her surprise, it bared its teeth and hissed at her, backing away.

13

'Good God!' Bruce said, 'I thought you were a cat person. Here, feller . . .' He picked the cat up in his arms, and it allowed him, still watching Jane warily.

'I am.' She frowned. 'Maybe I remind him of someone he doesn't like.'

'Be nice to the lady, Tommo. She's okay, really.'

Jane reached out, more slowly this time, and tried to stroke the cat's head. A second later, with a little cry of pain, she was staring at the bright red scratches on the back of her hand, already beading with blood.

The cat settled itself in Bruce's arms, rumbling a warning. Bruce was too astonished to drop it. 'You all right? That looks nasty . . .'

Jane almost snapped: 'It's nothing.' She moved away, following the party, surreptitiously holding a tissue against her smarting skin, and feeling even more humiliated than physically hurt. Animals didn't *do* that to her . . . Not wanting to appear to sulk, she smiled back deliberately at Bruce: 'Obviously you've got something I haven't.'

Bruce gave a humorous shrug, but still looked worried. The cat in his arms closed its eyes and began to purr. Insult to injury, Jane thought, and managed to smile at herself.

'This, ladies and gentlemen, is the Chapel. We don't know exactly when it was built, but the workmanship suggests early Tudor . . .'

The smile died on Jane's face. She put her hand on the chapel doorpost; for a moment she thought she was going to faint. Struggling to pull herself together, she told herself that it had been more surprise than anything – that sensation of an invisible barrier, of something trying to push her back, to prevent her entering the place . . .

She glanced around; nobody had seen her reaction. She and Bruce were in the doorway at the tail of the crowd, and Bruce's attention was on the Curator. Already her mind was seeking rational explanations – a moment of vertigo due to lack of sleep (no, last night had been interrupted, but not *that* much) – premenstrual nausea (don't be silly, you've

14

just finished) – delayed shock from the cat's attack (possible) – unevenness in the floor making her lurch . . . Yes, it could be that. The chapel was floored with flagstones, and the ones in the doorway *were* worn.

She took her hand from the doorpost, and concentrated on what the Curator was saying.

'The Montgris were a Catholic family, right through the Reformation – and, indeed, up to the last baronet. In Protestant times, they used to attend church in the village, as the law demanded; but it seems they always maintained this private chapel, and a family priest to celebrate Mass. The family letters show they came near to trouble over it more than once, especially under Cromwell. But apart from a fine or two, they were powerful enough locally to survive it. And remember, this was a strongly Royalist part of the Midlands.

'You will observe the particularly rich carving of the stone altar, which is larger than one would expect for a chapel of this size . . .'

Jane turned to Bruce and said quietly: 'This is the only room I don't like.'

'Neither does Tommo, apparently.' The cat was struggling in his arms as he stood on the chapel threshold. Bruce tried to calm it, but it jumped clear and paced up and down in the corridor outside. 'Extraordinary animal. You're both fervent anti-Papists, obviously.'

'No way. I hate prejudice.' All the same, something about the chapel oppressed her. The woodcarving, the stonework, the stained glass which had been ingeniously and unusually placed between the black oak uprights of the walls (for although much stone had been introduced, the basic structure was half-timbered like the rest of the house) were all unquestionably fine. But there was a claustrophobic heaviness about the place which Jane had not found in any of the other rooms. She had an open mind on psychic phenomena (otherwise she would not be here with the team), though she believed that she herself was not a

15

sensitive; but she decided, trying to make a silent joke of it, that for her this chapel had 'bad vibes'.

She looked upwards at the ceiling and caught the eye of a carved oak angel. Its face seemed vaguely familiar, yet inscrutable – as though it and she shared some dark knowledge, but it was watching, waiting, biding its time . . .

Jane threw off the fantasy, shuddering. Her imagination was running away with her. All the same, she knew an inrush of relief when the Curator finished his talk and the party filed out.

In her lightened mood, she was able to laugh when the cat sought out Bruce again as soon as he emerged from the chapel, and required to be picked up. So, even a cat-lover couldn't win 'em all. Tommo – or whatever his name was – liked Bruce and didn't like her, and that was that.

The tour ended back in the Great Hall, with the Curator asking his audience if they had any questions. The father of the noisy child put up his hand, as though he were in school.

'Yes. What about the ghost?'

Jane, Bruce and Ted watched the Curator with quickened interest. He seemed pointedly not to be looking their way.

'Every old house attracts that kind of gossip,' he said firmly. 'I have told you the history of Orley Grange as it is known and recorded. I am not here to perpetuate superstitious fairy-tales. Are there any other questions?'

Nobody dared. The visitors trickled out of the front door, murmuring their thank-yous. When the last had gone, the Curator locked the door and crossed to the staircase, saying over his shoulder: 'You have your own key, I think?' as he disappeared.

The team looked at each other.

'And that,' Bruce commented drily, 'puts us in our place, doesn't it?'

Councillor Trevor Cox, landlord of the Green Man, and local wire-puller whose enthusiasm had got the team from the Midland Psychical Research Society their permission to investigate Orley Grange, laughed at them across his bar.

'You mustn't mind old Charley Unsworth too much,' he said. 'He's like a mother hen about that place. Been a Council clerk all his life, and we made him Curator as a sort of semi-retirement cushy number when Pennington died on the job . . . No imagination, no nonsense – but he's a good caretaker, and he's learned his spiel to the tourists like a bloody tape-recorder . . . What else can we expect? The 20p tickets would hardly pay for a history professor, would they? Hiram Kolinsky left some money in trust to maintain the place, but it costs a bomb these days. We only just break even.'

'It's a beautiful house,' Jane said.

'It is that, Miss Blair. And it brings a steady trickle of trade to Orley, from Easter to the end of September. The odd conference during the winter, too.'

'A *practical* romantic, our Trevor,' Bruce murmured into his beer.

'Only thing to be, Bruce, if you run a pub – believe me.'

'Is that why you're sponsoring the ghost?'

Trevor Cox smiled. 'Hardly sponsoring. Your lot asked if you could look into it, and I spoke in favour and got the vote. If I'm sponsoring anyone, it's *you*. The Battle Maid doesn't need it – she can stand on her own feet . . . Okay, so a ghost brings in the tourists, whatever Charley Unsworth thinks. But that wasn't why I backed your application. I really am interested to see if you'll record anything.'

'The Battle Maid – is that what they call her?' Ted asked.

'I thought you knew the story?'

'Well, you know *I* do, being local,' Bruce explained. 'And Jane's read up on it. But Ted doesn't believe in cluttering up his mind with preconceptions. He's our electronics wizard. We tell him we're investigating a haunt story, he asks us when and where – and on the day, there he is with his boxes and wires. He's more interested in circuitry than he is in ghosts, really.'

17

'Not true,' Ted protested. 'I'd love to catch one.'

'Have you, yet?' the landlord asked.

Ted shook his head. 'Nothing concrete, if you can call a ghost concrete. One place, we recorded some odd temperature changes, and got what might have been a photograph – infra-red, you know. But it could have been mist. Hard to say.'

'But you still keep on trying.'

'Only way we *will* get anything, if there's anything to get . . . What *is* the story? Don't take any notice of Bruce.'

'Just this young woman in a kind of silver armour, with a sword in her hand. Long fair hair. The earliest known reference is in 1630, I think it was – Lady Clara Montgris – her diary's in the Grange library. Get Charley to show you . . . Several people claimed to have seen her, over the years, and it's always the same description. It was Philip Montgris who christened her the Battle Maid, in the eighteenth century, and it stuck. Bit of a poet, he was. Friend of Alexander Pope.'

Jane had her notebook out. 'Any modern sightings?'

Cox shrugged. 'Well, you know how it is. Always somebody wanting to jump on that kind of bandwagon, to draw attention to himself, and it's hard to know whom to believe. But there's two fairly sensible people in the village who'll tell you they've seen her. I'll fix for you to meet them, if you want to ask them questions.'

'Please . . . Have *you* ever seen her?'

'No such luck. But my grandfather did. Swore it to his dying day, and got very angry if anyone laughed at him for it.'

'How did he describe her?'

'Same thing. Fair-haired woman, about twenty-five, slim, and this silver armour – sort of close-fitting blouse and breeches, he said, not plate armour, you know, but like chain-mail. And she was carrying this sword – he described that, too. Plain cross guard, slender blade.'

'All that's pretty detailed, isn't it?'

'He only saw her for a few seconds, apparently, but he never forgot her. Hair falling over her shoulders, sword in her left hand . . .'

'*Left* hand?' Bruce repeated.

'Oh, yes – the Battle Maid is left-handed. Several people mentioned that.'

'Odd.'

'Not so much of the "odd",' Jane said defensively. 'Thousands of people are.'

'All right, Southpaw, we know *you* are. But it seems a bit unexpected in a ghost, somehow . . .' He turned back to Cox. 'Where did your grandfather see her?'

'On the Long Walk, east of the Grange. He was courting my grandmother; full moon, you know – the whole bit. The Long Walk's still a favourite Lovers' Lane.'

'Did she see her, too?'

'She always denied it, hotly. But I think she must have done, by the way it all happened. Grandpa said they came face to face with the Maid, and stared at her for a second or two. Then Grandma gave a little scream, and fainted. He turned to help her, and when he looked up again the Maid had vanished . . . Grandma maintained she just stumbled and twisted her ankle, and there was no ghost. Used to get quite worked up about it – only thing I ever heard them fight over. But then she was a very religious woman, and ghosts didn't fit into her tidy scheme of things.'

'Is that where it's always seen? The Long Walk?'

'Oh, no – several places, mostly inside the Grange. And most of all in the chapel, beside the altar. That's the favourite place.'

Jane felt an irrational spasm of unease. 'No wonder I didn't like the chapel,' she found herself saying.

Cox looked at her, interested. 'Didn't you, now?'

'Only room in the whole place that depressed me. I couldn't think why.'

'Well, it's not for me to tell you how to work – but it

19

sounds as though the chapel's the place to set up your stuff, isn't it?'

'If we do,' Bruce said emphatically, 'it'll be because that's the usual sighting place. *Not* because it gave Jane the jitters. That's the whole point of our method – going about it scientifically.'

'Contradiction there,' Cox suggested. 'You'd choose the chapel because it affected other people, but not because it affected one of you.'

'Of course. *We* have to remain detached.'

'We've brought in a medium sometimes,' Ted pointed out.

'That's different. That was to see if whatever the medium claimed to pick up correlated with our instrument readings in any way. The medium was another instrument, if you like. Not part of the investigating team.'

'Perhaps Miss Blair . . .'

'Jane,' she corrected.

'Perhaps Jane is a medium, without realising it.'

'If she were, she shouldn't be on the team,' Bruce insisted.

'Thank *you*,' Jane said drily.

'No, seriously, love. You're one of the team because you're a trained historian, and because you're interested in the scientific investigation of alleged psychic phenomena. Don't rock the boat by going all psychic on us yourself.'

Jane laughed. 'I don't think there's much danger of that . . . If you want a medium, try Tommo. It gave him the jitters, too.'

'Who's Tommo?' Trevor asked.

'We don't know his real name. The Grange cat. He came all round with the tour, but he wouldn't go in the chapel. He waited for us outside, in the corridor where all the armour and stuff's on show.'

'Oh, Bootsie. The resident tom . . . Interesting, because that's another Grange legend. That no animal will go into the chapel . . . He really wouldn't, eh?'

'Most insistent about it,' Bruce said. 'But then, he's a

20

funny beast. Friendly as you please with everyone, especially me – but he went for Jane, and she's a cat person.'

Jane held out the scarred back of her hand in corroboration. 'First cat who's ever done that to me.'

Trevor shook his head. 'Only thing I've ever learned about cats is – you decide you've discovered some rule about them, and the very next ruddy cat you meet will break it. You never know where you are, with cats. Except that in some queer way they always seem to know exactly what they're doing.'

Bruce laughed, and Trevor shook his head apologetically. 'Sorry, Jane – that wasn't very polite, in the circumstances.'

Jane liked the man, so she quickly reassured him and tried to smile. But for some reason the smile would not come.

CHAPTER III

Ted's 'boxes and wires' had, for Jane, a mildly exorcising effect. Helping him place microphones, temperature sensors, infra-red camera equipment and so on around the timber and stone of the chapel did not entirely remove the aura of menace she had been aware of yesterday; but it did seem to make the place more like a studio set for a sinister film, and less like the actual setting for sinister events, past or present. Besides, the sun was shining brightly through the jewelled, narrow windows, while yesterday had been overcast and oppressive. Today, Jane was almost ready to believe that her first unease had been a freak phenomenon, a chance coming-together of irrelevant subconscious associations.

Almost, but not quite. She still did not like the chapel, and she still could not say why. But at least the unease was manageable, like working in an office where the temperature was just a few degrees too hot or too cold. And being busy helped. Jane had deft fingers and a quick grasp of technicalities, so Ted soon gave up his first assumption that no woman could be trusted to secure a cable or call out an accurate dial reading. In fact she was better at both than Bruce, who had an excellent brain but ten thumbs.

Jane had got to know Bruce and Ted at the monthly meetings of the Midland Psychical Research Society, but this was the first time she had been on a field investigation team, and the first chance she had had to look at Ted's equipment.

'I'm impressed,' she told him sincerely as he explained it all. Ted grunted 'It'll do,' but was clearly pleased.

The heart of his system was a polygraph recorder which he had designed and built himself, with a fat roll of tele-printer paper moving slowly beneath a bank of fibre-tipped pens of various colours: red for temperature, orange for humidity, violet for graphic recording of sound-tracks, blue for barometric pressure, and green for a time-blip every sixty seconds – which also triggered off the infra-red flash and the single-shot 8mm cine camera. These coloured traces wove about black zero-lines which were inscribed by fixed pens ahead of the moving ones.

'Seven traces is all I can manage at the moment,' Ted explained. 'Two for temperature, two for sound, and one for each of the others. The traces are a bit too cramped already, for my liking. Can't read temperature changes of less than about a degree Centigrade, for instance. And if you get bigger changes than you expect, the traces overlap each other. That's why they're different colours, so that you can still read them separately even if they do overlap – look, I've got the two reds on opposite sides, and the two violets. But I'm working on a Mark Two model, with twin paper rolls. That'll give me much more scope.'

'Why have you doubled up on temperature and sound?'

'Because they're the two that can be different a few feet apart. This chapel, for instance – pressure and humidity will be the same all over, as near as dammit. But you could get localised temperature changes, and they could be important in what we're looking for. In fact, I'd like at least four or five local temperature readings going at once, if there was room on the paper. And if I had three microphones instead of two, I could pinpoint a sound source pretty accurately by relative volume. You know, like triangulation with three bearings on a map.'

'You'd have to make sure the three microphone circuits were exactly the same sensitivity first, wouldn't you?'

'Good girl – you're getting the idea. But that'll be fairly easy. Set up a whistler in the middle, with the three mikes equidistant from it, and calibrate them till they all give the

23

same reading, before you start.' Ted grinned. 'Then take away the whistler, of course. It might scare the ghost off.'

'Why record sound on paper, as well as on tape? I'd have thought the tape was all you needed.'

'Just to give a visual presentation of sound alongside the other ones. Makes it easier to spot any odd phenomena.'

'More important than a couple of extra temperature traces?'

'Bruce and I discussed that. We decided it was.'

Jane thought for a moment, and then asked: 'Why not sacrifice just *one* of the sound traces? You'd still have the stereo on tape, to help localise any sound source. And every sound would be on both channels – just the volume would differ. So one visual trace'd be enough for matching up the sound with the other traces.'

'Hang about...' Ted frowned in concentration. 'Hell, the girl's right. Why didn't I think of that?... Hey, Bruce – we can manage a third temperature trace ...'

Jane had more questions – for example, how Ted decided on the probable mean readings to fix the values of his zero-lines – but she saved them, enjoying her small triumph while Ted busied himself wiring up the extra temperature recorder and debating with both of them where it should be situated.

Jane was no women's libber; she had strong views on essential femininity and masculinity, holding them to be equal but complementary, and despising the all-too-general confusion between equality and identity. But she liked to make it clear that essential femininity did not imply inability to think logically. (Nor, she would add, that essential masculinity need imply lack of sensitivity.)

Suddenly, her own voice surprised her by interrupting her train of thought. 'Over there,' she found herself saying. 'About six feet from the altar, on that fluted column. That's where it should go.'

Both men looked up and asked 'Why?'

She managed not to flounder over the reasons she gave,

24

but she was aware they were not the true ones. She simply *knew* it was the right place, and she was relieved when her improvised arguments convinced them.

One up for essential femininity, she thought drily. Mustn't let pride of intellect swamp intuition, or I'll be out there with the bra-burners . . . All the same – *why* that particular spot?

All three of them went to sleep for a few hours in the afternoon. Their working sessions during the three weeks' investigation were all to be at night, both because (as Bruce put it) 'experience seems to show that it's in the night that ghoulies and ghosties *do* go bump', and because the chapel had to be open to visitors during the day.

So they had agreed on a working pattern. It was August, and darkness lasted from about 9.30 p.m. to 4.30 a.m. Trevor Cox, eager to cooperate, had arranged for them to have dinner each night at 6.30, and breakfast at 6.0. That would give them plenty of time to set up their equipment before dark, and to clear it away between dawn and a bath before breakfast. In bed by 7.0, and up for a light lunch at 2.0, would apparently suit them all.

In case anyone felt short of sleep, they would keep a couple of camp beds with their equipment at the Grange; these could be set up in the armour-display corridor just outside the chapel door.

'As long as one of us is on watch all the time,' Bruce said, 'he can wake the others if anything seems to be starting to happen. If we all want to sleep, we'll work a rota.'

'It won't be tiredness that'll make us want to sleep,' Jane predicted. 'It'll be sheer boredom. Six hours' bed is enough for me. But seven hours a night on watch, for three weeks, looking and listening for something that may never hap-pen . . .'

'We didn't have to join.'

'I know. I *want* to do it. But I'm not kidding myself it'll be exciting.'

25

She expected the first night or two to be the worst, while their metabolisms were still unadjusted to night-shift working. She was pleasantly surprised, therefore, to find that she slept like a baby on this first afternoon, waking refreshed and vigorous when her alarm clock rang at 5.0.

She ran herself a bath, and lay in it considering what she should wear for dinner.

Jane enjoyed dressing up in the evening. She was neither vain nor nymphomaniac, but she was confidently aware of herself as a woman, and saw no reason why she should not proclaim the fact. Dressing for dinner, making herself deliberately attractive without embarrassment, was her own ritual, her personal tribute to the goddess of femaleness – of whom every woman was (or, Jane felt, should be) aware within herself.

She *would* have been embarrassed to express that concept in words to anyone else, because although she thought of it in those terms, she was still uncertain whether such divine archetypes were mere symbols of forces at work in the unconscious, or in some way independent of the individual; so pending illumination on the subject, she was a proclaimed agnostic. But that particular goddess, whether symbol or self-existent entity, was real to her, as a principle which she had to express.

Friends and colleagues sometimes teased her about her evening elegance, about her unapologetic appearance in a long dress and bare shoulders when others wore jeans. But they had come to accept it as part of her personality, because there was about her a poise, a relaxed friendliness, which enabled her to display her sexuality without either taunting men with it, or implying criticism of other women. She had had lovers, and had rejected others; but she was neither promiscuous nor a tantaliser.

My God, it makes me sound a bloody paragon, and I'm not (she told herself as she made this conscious self-appraisal – a thing she rarely did). I can be selfish, I can be unkind, I can procrastinate and prevaricate. I can be a bitch –

26

though not, I think (no, I *really* think), a sexual bitch. I'm just thoroughly at ease being a woman, and I like it.

She got out of the bath and looked at herself in the long mirror, shaking her hair free from the shower-cap. That hair fell below her shoulder-blades (she always had to overcome an instinctive reluctance even for the necessary trimming of its ends) and was fair but not thick – if anything, she told herself, it was on the wispy side, though pleasingly fine and smooth. She was only five foot four, but her slimness, and her rather full breasts, made her seem taller than she was. She worried a little, sometimes, about the roundness of her stomach; but she knew it was due to the slight S-bend of her habitual stance, rather than to fat, and she remembered with a smile one boy-friend's description of it as her 'Botticelli pottibelli'. Her limbs, she knew, were good; lithe and well-carried.

All in all, not bad for twenty-six. And I'll not be bad at forty-six, is my guess. Acknowledging the goddess is a life-long thing, one way or another, or it's nothing.

And 'all in all' was what mattered, she knew. That same boy-friend (art master, now departed, at the school where she taught) had once snapped at her when she was criticising her own collarbones; 'For Christ's sake, Jane, stop looking at yourself piecemeal or you'll never *see* yourself. The Venus de Milo's got a hammer-toe – hadn't you noticed? Anyone can show what's wrong with a knee or a tit or an eyebrow. What matters is how they all relate to each other. And if you didn't fit together like a bloody daffodil, I wouldn't spend hours looking at you . . . Hell, what would Beethoven be without the planned resolving of deliberate dissonances?'

He had considered her for a moment, then said: 'Take off those clothes and I'll paint you.'

It was November and his flat was poorly heated, but she had complied, paying for it with a week of influenza; and she had been both disappointed and flattered when he had refused to give her the finished portrait because he wanted it

27

for himself. But she had learned the lesson, and had looked at herself differently ever since.

Stop reminiscing, get yourself dry, and decide what to put on. Half your luggage is evening things, so make the most of it.

She settled on a combination which had been the result of a happy accident. She had once, on the same shopping afternoon, lavished eight pounds on a gold bikini and picked up an evening dress at an Oxfam shop for two pounds which had fitted her perfectly. It was mandarin-collared and armless, of milk-chocolate lurex tissue that was dimly see-through. When she had got home she had tried on the bikini first, and then, through sheer impatience, left it on while she tried the dress. Her mirror had told her at once it was a successful dress, slimly elegant without being skin-tight. Then she had moved, and the light had changed – and she had become aware of the glints of girl and the glints of gold that appeared and disappeared under the dark gauze. The blend of austerity and subtle barbarity would have taken a genius to design deliberately, and Jane had been very pleased with herself.

She decided she was pleased with herself tonight, too. Ten minutes later she almost wondered if she had been wise. She was standing in the french window of the lounge, looking out, when Bruce's quiet wolf-whistle made her turn.

'I suppose you know how you look in that thing, against the light? Practically starkers.'

She moved away from the window. 'Sorry.'

'Who's complaining? Just that Trevor has some elderly guests, and you don't want to give them blood-pressure.'

'The lounge is empty – hadn't you noticed?'

He peered around, mock-dramatically. 'So it is. I was too absorbed to look . . . Drink?'

They both had a sherry, and the incident passed as a joke smoothly enough. But she had seen his eyes, and she worried a little. She enjoyed being appreciated; but with three weeks of serious and isolated work ahead of them – two men and a girl – she asked herself if she should have been more careful. If *that* kind of tension arose – if Bruce and Ted were provoked to compete for her, even subconsciously – it could jeopardise the whole project, and it would have been her own fault . . . Though Ted was so placid he seemed almost sexless. Maybe she was exaggerating the dangers.

'It's twenty-past six already,' she said. 'Ted's late.'

'No, Trevor gave him some sandwiches. He's up at the Grange ironing out the bugs in that third temperature channel. I think he's in love with that stuff.'

In a way I hope you're right, she thought. 'Will it work, Bruce?'

'Of course it will. The other two do.'

'Oh, I didn't mean that. I meant – *can* this sort of laboratory approach really pin down psychic phenomena?'

'Oh . . . That's an odd, back-to-school sort of question from a member of the M.P.R.S.'

'I don't see why.'

'Surely that's what the Society exists for?'

Jane smiled. 'To catch ghosts on camera and tape?'

'Well, oversimplified – but in principle, yes.'

'A lot more than that, surely. To find out what kind of evidence there *is* for psychic phenomena in general, by seeing if individual cases can be substantiated. Oh, I know we're scientific, or do our best to be – but the evidence isn't all *instrumental*. For instance, crisis apparitions – when somebody sees a close friend in the room, and it turns out later the friend was killed in a motor accident miles away at the same moment . . .'

'So? If we were trying to substantiate a claim like that, we'd look for proof that the observer couldn't have known about the accident or its likelihood – find out how reliably the time could be fixed – see whether the observer told anyone else, or said "Charlie, what are you doing here?" in someone else's hearing – that sort of thing. Straight detective work.'

'But Bruce – not *laboratory* work while the phenomenon's happening, like we hope to do at the Grange.'

'Sure, but what's the difference? It's all logical method. The sort of evidence you look for depends on the nature of the case, the particular circumstances. Just like police detection; some murderers get caught through eye-witnesses, and some through fingerprints or the analysis of bloodstains or X-ray proof that a will's been forged.'

'Ultra-violet, isn't it?'

'Or whatever . . . Point is, whether it's chemical analysis or Euclidean argument, it's all a question of factual proof. The principle's the same.'

'I just wonder if Ted's box of tricks is the right approach for this kind of case,' Jane said.

'If you wonder that, love, why are you here?'

'*Because* I wonder. It *might* be right, and the only way to find out is to try it.'

Bruce was silent through a couple of mouthfuls of grilled liver, then said: 'If ghosts do happen, outside our own minds I mean, I think it *must* be right . . . Look, say we're in luck and we see this Battle Maid – that means she's affecting our optic nerves. And anything that affects the optic nerves is instrumentally measurable. If we find it isn't, then we know she's just a hallucination, induced by our own mental state and our knowledge of the legend.'

'I just think . . .'

'And don't say "There are more things in heaven and earth, Horatio," or I'll clobber you.'

'I *was* going to say that if we saw her, but nothing showed on Ted's camera or his traces – she might still be a genuine phenomenon, but we might be misunderstanding the plane on which she happened.'

'When I hear that word "plane" in this context,' Bruce said sourly, 'I smell pseudo-science. Ditto with "aura" and "vibrations".'

Jane laughed. 'I'll try to be more careful. Will it do if I say "level of activity" instead of "plane".'

30

'Not much better – but go on.'

'Well, for instance – it'd be no good trying to measure sound with a thermometer, or to photograph radio waves, or to record a landscape with a radio receiver. They're all real phenomena, but each has to be recorded in its own terms. That's all I meant by "plane".'

Bruce frowned thoughtfully. 'Yes, that's fair enough. But if we . . . let's say *become aware* of the Battle Maid, it'll be through our eyes, our ears, or possibly our skin-sensitivity to temperature or humidity – though that'd be pretty subtle. And Ted has each of those "planes" covered.'

'There may be more,' Jane said, and immediately wished she hadn't. She knew Bruce's hostility to what he called "the mystical approach", and she could see his jaw-muscles tightening. She was too unsure of her own ground to do battle, so she disarmed her remark by adding, deliberately tongue-in-cheek: 'We might smell her.'

Bruce relaxed, innocently taking her cue, and grinned at her. 'Right, then. You're our historian. You are hereby briefed to do the necessary research, and to draw up a list of perfumes likely to be used by martially-inclined ladies between 1362, when the Grange was founded, and 1630, the first recorded sighting. You will also endeavour to obtain samples of these perfumes for comparison with any observed phenomena. You never know – we might even get a clue to her date.'

She matched his mock-seriousness. 'As a historian with some knowledge of the period, I think it likely that the predominant odour would be unwashed sweat. She might use perfume on top, but I doubt if it'd have changed much in those two-and-a-half centuries. It would have been in powder or water form, because they hadn't invented the spirit-based perfume yet. They used rose a lot – it was Elizabeth's favourite – damask rose in particular. Benzoin was the most popular gum resin; they called it "benjamin". And the animal scents were pretty prominent – ambergris, musk, civet . . . Historical perfumery – might be an interesting

31

project to keep my lot awake in class. Thanks for the hint. I'll think about it.'

'We might ask Ted to think about it, too. He'd probably love to design a ghost-catching scent-analyser.'

'Is circuitry all he dreams of?'

'That, and his Canadian girl friend. Believe it or not, he's got one. He writes her a long devoted letter every week. He's going to emigrate and marry her when he's got his degree...' Bruce waved a hand towards Jane's dress. 'Don't be offended, love – that outfit of yours'd be enough to inflame any red-blooded male, but Ted wouldn't even notice you were wearing it. You exist for him as a good pal, but not as a woman. No one does, except Angela Sowerby of Montreal.'

'I hope Angela Sowerby feels the same about him.'

'One gathers she does.'

The meal continued happily, Bruce hopping from subject to subject with increasing good humour, and Jane feeling considerably more relaxed. She found Bruce attractive, with his dark untidy good looks and his quick mind, and now that she knew about Ted's Angela, she could treat Bruce's obvious interest according to the normal spirit of the game, without anxiety over possible trouble... She was certainly drawn to him, yet she was aware of one alienating factor; intuition was important to her, an essential ingredient of her reaction to her environment – but to Bruce, she sensed, intuition was anathema, a fogging of the intellect. She would have to watch her words if they were to stay friends.

Hell, what am I worrying about? This is a holiday relationship. It isn't as though I wanted to *marry* the man.

She accepted a second liqueur before going upstairs to change into slacks and sweater for the night's watch.

When they joined Ted in the chapel, she began to wish she had stayed in her dinner outfit, inflammatory or not. Though the sun had already set, Ted's temperature traces still showed over 23°C; and while the humidity figure meant nothing to her, Ted confirmed that it was high. Her sweater was thick, and her skin prickled. She was tempted to take the sweater off; but her bra was translucent to say the least, and there were limits. Besides, there was always the possibility that the Curator might look in on them, and he was disapproving enough already.

She hoped the night would grow cooler.

While they made the final adjustments to the equipment, they kept the chapel lights on. They were surprisingly bright, and seemed to Jane to be directly opposed to the true nature of the place. She guessed that they had been installed by the Curator himself, for purely practical purposes and without any sense of drama. They baldly illuminated corners that the lighting-cameraman of a horror film would have left in shadow, and flattened details that he would have thrown into menacing relief. Jane did not mind at all. This operating-theatre lighting killed the place stone-dead, and she preferred it that way.

Ted produced three folding garden-chairs, and asked: 'Where shall we sit?'

'By the door, and facing the altar, I think,' Bruce suggested. 'According to Trevor, it's beside the altar that it all happens. Several people say they've seen her there.'

Ted said 'Right' and set up the chairs. 'The camp beds are outside, if anyone wants to sleep . . . Jane?'

She knew he was merely being gentlemanly, and she answered: 'I'm wide awake, thanks.' She realised she was dreading the lights going out, and she felt a sudden almost panicky desire to escape into the safe neutrality of the corridor; but she was determined not to show weakness, since the two men seemed unconscious of anything that one might show weakness about.

Bruce and Jane sat down; Ted took a last look at his faintly humming polygraph, on the floor beside his chair, and then turned out the lights.

Jane smothered a gasp.

The moon was almost full. It streamed through the stained glass, casting pools of blood and ice on the pale stone. The altar stood out like a focus of evil, ablaze with dripping red fire and blue malevolence and green poison. At first the surrounding blackness revealed nothing, but as her eyes adjusted, details began to emerge, lent sinister distortion by the reflected moonlight. Carved foliage took on animal shapes. The roof angel above the altar grinned with a skull face. Sloping beams reached out like the arms of predators . . .

'Dramatic, isn't it?' Bruce remarked, in an everyday voice.

She said 'Yes', hoping she sounded calm, and seizing with gratitude on the sheer ordinariness of his comment. She struggled to pull herself together, to be objective. Yes, if *she* had been lighting a horror-film set, *that* was how she would have done it. The formula was simple, almost banal. She mustn't fall for it. It was just too naive.

She realised her teeth were clamped painfully together, and she deliberately unclenched them, breathing slowly and deeply.

She wished they had something to do. There was nothing, except this silent motionless vigil.

She tried to think herself into the role of the imaginary lighting-cameraman, analysing and calculating each effect, imposing detachment on herself, reducing the chapel to a mere film set, a contrived visual trick.

At first she seemed to succeed. She became less aware of emotional distress, and correspondingly more aware of her physical discomfort, of the hothouse prickling of her woollen sweater. *That* was real, explicable, and by contrast almost a relief. She listened to the tiny hum of the polygraph, the minute-by-minute click of the camera shutter.

Pleased with her regained control, she let her mind wander back to the thoughts of the day, and smiled at herself. One up for Bruce, though I'd never tell him. This is no time for 'essential femininity', for the treacherous bog of psychic

34

awareness. This is a time for my male aspect – for cool intellect, for detached observation . . .

The very thought betrayed her. Psychic awareness, like a fractious child ordered to sleep, yelled its refusal.

She was unaware of having stood up until she was half-way to the altar, walking with a slow compulsion. She heard Bruce's muttered protest, but it seemed distant, muted, unimportant.

She stood over the altar, curiously and fearfully aware of dim entities surrounding her, their message urgent but obscure. The altar-top pulled at her like a marriage bed.

But the bed was accursed, the marriage an obscenity . . .

She spun round with a mighty effort, turning her back to the altar, panting with fright and unable to take a step away from it. The heat was unbearable, like warm acid eating her skin.

She heard herself cry out: 'I can't stand it!' Then she was grabbing at the sweater, pulling it over her head and fling-ing it halfway down the chapel. She leaned back, bracing her arms against the altar, as the shapeless entities pressed towards her. Beyond them, she saw Bruce and Ted jump to their feet, but they were only half real.

Her arms lost their power, and she felt herself falling backwards. She lay sobbing with her back on the stone, helpless against the looming shapes, against the cruel moon-light staining her flesh.

Only the blaze of light as Ted threw the switches saved her from losing consciousness.

CHAPTER IV

'But the temperature was going *down*!' Bruce protested. 'On all three traces. Partly because we'd lost the heat of the lights, of course, but that was less than a kilowatt – and anyway, the cause doesn't matter. It was going *down*.'

'Let her be, Bruce,' Ted said. 'She's had a shock.'

Bruce muttered something that might have been an apology, but still looked puzzled and angry. Ted poured a beaker of coffee from the thermos flask and brought it to Jane where she lay, shivering and pale, on the camp bed. She propped herself on one elbow and accepted it.

'Thanks, Ted.'

'How're you feeling?'

'Cold, now. Your traces must be right . . . Could I have my sweater back?'

Ted fetched it for her. She pulled it on gratefully, finished the coffee, and lay down again. The two men stood watching her.

After a while Bruce said: 'Well?'

She did not answer at once. Her mind was clear now – it had been, from the moment they had helped her out of the chapel into the corridor – though her body still felt drained of energy. What to tell them? If she were less than honest with them, and pretended to rule out any psychic explanation, she would be condemning herself as nervous, suggestible, hysterical; inviting Bruce's sarcasm. On the other hand, if she described her experience as exactly as she could, insisting that it had been as real as it was terrifying . . .

'Did the traces show anything else, Ted?' she asked, temporising.

Ted disappeared into the chapel for a minute, while Bruce stood fingering a flintlock on the wall and saying nothing.

'I'll have to study them more carefully,' Ted told them when he returned, 'but there does seem to have been a temperature drop of about two degrees in less than a minute, just about the time Jane went to the altar, And I *think* the drop was biggest on the recorder nearest the altar, though it's hard to say without comparing measurements . . . Nothing noticeable on pressure or humidity.'

'Two degrees Centigrade in less than a minute – isn't that a hell of a drop?' Jane asked.

'In still air, it would be. But we've a couple of windows open. A puff of wind could do it.'

'Did *you* feel one?'

'No – but my attention was on what you were up to.'

'We're dodging the bloody issue,' Bruce broke in roughly.

Too right we are, Jane thought. And since I will *not* be called a hysterical female, I might as well take the plunge.

'And what is the issue, Bruce?' she asked.

'What *you* think happened, of course. Why you behaved like that.'

Jane sat up. 'I'll tell you what happened. I *had* to go to the altar – I was halfway there before I even realised I was moving. It pulled me, but it was utterly evil. When I got there, I could *feel* two . . . people, beings, whatever, but two of them, hovering close to me, in front of the altar. They were interested in me – I don't know how else to describe it . . . It took all the strength I'd got to turn round – and when I tried to stop falling backwards, I had no strength at all . . . It wasn't my muscles, because I got that sweater off smartly enough.'

'Smartly? You *tore* it off.'

'I had to, Bruce. The heat was killing me. It was as much a compulsion as falling on to the altar after I'd done it . . . And after I fell . . .'

'You looked as though you were going to pass out,' Ted put in. 'That's why I ran for the lights.'

'Thank God you did. It would have been worse than just passing out.'

'What do you mean worse?'

'I . . . I don't know . . . Just that it *would* have been. Like . . . losing the boundaries of my identity . . .'

She knew she was floundering; the concept was there, and heavily charged, but it hovered on the edge of consciousness, defying definition. She could see Bruce losing patience.

'For Christ's sake,' he almost shouted, 'you're supposed to be a historian, a scholar, you're supposed to have a brain! And you let yourself be bloody-well hypnotised by a spooky atmosphere! We're here to *find* ghosts, if there are any – not to *invent* them out of our own fevered imaginations . . .'

'Who says she's inventing?' Ted interrupted. 'We're looking into an alleged psychic phenomenon. If it's not just "alleged" – if it's really here – why shouldn't Jane be psychically aware of it?'

'That caper of hers wasn't psychic. It was psychological.'

'Don't you mean psycho-pathological?' Jane asked, stung.

'You said it. Not me.'

'And *you* said we were supposed to be scientific,' Ted reminded him. 'Cool off, both of you. Stop slinging long words at each other like custard pies.'

The phrase was so unexpected, coming from Ted, that it broke the tension. Jane laughed, and Bruce grinned a little sheepishly.

'I'm sorry, love – I guess I was a bit rude. You *have* had a shock, whatever the nature of it was . . .'

'It was real, Bruce. *Whatever* it was, it came from outside me. I'm sure it did.'

He went on much more quietly: 'I'm sure it *felt* real. I'm not doubting your sincerity – or your sanity, honest. But

38

you're an educated woman – you must have read enough psychology to know how delusions like that can be triggered off even in normal people. And how real they can seem . . .'

She listened to his reasonable voice, summing up (remarkably well, she had to admit) the known mechanisms of hallucination and auto-suggestion. She let him go on, agreeing, with her brain, to every word he said. And yet she *knew* . . .

'You could be right,' she told him resignedly.

It was Ted who would not let it rest. 'That's all very well, Bruce – and sure, you *could* be right. But I don't see how we can be *certain* you are. The experience would *feel* the same to Jane, whether it was genuinely psychic or merely psychological. Shouldn't we just say we don't know? Pending further evidence?'

Bruce did not answer for a moment; he looked slightly embarrassed, Jane thought. 'All right,' he said at last, 'I can't deny that. But if Jane *is* psychic, she ought to stay clear of the experiment. She can do all the library work, all the research and interviewing – but she ought to stay away from the chapel while we're trying to record. We can't use both approaches. If Jane keeps going into a trance, or feeling compelled to rush around, it'll only confuse the issue. Your instruments might just as well not be here.'

'I don't see why . . .'

'Besides,' Bruce went on, 'the state she was in just now, I'd say it could be bloody dangerous for her.'

Jane had been about to protest at her banishment, but the concern in his last remark was so transparently genuine that she was disarmed, and allowed her silence to be taken as acquiescence.

But of one thing she was sure. Whatever Bruce's resistance, and however frightened she had been and might be again – nothing on earth was going to keep her away from the chapel until she knew what it had to tell her. *That* was a compulsion as irresistible as the force which had pulled her supine and half-naked on to the altar.

The knowledge fascinated and terrified her.

She did not want to make an issue of it straight away, so she agreed readily enough when Bruce suggested she should go back to the Green Man and to bed, while he and Ted continued the night's vigil as planned. It was only 10.0 p.m., so she could have a full night's sleep – and she was not lying when she told Bruce she was exhausted. Her experience in the chapel had taken from her all the benefit of the afternoon's rest, and more.

She did not enter the chapel again, but stood in the doorway talking to them as they reset the equipment. When they were ready, Ted stood by the light switches but did not move to touch them. She caught his diffident glance, understood, and smiled her thanks at him.

''Night, boys. Good luck with it.'

She made her way by torchlight down the long corridor of armour and weapons, and it was not until her footsteps sounded on the staircase at the end that the glow from behind her vanished, telling her that Ted had cut the chapel lights. Dear Ted – she had certainly underestimated his sensitivity. He wasn't going to expose her to the terror of the darkened chapel again, and had waited till she was well clear.

Nice of him, but it doesn't matter anyway. Nothing more will happen tonight. Not even on his precious traces.

Now *why* do I know that? Am I some kind of medium, God help me, so that whatever's in the chapel can't manifest without someone like me to give it a channel? Someone like me, or me in particular? – no, surely that would mean that Bruce was right, and the whole thing came from my own subconscious . . . Or would it?

She left the house by the door that led to the Long Walk, still pondering the problem, with the various possibilities chasing each other in circles, each casting doubt on the one before.

Problem or not, she found she was much calmer; tired, drained even, but oddly at ease now. She was not frightened any more, even by memory. She could look at the bright moonlight that bathed the Walk and the flower-beds and the tall beeches – know that it was the same moon that had spilled poison on the altar – and be undisturbed.

Puzzled anew, she slowed her pace, and sat down on the limestone bench that flanked the middle of the Long Walk.

Ten minutes ago, when I realised that I must go back to the chapel on other nights, I was afraid. Now I am not. Why?

There are things going on inside myself I don't know about – processes of distillation and resolution which present their strange answers to my conscious mind, unexplained, in the form of moods, of apparently baseless certainties – and I'm not sure that I like it . . .

Come off it, Jane Blair. You can't have it both ways. You can't cherish your intuition as long as the going's easy, and then run away from it when the going's rough. So take a good look at what you really are feeling.

I am unafraid – out here, at any rate; but do I smell danger? . . . In a sense, yes; but as the war-horse smells it. He mocketh at fear, and is not affrighted; neither turneth he back from the sword . . . He saith among the trumpets, Ha, ha; and he smelleth the battle afar off, the thunder of the captains, and the shouting . . . Good old Job; the struggles he had with his intuition!

Right, then; there is fear, but I mock at it, I am not affrighted. Battle . . . Battle against whom, against what?

She plucked idly at a sprig of lavender that overflowed the bench, and sat twisting it between her fingers, trying to still her thoughts and make herself receptive.

The lavender is fair, this year.

Jane was startled. The voice had been so clear – her own voice, and yet not her own. Her vocal chords had not moved, but the voice – and the thought – seemed to have come from within her.

A petty, irrelevant thought; but clear, and somehow warm. She was *pleased* that the lavender was fair – its condition was her concern... Fair, her brain asked? Rather a grudging word; nothing to be warmly pleased about... It's true, too, she told herself, looking at the sprig in her hand; only *fair*. Sparse and stringy. This can't have been a particularly good year for lavender.

But suddenly she knew she had it wrong. Her voice had meant *fair* in the old sense – 'excellent, beautiful'; not in the modern sense of 'average'. The old sense was not natural to her, to Jane Blair, but it had been natural to the voice. And it *had* been a good year for lavender; not like this . . .

Intrigued and a little excited, she tried to grasp at the uncanny moment; but her very excitement drove it away. The moonlight was only moonlight, and the sprig in her hand was this year's.

Sighing, Jane got up from the bench and descended the hill to the Green Man.

She would have no real need to get up for breakfast at 6.0, so she looked in at the bar to tell Trevor Cox. He was not there; the barmaid who was on duty said she would find him on the terrace with Dr Stoneleigh.

Jane bought herself a lager – the night was still hot and her throat was dry – and took it out on to the flagged terrace that overlooked the garden. Trevor sat at one of the tables, talking with a tall thin man, who stood beside him as though he were on the point of leaving.

He called to her: 'Hullo, Jane – come and join me . . . This is Keith Stoneleigh, from the hospital. Jane Blair – one of our ghost-hunters.'

'Miss Blair.'

'Doctor.'

He shook her hand, formally but firmly, and looked at her with narrow bright eyes. 'Trevor's been telling me about your experiments. I'm very interested. Do you think I could see your equipment some time?'

'I'm sure Ted Harris wouldn't mind. It'd have to be about half-past eight or nine one evening, before they start monitoring. I'll have a word with him if you like.'

'I'd be very grateful. The Battle Maid intrigues me . . . I've always thought someone ought to do a proper investigation – either by your approach, or with a good medium.'

'Have *you* ever seen her – the Battle Maid?'

'No such luck.'

'But you believe she exists?'

'*Something* does. I had to treat a hysterical girl in Casualty last year – an Austrian au pair who swore she'd just seen her in the Grange drive. She'd never heard the legend, but her description tallied, sword and all . . . If I hadn't had a few words of German, I wouldn't have known what the hell was up with her.'

Jane asked quickly: 'Is she still around? Could I talk with her?'

'Afraid not. She went home the week after. She was a devout Lutheran, and she convinced herself Orley was an evil place . . . Oh, well, I must be off. Night duty this week.'

When Dr Stoneleigh had gone, Trevor waved Jane to a chair and asked: 'I thought you were on night duty, too?'

'The boys are doing it tonight. I've got some research to do tomorrow, so I'm going to sleep.'

'When do you want to interview my two witnesses? Mrs Cannon and Geoffrey Withecombe?'

'Well, I could do one tomorrow, if it can be fixed . . .'

'Okay. Geoff's in Manchester all day, I think, but Mrs Cannon'll probably be at home. We'll ring her in the morning and you can make a date.'

'Thanks, that'd be fine.'

Trevor sipped his drink, then asked almost too casually: 'You must have been there for the first hour or so. How did it go?'

'Everything seemed to be working.'

43

She knew the answer sounded wary, and without looking up she could feel him watching her.

'Want to tell me?' he asked at last.

'Tell you what?'

'Why you're disturbed ... Sorry, I'm being nosey. It's no business of mine.'

'No, don't apologise ...' Maybe it's disloyal to the team, she thought, but I do need an ally – I need someone level-headed like Trevor to tell me I'm not being fanciful, or at least to encourage me to find out if I am – someone who has an interest in the experiment, but no preconceived ideas about how it should be carried out ...

'I've been banished from the chapel,' she said. 'Sounds like a Welsh excommunication, doesn't it? ... Bruce insists I confine myself to research and interviews and so on. No more night watches. I'm a disruptive influence ...'

She told him everything that had happened to her, as dispassionately as she could, and he did not interrupt her once. When she had finished, he said: 'I thought something like this might happen. I could see Bruce was pretty rigid about method, and that you and he might clash ...'

'Why me?'

'Because the chapel affected you, and you said so. If anyone was going to pick up anything, my money would be on you rather than Ted's instruments ... What are you going to do? Stay clear, like Bruce says?'

'I can't, Trevor. I've got to go back.'

'Yes, I can see that . . . Would you like a brandy or something?'

Jane laughed. 'Do I look so shattered?'

'Stop being defensive! I'm having another myself, that's all.'

'Sorry . . . Yes, I'd love one.'

He went to fetch them, and for a minute or two after he brought them back he only talked inconsequentialities. Then he said suddenly: 'It could be dangerous for you, you know.'

44

'That's what Bruce said. But even if it's true, it doesn't make any difference. It's like a challenge I can't run away from . . . That sounds awfully brave. I'm not really. It's . . . Oh, I don't know. I can't describe it. But I'm going back there. Tomorrow night. I'll have trouble with Bruce about it, that's for sure.'

'You'll cope with that.'

'What makes you think so?'

'Because . . . No, this *is* an impertinence.'

'Never mind. Say it anyway.'

'Because all's fair in love and war – and Bruce is vulnerable to you. Very.'

Jane laughed again. 'That's not impertinent. It's just plain unscrupulous.'

'This thing's important to you,' Trevor said. 'And not just to you, I feel. It's important – period. So I shouldn't be too choosy about your weapons, Battle Maid.'

'Why do you call me that? I'm no ghost.'

'Anything but. Just that you have a lot in common with her.'

'She's real to you, isn't she? Even though you've never seen her?'

'Maybe I haven't,' Trevor said. 'But we've been neighbours all my life.'

The night remained close and humid, and even though it was Jane's habit to sleep naked, she still had to throw off all the bedclothes except for a sheet and the thinnest blanket. She set her alarm for 7.0, turned off the light, opened the curtains, and went to bed wondering if she would be able to sleep.

She need not have worried. The next thing she knew was that the sun was streaming in the window, her clock read 6.27, and she was wide awake. She went to the toilet, cleaned her teeth, splashed her face, and went back to bed, content to rest till the alarm went.

She felt calm, relaxed, and ready for whatever the day

45

might bring. One thing was certain – it was going to be hot; she could see through the window that yesterday's overcast had vanished. She pushed the bedclothes down to her waist and shut her eyes, letting her mind drift.

Her conversation with Trevor came back to her. She was glad she had told him, and he had been sensibly understanding – although (she smiled to herself) his prediction about how she could deal with Bruce was . . . Well, anyway.

She was almost asleep again when she became aware of the footsteps on the landing. One of the boys going to bed, she thought mistily.

The footsteps halted, and somebody tapped gently on her door.

Let him think I'm asleep. I can't be bothered.

'Jane?' It was Bruce's voice, quietly concerned.

She did not answer, did not open her eyes, did not pull up the bedclothes. She felt almost detached from herself; she could picture herself, naked to the waist, long hair tumbling over the pillow, half-open hand lying palm upwards. A seductive image, innocent in the flush of sleep.

Jane Blair, what the hell are you up to? . . . but she did not move.

The door opened softly; Bruce was looking inside. It stayed open for quite a time.

The alarm broke the silence. Jane stirred, feigning a slow awakening, and keeping her eyes shut till she heard the door click.

She laughed quietly to herself as the footsteps moved hurriedly away; then she jumped out of bed and ran to the shower, still laughing.

Jane Blair, you should be thoroughly ashamed.

That was quite deliberate – to make him more vulnerable, easier to manipulate. And only yesterday you were telling yourself you were not a sexual bitch . . . So what? I'm not leading him on with the *intention* of refusing him. Maybe I won't refuse him . . . That won't do, Jane Blair. You weren't thinking about that when you waited for him to open the door. You were thinking of Trevor's words: *This thing's important. So I shouldn't be too choosy about your weapons, Battle Maid* . . . Maybe I was; but I have to get back into that chapel, at night, no matter what I have to do to achieve it.

She dressed and went down to breakfast, trying without conviction to feel ashamed of herself.

She ate heartily, and took her time.

CHAPTER V

Mrs Cannon's voice on the other end of the line was old, chintz-curtainy, and kindly. She sounded like everyone's favourite great-aunt, Jane decided. Ninety if she was a day, but perkily alive.

'By all means come and see me, my dear. I don't know whether I can be a great deal of help . . .'

'I'm sure you can, Mrs Cannon. You've actually seen the Battle Maid, Mr Cox tells me.'

'O, indeed I have. Three times. The first time was when I was a young gel – the Christmas after the old Queen died, I remember, because that was the year my brother Robert was ordained, and he came home to spend Christmas before taking up his first curacy, a disaster that was, because he had to do all the work – the Rector drank, you know – and Robert was *quite* inexperienced . . . His next parish was *much* more suitable.'

'I'm glad,' Jane said, a little faintly.

'Yes, well, where was I? Oh, of course. Yes, Robert and I were taking a walk along the Upper Lane, you know, along the Grange boundary, we'd been out too long really, because it was dark by then, young people just don't *think*, and there she was. Robert saw her too, he was a bit of a prude, to be quite honest, he was more put out by her wearing *breeches*, indelicate for a woman, he called it, than he was by her being a ghost. I said you couldn't call chain-mail quite the same as breeches, and he reprimanded me rather sharply, I couldn't think why at the time, she was a *striking* gel, and in those days no gel of her age wore her hair *down*, of course, but *she* did. Striking, yes . . . We were late for tea.'

'Oh.'

'Yes, a prude I'm afraid, but then he *was* only just ordained – he mellowed later on . . . Well, now, the second time was in broad daylight – did I mention there was a moon the first time? No, well, there was – but this time it was about three in the afternoon, about August it would be, like now, and I was an old married woman by then, thirty-two – no, thirty-three, because *young* Robert – that was our eldest, we named him after my brother, I sometimes wondered why, but there it is – *young* Robert was on his first summer holiday from Rugby, and that would make me thirty-three, wouldn't it?'

'Er . . .'

'He saw her first, as it happened. I can remember him asking me – did I say we were in the Grange grounds, walking along the river bank? – well, I remember him asking me: "Mater, why is that lady wearing trousers?" Naturally I turned round, and there she was, looking down at the river, with the sword in her hand. Her *left* hand – it's always her left, everyone says so.' Mrs Cannon chuckled. 'Do you know, *that* upset Robert – the older one, I mean, my brother – that upset him almost as much as the breeches? He seemed to think it wasn't quite ladylike to be left-handed . . . Anyway, I looked at Robert – my son, I mean – to answer him – do you know, I can't remember what I said? – and when I looked back she'd gone. Now the *third* time was much later, only three years ago. Since Arnold died – that was my husband – I haven't got out very much, and lately not at all, well hardly, just down to the shop – but up to a year or two ago I used to like taking a little stroll to the Grange and resting on that seat in the Long Walk – you know it?'

'I was sitting on it only yesterday.'

'Charming, isn't it? Well, it was mostly in the afternoon of course, but three years ago, that very fine summer, you remember, I was there one evening just after sunset, all by myself. At least, all by myself until *she* was there all of a

49

sudden, looking at me, poor gel, that was the only time she troubled me, the other times I'd just been curious, you know, perhaps because I wasn't alone, but this time, face to face with her – she looked *distressed*, poor thing, well, no, I'd say *horrified*, as though it wasn't me she was looking at but someone else, and it was a shock to her . . . I even spoke to her, I said "What *is* it?" – foolish of me, of course, I mean she could hardly answer, could she, but the way her face looked, I felt I had to say *something*. Would eleven o'clock suit you?'

Jane realised the question had been addressed to her and not to the ghost, and recovered her breath in time to say that eleven o'clock would be perfect. Mrs Cannon said 'Splendid, splendid,' and rang off.

She felt she had probably heard all that Mrs Cannon had to tell, though from such a grasshopper narration there was no certainty something vital had not been missed, and if so it might emerge almost casually from a second telling. Besides, it would be only polite to visit the old lady; she was very probably lonely.

Mrs Cannon's house was at the end of the village street, only a couple of hundred yards from the Green Man. Jane knocked on the front door at 11.0 precisely, guessing that Mrs Cannon had been brought up to observe, and to expect, good manners and punctuality. The house certainly suggested a Victorian middle-class meticulousness. Foursquare, modestly prosperous; the curtains *were* chintz, many years old by Jane's guess, but spotless and drawn tidily open. The garden was obviously tended by a gardener, and the front door was opened to Jane by (of all things, these days) a uniformed maid. Arnold must have left his widow comfortably provided for.

The maid ushered her into the drawing-room, announcing her formally. Mrs Cannon, a tiny white-haired sparrow of a woman who looked exactly like her voice, began to rise courteously but with difficulty from her very upright armchair.

50

Jane said: 'Oh, please don't get up,' and hurried forward to take the offered hand.

'Thank you, my dear.' Mrs Cannon subsided into her chair, smiling at her short-sightedly. 'I get quite exasperated with myself, being so feeble. I've always run around like a two-year-old, and I just can't get used to being an old woman . . . Would you like some sherry?'

'That would be lovely.' Jane did not like morning drinking; but in a house like this, one surrendered to the established ritual. The maid (whom Mrs Cannon addressed, to Jane's amused delight, by her unadorned surname) brought a sherry decanter, two crystal glasses, and a doyleyed plate of biscuits on a silver tray, placed them on a table at the old lady's side, and withdrew silently.

'It was so nice of you to come and see me. You're a schoolteacher, Mr Cox tells me?'

'That's right, Mrs Cannon. I teach history.'

'And you've come to Orley to find out about the Battle Maid. Very enterprising of you. I'm sure you'll find a great deal to fascinate your gels with when you go back. Orley has almost too *much* history.'

Jane smiled at the assumption that a lady taught 'gels'; coeducation did not exist for Mrs Cannon except in primary schools. 'It can't have too much for me.'

'Well, to tell you the truth, my dear, I feel the same myself. I love this village – my father was Vicar here, you know, dog-collars run in the family, though I didn't marry one, Arnold was a solicitor, but then I've told you that already, haven't I?' She hadn't, but Jane let it pass. 'Sign of senility, repeating oneself, bad habit. Tell me if I do . . . I wonder if you'll actually *see* the Battle Maid? She's a strange creature, so unpredictable, I mean there are people who've lived in Orley all their lives and never seen her once, and a foolish woman like me sees her three times, not really fair, is it? – but perhaps she knows you've come here specially on her account, and she'll make a point of meeting you.' She laughed happily at her own joke. 'After all, it would be only

51

polite, wouldn't it, and she looks a lady, in spite of her tin breeches.'

'Is that really how they looked to you?'

'Dear me, no, I used to call them that to tease Robert, he was a bit pompous, did him good to tease the stuffing out of him now and then. Tin breeches!' She laughed again. 'Really it's chain mail, I suppose – anyhow, silver and close-fitting, her tunic thing as well – I'm not surprised Robert was upset about her.'

'Oh – why?'

'Well, I told you he was a prude, didn't I? – when he married Georgina I often wondered if they blindfolded themselves to go to bed. You mustn't mind me, I'm a wicked old woman. But to be truthful, she has a *very* good figure. The Battle Maid, I mean, not Georgina, she was like a sack of potatoes. You must be *dying* of thirst and I go on chattering like a magpie.' Her hand wavered vaguely over the decanter, and then she gave a little shrug and took a spectacle-case from the handbag on her lap. 'I really should wear these all the time, blind as a bat without them. Sheer vanity, and at my age!'

'I only hope I look half as pretty when *I'm* your age.'

'You're a sweet gel and I *like* you lying to me. Vanity again.' She turned sideways towards the tray, put on her spectacles, and carefully filled the two glasses. 'I do hope you like really dry sherry . . .'

'I prefer it.'

'Quite right, all this nonsense about women preferring sweet wines, pure fairy-tale, it's the *men* in my experience, no palates most of them. This is a Manzanilla, splendid, splendid, tastes of the sea.'

She picked up one of the glasses and turned to face Jane, holding it out to her.

The moment their eyes met, Mrs Cannon gave a little cry, and the glass of sherry slipped through her fingers to the floor.

Jane was on her knees at once, picking up the frail crystal

carefully, while the old lady babbled incoherent apologies.

'Don't worry – it's not broken, Mrs Cannon. The carpet saved it.'

The maid must have heard Mrs Cannon cry out, because she was in the room at once, mopping up the spilled sherry. Mrs Cannon diverted her apologies to the maid, who uttered little soothing noises in return, fetched a clean glass, and poured another drink for Jane herself. Jane tried to calm her hostess by tasting it at once and saying that it truly was splendid. Mrs Cannon clutched at her own glass and drank hurriedly, as though she needed it.

The maid disappeared as silently as before.

'Are you sure you're feeling all right, Mrs Cannon?'

The old lady did indeed look pale, but she tried to smile. 'So clumsy . . . I really am getting decrepit.'

'Nonsense – it could happen to anyone. I'm just glad it didn't break. They're beautiful glasses.'

'Yes. Wedding present. Dozen. Still got them all.'

'Then I'm *very* glad. It would have been a shame.'

That must explain the shock, Jane thought; because Mrs Cannon really did look badly shaken, though she was struggling to do her duty as a hostess. Before she dropped the glass she had clearly been enjoying herself; now she was equally clearly in distress.

Jane left as soon as she decently could. Mrs Cannon, courteous to the last, begged her to come again, but the myopic eyes looked almost afraid.

It's easy to forget how little reserve of energy the very elderly have, Jane thought as she walked away from the house. That old dear was so full of life – and then a little incident like a spilled sherry just sent her to pieces. She looked *ill* . . .

But wait a moment – her shock came *before* she dropped the glass – it *made* her drop it . . . She put on her spectacles and saw me properly for the first time, and it jolted her. Badly . . .

I wonder if I'm the spit image of a dead daughter, or

something? But if I am, why didn't she say so? Perhaps the memory was too painful.

Poor old thing. I like her. And I'll probably never know.

Jane still had a couple of hours to spare before she joined Bruce and Ted for lunch, and she decided to spend them introducing herself to the Grange library. She went and found the Curator, who was resting between tours in his little office just off the Great Hall.

'Good morning, Mr Unsworth – I'm sorry to bother you, but could you let me into the library?'

His eyes were still hostile. 'The next tour starts in ten minutes, I wouldn't really have time to show it to you.'

'I know, but . . .'

'The library has some very valuable papers in it, Miss Blair. Quite irreplaceable. And some of them are fragile. I should be there whenever they are touched. They are my responsibility.'

'I do have a history degree, Mr Unsworth. I'm quite used to handling old documents. It's part of my profession.'

For the first time, the Curator's hostility thawed a little; that was plain from his hesitant 'Well . . .' Jane sensed that she had found a chink in his Council-clerk armour. If she had letters after her name, ghost-hunting crank or not, that moved her up several places in Charley Unsworth's pecking order.

'Oxford,' she added, shamelessly completing her victory. Mention of the senior university was the *coup de grâce*. The Curator actually smiled – still frostily, as though his facial muscles were unused to it, but a smile none the less. In Mr Unsworth's tidy cosmos, an Oxford or Cambridge graduate was, by definition, a responsible person, entitled by rank to a little eccentricity.

'Oh, in *that* case I'm sure it'll be all right.' He rose and took a key from the wall-board. 'Please come with me, Miss Blair.'

He led her to the library on the first floor, and showed her

54

where the Montgris papers were kept. They had been arranged roughly in chronological order by some well-intentioned but inexpert hand; Jane noticed that several documents in lawyers' Latin had defeated the arranger, and been wrongly placed. She made one or two comments, not deliberately intending to impress the Curator, but succeeding in doing so nevertheless.

'I'll leave you to it, then, Miss Blair . . . If you want to come here at any time and I'm not in my office, the library key is the fourth from the left on the board.'

Victory indeed. 'Thank you very much, Mr Unsworth. I'll lock up and put it back there, when I've finished.'

He smiled again, almost humanly this time, and went out.

Jane loved original sources, and had to resist the temptation just to browse for the fun of it. She had to be methodical; the first thing to look for was the diary of Lady Clara Montgris, who had apparently been the first to mention the Grange ghost, in 1630.

The journal was not hard to find, for Lady Clara had been a prolific, not to say compulsive, diarist. Not all of her volumes had survived, but the haystack was still big enough to make needle-searching quite a task. Family arguments, recipes, local gossip, political comment, fashion notes, pleas and admonitions to St Barbara (who for some reason seemed to be Lady Clara's personal contact in Heaven), and scorn of her mother-in-law's hypochondria, ran from her pen in inconsequential profusion. Jane spent twenty minutes failing to find any reference to the ghost under 1630; Trevor Cox had only said 'I think it was', and must have been wrong.

She started on 1631, and found it almost immediately. It seemed, unfortunately, to be a second reference; and since the earlier volumes only covered 1623 to 1626, the original reference was probably lost. A nuisance, because it presumably contained a fuller description. Still, this was something.

17th Feb. – Again have I met with the Specter wh. frequenteth the Chappel, not seen these severall Yeares. But still my Husbande will none of it, declaring the Armour wh. I protest she weareth to be not natural, either today or in earlier Tymes; to lend Veritie to wh. Argument he hath led me to the Gallerie where many such Curiosities are kept, to the ill Use of needful Room and the Tyme of Servants in the Cleaning thereof, if alle be not to rust away. And theer hath he been much concern'd to shew me that the Specter's Accoutrements should not be as I describ'd them, in much learn'd Exactitude, arguing moreover that he being the Soldier and not I, was better vers'd in such Matters. Certes, Husbande, say I, I must bow to yr Knowledge, but my verie Ignorance surely supports my Claime; for if as you aver the Specter is borne of my Fancie, would I not hv. cloth'd that Fancie in that wh. is familiar, the more so for gathering a Plague of Duste in my House? Yet hv. I encounter'd her twice, & each Tyme dress'd as I hv. describ'd; therefor must her Accoutremt. be of its own Nature, & not of my Fancie. But he still unpersuad'd.

It sounds just like Bruce and me, Jane thought. A very intelligent woman, the Lady Clara; and I sympathise with her about the dust. All that ironmongery must have been murder without a vacuum cleaner.

'Interesting, that,' Bruce said when she read the copied-out passage to them over lunch. 'I wonder if he was right about the Battle Maid's armour being incorrect?'

'There's no way of telling. Maybe he was just a seventeenth-century male chauvinist pig, trying to blind his wife with science.'

'Could be. Ex-service bores are like that – my Dad's one. You know: Tobruk's a holy word, and no civilian can tell a cartridge from a bullet or a Bofors from a beanpole. Mother says she learned that in 1945, in the first month after his demob. On military matters, even if she was right she had to be wrong.'

56

'Thought you told me she'd worked in an arms factory?' Ted said.

'So she had. She could have stripped a Bren gun in her sleep and reassembled it with one hand. But that didn't count. Dad had been a *Sergeant* . . . Anyhow, back to Lady Clara. It's possible that he *was* right, and that she'd just described it wrong.'

'I doubt it,' Jane told him. 'I've only spent an hour with her so far, but I get the feeling she was a pretty accurate observer. Her descriptions are very precise, and well larded with measurements.'

'Too bad we haven't got her first description of the Battle Maid, then.'

'Well, we might have. I'll go on hunting . . . But she had a point, you know. If she *had* dug up an armoured ghost out of her subconscious, she'd have dressed it in correct armour – the stuff she was fed up with dusting. But she didn't. *Ergo*, the ghost was an independent phenomenon.'

'All right, accept that for a moment. I'm still bloody curious to know why the Battle Maid wore armour which a military expert insisted was wrong.'

'So am I. But it must have been something that *looked* like chain mail, because that's how every witness has described it – including the ones who saw her before they knew the legend . . . Okay, I know we've only got their word they *didn't* know the legend, and some of them may have heard it and forgotten they had. We've no way of checking. But it's still odd.'

'The fact that she carried a sword may have made them *see* whatever–it–was as armour.'

'There's that, too.'

They ate for a while in silence, and then Bruce asked: 'What's your next step, when you've finished searching Lady Clara for the earlier reference? Work forward through the other sightings, I suppose.'

'No,' Jane said, with the familiar sensation of surprising herself by her own words. 'Backwards.'

'Why, for God's sake? All the other references come later.'

'Just a hunch,' she admitted, unwisely. She could see Bruce's jaw muscles tightening.

'Jane, Jane – we've got to have *method* . . .'

'A *professional* hunch,' she amended. 'You can trust those, Bruce.'

He looked at her, only half-convinced. She smiled in his face, with calculated intimacy, and he actually blushed.

'All right,' he said. 'Sorry, love. I guess you know your own job.'

My God, she thought. Trevor's right. It works.

CHAPTER VI

Jane was determined to be awake and on her toes all night and that meant going to sleep all afternoon. But if she did she would reveal her intention before she was ready . . .

She considered going off into the woods and sleeping in the open; but her skin was sensitive to insect-bites, and in this weather the woods were alive with them. She considered sunbathing in the Green Man's garden, which would allow her to fall asleep without anyone being surprised; but that meant either lying in the shade, which would look silly, or getting scorched. She considered taking Trevor into her confidence again, borrowing another bedroom for the afternoon, and simply disappearing, but she felt diffident about that. Trevor had frankly recommended her to be devious, and she was reluctant to let him see how right he was.

Fortunately Ted solved her problem for her. The microphones which he had been using for his two sound traces were a matched pair; but now that he only had one channel, he wanted to use a higher-quality single Sennheiser which he had at home in his Manchester flat, and he proposed to drive up and get it.

'Want to come, you two? We'll be back in time for dinner.'

'Sure,' Bruce said. 'I want to go to a decent bookshop for the new Lyall Watson.'

'Jane?'

'Thanks, Ted, but I think I'll try to see my other witness,' – whom she knew to be out, so that fixed that.

59

The men hurried off without even waiting for coffee; Jane went straight to bed and slept like a baby.

She woke to the alarm at 5.45, sang in her shower, and set about dressing up for the disarming of Bruce without even a twinge of conscience. She observed her own state of untroubled determination, and decided that her subconscious had been at work on the problem while she slept, exorcising her qualms.

Well, that's okay by me. I'm going to do it anyway, so why waste nervous energy?

The lurex-and-bikini outfit had obviously rung the bell; now to hit him with a complete change. That had been mistily revealing; how about something figure-hugging?... Her best thing for that, she decided, was a gunmetal lamé trouser suit, its grey glitter subdued but effective; wrap-over long-sleeved blouse and ground-brushing pants, the whole thing skin-tight from shoulder to knee, with a flash of bare waist when she bent.

Last night her hair had been sleekly bunned, to contrast with the softness of her dress. Tonight she brushed it loose, to set off the metallic clarity of the trouser suit.

She studied the effect in the long mirror.

O-*kay*.

When she joined the men downstairs in the lounge, Bruce's very silence confirmed her success. Last night he had made flattering jokes; tonight he just looked, and went on looking. Even better, he tried to hide the fact that he was looking.

Ted seemed not to notice, plunging straight into technicalities about his Sennheiser. That Angela Sowerby must be quite something, she thought – and rebuked herself for her own conceit; but the rebuke was half-hearted; she *knew* she looked good. Whenever Ted's technicalities touched on something she understood, she put in a comment or a question to keep him going, and left Bruce to his silent

60

inspection; she was thoroughly aware of him, though her eyes were on Ted.

After a while Ted seemed to be drying up. 'Is the Sennheiser directional?' she prompted him.

He launched into another five minutes on the shape of the response-lobe in relation to the shape of the chapel, and on how he could place the mike to the best advantage.

'How about dinner?' Bruce asked suddenly.

Jane led the way, and heads turned as they entered the dining room. She saw it without looking, just as she could feel Bruce's eyes on her back, and she purred.

Bruce handled her chair for her when they reached their table; he had never done so before, and the little gesture brought back her qualms with an unexpected rush. She was exploiting him quite unfairly, for her own ends – and it was no use pretending to herself that her aim was honestly sexual, within the rules of the game. She found him attractive, yes. But if she did envisage a natural end to her behaviour, that was only a sop to her conscience; it was not *why* she was leading him on. She was using her sex and her charm and his vulnerability for one reason only – that he was the obstacle to be overcome if she was to get back into the chapel for tonight's session. And, by hook or by crook, get there she must.

She was being a bitch.

Bruce handed her the menu, and she smiled her thanks at him, her sudden guilt making the smile warmer than she had intended. She wanted to say something, anything to reduce the charge in the atmosphere, but she was dumb.

'Did you get your other witness?' Ted asked. 'Whatsisname – Geoffrey Whitcombe?'

She seized on the diversion gratefully. 'Not Whitcombe – Withecombe . . . No, he was out. *He* was in Manchester, too. I'll get him tomorrow, probably.'

'What did you do, then? Library'

Might as well face it, get it over with.

'No. I went to bed.'

61

Ted looked sympathetic. 'On an afternoon like this? Last night must have taken it out of you even more than we thought.'

'It wasn't that.' They both looked at her, questioningly, and she went on: 'I wanted to rest, because I'm coming back in the chapel tonight.'

She did not look directly at Bruce in the few seconds' silence which followed, but she could feel him tensing up, his mind changing gear; almost share the effort with which he tore himself away from erotic speculation to angry denial. Her own mind, too, was in turmoil. The guilt remained; she felt naked and ashamed; but like a swordsman reacting instinctively to the enemy's intention, she was preparing her parry and riposte for the moment when the thrust should reveal itself. Victory was all, shame was the mere pain of a non-mortal wound already suffered.

'Like hell you are,' Bruce hissed at her.

She looked him in the eyes now, but before she could reply Ted cut in with: 'Easy, Bruce, easy . . . Jane, do you think that's wise?'

'Yes, I do. We came here to hunt a ghost, and we've picked up the scent. Or *I* have. I don't claim any special credit for that, it just happened that way. I picked up *something*, like it or not, and it's up to me to pursue it, if I can. I think Bruce is too hung up on this detachment thing. Your instruments are fine, Ted – I mean that, they're beautifully thought out, and they're a vital part of the experiment. But I don't see why it should be the Law of the Medes and Persians that they're the *whole* of it.'

'Because that's what we're after,' Bruce said, a little more calmly. 'We're not here to convince *ourselves* that there's a ghost. We're here to see if we can get recorded, measurable evidence of some phenomenon that can't be explained by so-called "normal" rules. Objective evidence – not subjective. Evidence that'll be just as valid for other people as it is for us. And whether Jane's experience came from inside herself or outside, as evidence it's still subjective.'

'That's not quite the point,' Ted objected.

(Good. Let them fight it out between them till I choose the moment to jump in.)

'Of course it is. Look . . .'

'No, *you* look, man. The point is *not* whether Jane's carry-on last night, and anything else she might pick up, is conclusive evidence *in itself*. The point is – does it tie in with the recording experiment, or does it interfere with it?'

'It *must* interfere with it. How can we observe any phenomenon if we're observing Jane at the same time?'

'Because Jane's reaction may be part of the phenomenon.'

(Nice one, Ted.)

'And it may be pure hallicination,' Bruce retorted, 'with Jane blundering about and cocking up the sound track, and you switching lights on . . .'

'Or it may not. And if we get marked temperature changes at the same time (we'll keep the windows shut this time, by the way), or humidity changes, or something odd on camera, that'll suggest Jane *is* reacting to the phenomenon, and *not* just hallucinating.'

'Changed your tune, haven't you? You were agreeing with me when we went to bed this morning.'

(Still on about it then, were you?)

'I've slept on it since.'

'Talking of lights,' Jane found herself saying, with a tremor of fear but inescapably, '*don't* switch them on if it happens again, until I actually tell you to. Let whatever-it-is take its course.'

'You're taking it for granted you're coming back, and that it'll happen again?' Bruce challenged.

She smiled at him. 'Yes to both. I'm coming, and I've got a . . . I know you don't like the word, but *hunch* . . . something more will happen.'

'If you're convinced in advance, of course it will.'

'Depends whether the conviction comes from inside or outside.'

'Oh, for Christ's sake, Jane . . .'

63

'I'll admit that's the one thing I don't like,' Ted interrupted again. 'Jane's got guts, but it still could be dangerous for her.'

She leaned back deliberately in her chair, clasping her hands behind it, and still smiling at Bruce. 'I'm a big girl now.'

Laughing inside herself, she saw his eyes flicker.

The waiter arrived to take their order. Jane was pleased, knowing that the argument had been broken at just the right tactical moment; and she prepared to keep it that way for the time being. As the waiter left, she turned to Ted.

'I've been wanting to ask you. How do you decide on the mean reading, the zero line, for each of your tracks?'

Ted reacted to the stimulus like a Pavlovian dog. 'Well, sound looks after itself, of course – zero is silence. But temperature, humidity, pressure – you have to watch the Met forecasts and guess an average; but of course in a place like that chapel you're dealing with microclimates, so you use your first night's readings as a guide to correcting your guess . . .'

He was soon riding his hobby-horse at full tilt, and Jane kept feeding him questions. Bruce, taciturn at first, was gradually drawn in. Jane relaxed, cautiously.

Ted, eager as ever, left for the Grange as soon as dinner was over. Jane was alone with him for a moment in the hall while Bruce went up to his room for cigarettes, and he turned to her questioningly.

'You'll be up there, then?'

'I'll be there, Ted.'

'Bruce hasn't said yes, yet.'

'Who's the boss around here?'

Ted grinned suddenly, glancing up the stairs and then back at her. 'With your assets I guess you are, love. It's not fair, but it works. Good luck.' He gave her a thumbs-up, and left.

Well, well, well. Rule No. 3(b): stop underestimating Ted.

She wandered out on to the terrace, where Bruce soon joined her. They stood in silence watching the lengthening shadows on the lawn, till the silence, too, had lengthened to the point of awkwardness. To escape it, Jane began to walk through the garden, and Bruce fell into step beside her.

'You're still set on coming?' he asked at last.

'You know I am.'

Another pause, and then: 'Hadn't you better go and change, then?'

'What for? I was too hot last night. This'll do fine.'

Bruce halted, turning to face her. 'I still don't bloody like it. I *wish* you'd stay out of it.'

His tone was almost plaintive, and it left him wide open for the *coup de grâce*. She put her hands on his shoulders, looking up at him with calculated reproachful mockery.

'Now, *Bruce*.'

He kissed her, of course, and she melted against him, at least half-spontaneously; his attraction was real, and but for her guilt she would have enjoyed it. Then he broke free, his eyes hurt and angry, accusing her without words: *You bitch, did you have to work it that way?* She seized his hand, trying desperately to convey warmth, to make the moment genuine in retrospect. The anxiety in her face must have spoken to him, too, because he sighed and gave her a half-smile, squeezing her hand before he let it go.

'See you up there, I suppose,' he said, and walked away.

Involuntarily echoing his sigh, Jane watched him go.

She paced around the garden, edgily, for a while, until a party of diners came out on to the terrace; they all seemed to be watching her as though she were an after-dinner floor show, and embarrassment drove her indoors and up to her room . . . Let the boys set up their equipment by themselves. She would join them when it got dark.

She lay on her back on her bed, staring at the ceiling. Her mind was curiously static, as though guilt and triumph had reached an equilibrium and called a truce. She found herself drifting towards sleep, but she did not want that, so she turned on the bedside light and reached for a book. It did not absorb her, but it filled the time in a neutral sort of way.

When the square of the window had grown black, she put down the book, jumped up with a sense of relief, and gave her loose hair a few minutes' satisfying brushing. She wondered for a moment whether to change, but she had been right; it *was* still hot, and she felt perfectly comfortable as she was. In any case, she had a cardigan up at the Grange, so it didn't matter if the temperature dropped later. Methodically, she had left a bag with Ted's equipment – toilet and makeup things, a couple of paperbacks, spare cigarettes, and so on; no point in carting stuff back and forth every day.

Time to go.

She walked out of the Green Man, empty-handed and free, feeling relaxed and ready for whatever the night might bring.

The moon was already topping the far trees, but Orley's few street-lamps had not come on yet. Jane made her leisurely way up the village street towards the Grange gate.

A light glowed through the chintz in Mrs Cannon's drawing-room window. The old lady was doubtless enjoying an after-dinner liqueur out of yet another wedding-present glass. Or more probably brandy, with her dry palate . . .

No, she wasn't. She was taking an evening stroll in her front garden, wrapped in a fur coat and moving carefully with the help of a walking-stick.

As Jane drew level with the front gate, she was about to call a greeting to the tiny moonlit figure; but at that moment Mrs Cannon caught sight of her, and her sudden change of expression left Jane speechless.

After their last meeting, Jane would have been ready for the old lady to show confusion or embarrassment. But instead, Mrs Cannon seemed transfigured. She stared at Jane with radiant delight, stopping in her tracks, the small hand on the stick-handle quivering with excitement.

Jane dared not open her mouth to break the spell. Poor

old soul – she doesn't think I'm real – I must have been right, she's looking at a vision of her dead daughter, or of somebody she loved. God, I'll have to be careful . . .

She smiled at the old lady and blew her a silent kiss.

Mrs Cannon gave a little gasp, and waved her free hand feebly in reply. Her eyes were still alight; she still saw her vision.

Almost on tiptoe, Jane went on her way. She found that she was treading softly till the street curved and she knew she was out of Mrs Cannon's sight. She wished she knew what lay behind it all . . . A sudden thought occurred to her: 'tin breeches'! She looked down at her own legs, and laughed. Maybe the aged eyes, in poor light, had seen the lamé suit and mistaken her for the Battle Maid. Oh, well. At least she'd seemed pleased about it. She must be careful not to disillusion her, if they met again.

Jane entered the Grange gate, and turned right past the lodge cottage towards the Long Walk.

Everything was very quiet under the rising moon, and the motionless heat made the air heavy with the odour of flowers. She was aware of the briar-rose that spiralled up a nymph's pedestal, of the night-scented stock that bordered the Walk, of the lavender flanking the limestone bench.

The limestone bench . . . Somebody was sitting on it. Somebody robed and hooded in black.

All of Jane's senses came doubly alive. The lavender-scent was overwhelming, the moonlight dazzled, the growing things seemed to whisper in the soil. She stood stock-still for an instant, and then found herself drawn forward by the same compulsion that had forced her to the altar last night.

She knew fear, but under the fear there was a burning anger; part of her mind noted it, and wondered. She moved inexorably towards the dark figure and stood challengingly before it.

Her voice (*her* voice?) spoke out, trembling with hatred and disgust: 'Father Gadd!'

67

The hooded figure looked up, revealing the gaunt face. It reflected her own hatred – and it *was* Father Gadd.

Vertigo gripped Jane, and she thought she screamed. Father Gadd? *Who* was Father Gadd? What . . .

The figure was no longer there. The bench was empty.

She stumbled a pace backwards, falling to the grass. She did not faint, but sat gasping on her haunches, refusing to be defeated. She was numb, but at least now she knew what she faced.

The Dream.

Every detail of it had burst through into her consciousness, after its unreachable years below the threshold. She could see the chapel, see herself-not-herself spreadeagled naked on the stone altar, see the remorseless Gadd bending over her with the desecrated Host in his fingers, see the frightened but fascinated figure of her young husband – no, Katherine's husband – hovering beside him . . . *Hal, save me!* her mind cried out, but Hal was as helpless as she . . . *Suproc tse coh* . . . The stench of asafoetida in the black candles, blending with the musk and jasmine that anointed Katherine . . .

Jane cringed, clasping her loins in sympathetic protest. Sympathetic? No, more than that – an overlapping, a merging, a resonance of identity . . .

Tse assim . . .

Jane stood up. She felt shattered, but was amazed to realise that the anger had almost swept aside the fear.

She could not see the shape of it all yet; but somewhere inside herself, she knew what she had to do.

CHAPTER VII

During the rest of her walk to the chapel, Jane regained control of herself. The shock had been great, but it had also brought release. Only now did she realise what a burden her failure to reach the Dream had become, over the years. She had always been aware that it troubled her, but the apparent impossibility of solving the problem had made her, defensively, undervalue the strain it created. Now she could admit how deep her frustration had been, because at last it had been swept away.

She asked herself if she was also undervaluing the implications of the Dream, now that it had broken through into consciousness; if, in the wave of relief she felt with the collapsing of the dam, she was underestimating the threat which the released flood posed to her psychic landscape. Wasn't it significant that she had thought of the blockage as a 'dam'? A dam was not a mere obstruction; it had a protective purpose. Downstream of its bastion, fields and villages and towns could flourish secure . . . As the flood gathered momentum, what would be wrecked, what swept away, what buried under malodorous silt?

But no, it wasn't like that. She *knew* it wasn't like that . . . Jane Blair, you're leaning over backwards to be analytical, straining at metaphors because your brain's afraid to trust your gut. Cool it, brain; listen to what gut has to say.

Gut says: the dam *had* a purpose, but it's over. Here at Orley, it has become due for demolition.

Why?

She still had the sense of unrevealed purpose that had come to her in the wake of her experience by the bench; but she felt no frustration or impatience. The curtain had gone up, and the theme of the drama would unfold at its own pace.

Meanwhile, just how much did she know of the content of the Dream?

It all took place in the chapel – it always had, before she had ever seen Orley Grange. She was familiar with the deep stone altar, the narrow many-coloured windows between the timbers, the brooding angel in the roof . . . She considered the possibility that she had projected the reality of the chapel on to the memory of her Dream, but she dismissed it at once. Her unexplained revulsion when she first entered the chapel had been *prompted by* recognition . . . A Black Mass had been celebrated in that chapel, and she, Jane Blair, had somehow witnessed it across the centuries. How many centuries, she could not tell; the naked girl, and the two timelessly-robed men, gave no clue . . . But she knew their names, beyond all doubt. There was Father Gadd (again that surge of anger and hate), the evil celebrant. There was Katherine, terrified and sickened by the rite, but somehow captive – the thought, 'of her own love', came to Jane, but she could not yet unravel it. There was Hal – Sir Henry – immature, mesmerised; captive too, but in a different way . . . The two young ones were Montgris, lord and lady of this manor; but when?

And why did she know their names with such an intimate, personally-experienced certainty?

That question she *could* answer. It was through her resonance with Katherine, the almost vertiginous merging and unmerging with her that Jane had experienced every time she had dreamed the Dream. When she and Katherine merged, she thought of them all by name – and she remembered it afterwards. As simple as that. (Simple? My God!)

She probed for more details, but they would not come . . . In the chapel itself, they might. So on to the chapel . . . Momentarily, the fear returned; would she be able to cope?

It made no difference. She had to go and find out.

70

Strange, she thought. We came here to investigate one ghost, and instead, we – or I – have found three others. No sign of the Battle Maid as yet. Where does she fit in, I wonder?

'That Sennheiser works a treat,' Ted said. 'Next pay-day, I'm going to get another and pair them up.'

'How can you be sure, just from the trace?' Jane asked. 'Don't tell me you can judge sound quality from a wavy line.'

'In theory, no.' Ted grinned and jerked his head towards Bruce, busy with cables at the other end of the chapel. 'Don't tell *him*,' he continued in a whisper, 'but I look at that trace, and get what *you* call a professional hunch.'

Jane laughed out loud, and the laugh did her good.

She helped for a while, securing cables and checking dial readings – the men had been less advanced with setting-up than she had expected, because a fault had developed in the paper-moving mechanism of the polygraph and it had taken them half an hour to correct it. She felt calm but excited, and as soon as Ted no longer needed her help, she wandered out into the gallery and browsed among the armour and weapons. It was an excellent and comprehensive collection, which had clearly been added to right up to the last baronet's time. The Lady Clara would have had a lot more dusting to moan about by then.

Jane liked all the armour, but she decided that gunpowder had taken all the fierce beauty out of weapons – out of personal ones anyway. There was a certain terrifying elegance about a modern anti-aircraft gun, and a Taurean dignity about a Crimean cannon; but only clumsiness in an arquebus, and only functional brutality in a revolver.

A sword was something quite different.

She fingered the blade of a mighty two-handed sword from the fourteenth century, and tried to imagine the blacksmith-muscled Montgris who must have wielded it . . . In *his* time, man faced man, and by and large the better man prevailed. Came gunpowder, and any sharp-eyed runt could fell a Hercules.

Romanticising, was she? Maybe. But if men had to fight, let it be face to face. A blade was a man's ally; a trigger was his hired assassin.

Her eye lighted on a beautifully simple weapon that hung by the chapel door. Its scabbard was of finely-chased damascene, glowing but unostentatious; the hilt a graceful ellipse, the guard a plain steel cross with the ends furled like fern-shoots. A gentleman's sword, as expensively modest as a well-cut suit. She grasped the hilt and slid the blade out of the scabbard; long, slender, bright.

She thrust and parried with it once or twice, and carried it into the chapel, savouring its beauty.

'Don't kill the pianist, he's doing his best,' Ted joked, and she smiled, feinting towards him as he cowered in mock fear. But the joking was on the surface; the pleasant triviality of friendship. Something about the sword in her hand pleased her, gave her an inner satisfaction. She went on carrying it.

'That's rather nice, that one,' Bruce said, coming down the chapel towards her. His almost prim remark was, she knew, a kind of peace overture. She smiled at him, trying to make the smile sexless and sisterly, and flicked a salute at him with her blade.

'Yes, it is, isn't it?'

It was so slim and clean, and yet so masculine, she wanted to dance with it, to pirouette through the chapel while it flashed and weaved around her. She must control herself. She rested the tip on the floor, reluctantly.

'All set,' Ted said. 'Shall we begin?'

He placed the three chairs, and Bruce sat down while Ted started the polygraph and went to the light switches. Jane remained standing by the wall, and Bruce threw an anxious glance in her direction, but she just nodded reassuringly.

Ted put out the lights and sat down.

The multicoloured moon flooded the altar; the rest of the

72

chapel vanished into blackness, and then dimly re-emerged as their eyes adjusted. Jane studied it warily. The undertone of malevolence was still there; but this time she felt, not the helpless terror of one who faces the unknown, but the tension before zero hour, the constructive fear that surveys the battlefield for threats and openings.

But what battle? What threats, what openings – and what enemy? The shadow of things long dead?

The Dream might have broken through into consciousness; its meaning still had not. But Jane's silent reconnaissance went on in spite of herself, as though deep within her there was a battle headquarters which understood the significance of the incoming reports and laid its plans accordingly.

'Temperature's dropping,' Ted murmured. 'Want your woolly thing, Jane?'

'No thanks, Ted.'

'I can't feel it yet,' Bruce said.

'It seems to be localised. At the altar.'

'Windows?'

'No, they're all sealed. I checked. It's not a draught.'

All was still for perhaps a minute. Then Ted whispered; 'The altar's nearly three Centigrade down, and still dropping. But No. 2 sensor's moving *up* . . . I don't get it.'

'Which one's No. 2?' Bruce asked.

'The one by the triangle,' Jane told him.

'Triangle? What triangle?'

'You know. Left of the altar. The one marked on the floor.'

'There's no triangle, Jane.'

'Of course there is. Look . . .' She walked up the chapel and pointed her sword at a spot on the stone floor, a few feet to the left of the altar. 'Right there.'

She stepped on to the spot she had been pointing at, and turned.

Where she stood, the moonlight bathed her, clear and uncoloured from a high plain window. Ted and Bruce

73

gazed at her, transfixed; silver-slim, long-haired, the sword glinting in her left hand.

'Good God,' Ted breathed. 'The Battle Maid . . . Bruce, Jane *is* the Battle Maid!'

'You're crazy!' Bruce's voice sounded a little wild in the stillness. 'It's a weird bloody coincidence, that outfit – but for Christ's sake, don't get carried away!' He called, urgently: 'Jane!'

But Jane neither heard nor saw them. She saw, and heard, the Dream.

CHAPTER VIII

Jane knew a long moment of detachment when not only the scene before her, but even her emotional response to it, stood still. During that suspension, which seemed outside any measurement of time, she examined what she saw with an undercurrent of excitement but without fear.

She knew well enough when the fear would come; it would be when she reached out the tendrils of her mind to link with Katherine's. She knew she could make that link, and knew, too, that she could withhold it till she was ready. The knowledge strengthened her, easing the anticipation of the fear. Though whether she could break the link, once made . . .

Katherine – the Lady Katherine Montgris – was the focus and centrepiece of the drama; deliberately, and by Father Gadd's design, it was around her beauty and her terror that the drama revolved. Beautiful she certainly was. Jane, detached from modesty as from time, saw that Katherine could have been her sister; not her twin (a year or two younger, perhaps) but startlingly akin. Jane studied her as she lay face-upwards on the altar, knees folded and feet hanging loose over its front edge, thighs wide open to the coming desecration; hands clasping the chalice where it stood upright on her flesh midway between breasts and navel. Although the scene seemed frozen, Jane thought she could see the chalice trembling.

Many-coloured moonlight moulded the pale naked body, and the glow from the candles (black, yellow-flamed) suffused its shadows. The hair, fanned out over the stone, was as long as Jane's, but chestnut-coloured and thicker; but from the planes of the tense face to the pendant toes she *could* have been her sister. Shoulders a little narrower, perhaps, and pelvis a little wider; the same small hands clasped above the same waist; nipples more prominent (though what strange things might terror do to those responsive buds?) but rising out of familiar breasts . . . And the loins, the wedge of curling hair, the secret cleft – *my God, I see my own* . . .

The instant of intimate resonance shocked time into motion; gripped by vertigo, Jane almost merged with the supine body. She dragged herself back with an effort, gasping, and time froze again. She was not ready for that, yet.

Father Gadd; look at Father Gadd; look away from Katherine.

If Katherine was the focus of anguish, Gadd was the focus of evil. He towered before her, a foot from her bent knees; his raised arms let the dark robe slide back, revealing his skeletal forearms and his cruel hands. Of the face, little could be seen within the hood; only the aquiline nose, the thin lips motionless in the middle of some blasphemous phrase, the shadowed caverns of the eyes.

The mental curtain lifted a little further, and Jane knew suddenly that the man she looked on was an unfrocked priest; the title of Father long forfeit, but the inalienable power retained, perverted to terrible ends . . .

Long? How long? *When* were the things she looked upon?

The scene wavered briefly, then steadied, as real and overpowering as before. But as though the very thought of time had conjured time up, Jane knew that its suspension was coming to an end. Soon she would be caught up in the drama itself . . .

She glanced down at the triangle in which she stood, clearly marked on the chapel floor, and knew somehow that it gave her a measure of protection; that it was part of Gadd's plan of which she could take advantage. Reassured, she turned her attention to the third figure in the chapel.

Young Sir Henry was shrouded in black like Father Gadd, and stood a pace behind him and to one side; but although the robes were indistinguishable, in some way there was no mistaking the difference. Hal was as frightened as Gadd was exulting, as hypnotised as Gadd was commanding, as trapped as Gadd was wickedly free . . . As trapped as Katherine . . .

With the new thought of Katherine, the timeless moment of detachment broke. Jane almost screamed as the maelstrom of feeling engulfed her; she gagged on the unborn scream, fighting to hold on to consciousness – for without consciousness she would fail the challenge.

Physical and spiritual terror; a vast, contemptuous pride; the corrosive miasma of sacrilege – all were there, enveloping her. But pervading and overwhelming them all, the almost tangible pressure of psychic evil – of the whole ancient power of the pit of Hell, conjured and released by a black Adept who knew what he did and mocked the consequences.

The sword in Jane's hand seemed a talisman, fending off the evil. She gripped it harder.

As she regained control of herself, the first thing that hit her senses was the smell.

Strangely, because of the vividness of what she saw, she had not noticed till now that she heard and smelt nothing. But now, with the rebirth of time and movement, although she was still deaf, the obscene stench of asafoetida burst upon her nostrils; she knew it was blended into the wax of the tall black candles. There were other scents, too. A touch of frankincense, in ironic counterpoint to the blasphemy of the asafoetida. Even the night perfume of the garden (*the lavender is fair, this year*) wafting in through some open window. The smell of the sweat of anguish which bathed Katherine's moonlit skin.

But still, emphasising the horror, that hissing wordless silence. Gadd was mouthing his ritual, Katherine was visibly panting with fear; but Jane could hear none of it.

The silence was like a signal – the next stage of the challenge, drawing Jane on. She knew – the silence told her – what she had to do.

Fixing her eyes on the supine Katherine, she reached out for the girl's mind.

There was an instant of sliding, of multicoloured disorientation; then her vision cleared, and Jane and Katherine were one. She braced herself as the observed terror became a shared terror; cringed from the cold of the altar-stone against her back; felt the trickle of spilled wine as the chalice shook; gazed beseechingly up at the angel in the roof, mute in its oaken indifference.

The silence remained, but it was peopled with Katherine's thoughts. *Suproc tse coh*, the phrase repeated itself on the edge of awareness, *suproc tse coh*, as though Katherine longed to be rid of it, *suproc tse coh*, but was obsessed by her revulsion, *suproc tse coh* . . . Gadd's voice as remembered by Katherine's ears, resonant yet grating: *suproc tse coh* . . . Infected by Katherine's obsession, Jane fought to understand . . . then in a flash, dredged up perhaps from Katherine's own understanding, came the meaning: the *hoc est corpus*, 'this is the body', of the Latin Mass, reversed and desecrated . . .

But there was fight in Katherine, too. As Jane became more attuned to her confused stream of thought, she found she could grasp, at the same time, the girl's awareness of Gadd's purpose and her almost hopeless, but desperately stubborn inner cry for help.

Ave Maria, gratia plena, Dominus tecum, benedicta tu in mulieribus . . . *Holy Mother of God, blessed helper of women, save us* . . .

But Gadd was summoning Marbas . . .

Or if I am damned beyond redemption, save Hal, Holy Mother, save him, he is but weak, not wicked, Gadd has enthralled him . . .

Marbas . . .

Mary, Queen of Heaven, Thou knowest of love and sacrifice . . .

Marbas, a Prince of the Infernal Legions, empowered to inflict or cure diseases . . .

Ave Maria, gratia plena . . .

Summoning Marbas to the Triangle . . .

Thou knowest of love, Thou knowest I love him beyond my life – Hal, my beloved, my heart . . .

To save Basil . . . Basil? . . .

I am damned, I have submitted to this dreadful thing, I have suffered the Body of Thy Son to be defiled by the instrument of mine own body . . .

Who is Basil? . . .

But Thou, Holy Mother, Thou knowest I submitted only through love, to stand beside my husband even in the fires of Hell . . .

I see a sick boy . . .

Mother of Love, Queen of Heaven, Thou knowest these things – be my sin as foul as night, my love is pure, my love for Hal – this is pure if nought else . . .

Gadd is desecrating the Mass in honour of Marbas, to summon him into the Triangle . . .

Save Hal, Holy Mother, he is enthralled, he knoweth not – if it must be, let my soul be the price of his . . . CHRIST IN HEAVEN, NOW IT COMETH . . .

As Gadd loomed over the altar with the dish of musk and jasmine oil in his hands, Jane's identification with Katherine became complete. She was imprisoned in Katherine's body, and Gadd's fingers were inescapable, anointing the gate of her vagina with a cruel and lingering gentleness. Prepared by the awful familiarity of the Dream, and with no control over the body she shared, Jane was paralysed by the inevitability of what was happening. She knew, too, that worse was to come; knew that as Gadd moved away momentarily from between Katherine's knees, it was to fetch the Host.

Suproc tse coh . . .

The captive Jane would have panicked, fought to escape, but a sudden loyalty held her. She could not, at this most dreadful moment, abandon her sister, her other self . . . She must stay, must give her the strength of two . . .

Heaven grew dark, and the anointed path was helpless against the sacrilege. Gadd's fingers took the wafer right to the mouth of her . . . their . . . womb.

Avemariagratiaplena . . .

Their head turned sideways on the stone, watching Gadd as he carried Host and chalice to face the Triangle. He held them up with an exultant flourish, and Jane heard his call echoed in Katherine's mind.

'Marbas, Prince of Plagues, by this sacrifice of the defiled Body and Blood of thine Enemy, I summon thee to the Triangle, to do my bidding!'

Katherine's inner voice rose to a scream. *Holy Mother of God, prevent him! Prevent him! Send* Thy *messenger!*

Then Jane lost her hold.

She knew an instant of blinding light, of dimensionless being, and at once she was in the Triangle.

She knew that they saw her. She would remember that moment for the rest of her life: the stunned anger in Father Gadd's face, the bewilderment in Hal's, and the incredulous dawning of hope in Katherine's.

And still with part of herself, through Katherine's eyes, she saw herself as they saw her; the silver-clad Battle Maid, with the sword in her left hand.

Time stood still, and then disintegrated, together with the chapel and everyone in it.

CHAPTER IX

Someone was grasping the wrist of her sword-hand as she drifted back to consciousness. Instinctively, she pulled her arm away.

'Take it easy, now,' a man's voice said, gently professional. Jane opened her eyes and looked up into Dr Stoneleigh's. From the other side of the bed, Bruce murmured 'Thank Christ!'

'Hospital?' Jane asked, puzzled.

'Yes. Orley Cottage Hospital. But you're all right. There's nothing to worry about.'

She moved to sit up, but Dr Stoneleigh eased her back on to the pillow. 'I'm not worried,' she told him. 'I feel okay. Just surprised. I don't remember getting here.'

'We called an ambulance,' Bruce said, his words coming in a rush of relieved tension. 'You were out cold. Your heart seemed to have stopped. God, I was scared! We thought you . . .'

'That'll do,' the doctor said sharply, frowning across at him; Bruce bit his lip, and was silent. Dr Stoneleigh smiled at Jane and went on: 'It did *not* stop, you know. This really isn't the time to discuss symptoms – but since it's been mentioned, let me reassure you. I was there within ten minutes, and your pulse was faint and slow and your breathing shallow, but both perfectly regular. I've seen the same effect in trance mediums, and they come to no harm . . . Their body temperature drops, too, and so did yours. And now they're all three normal. What *you* could do with is a cup of tea.' He went to the door and called: 'Nurse Monaghan!'

Jane took advantage of his brief withdrawal to sit up, waving aside Bruce's nervous attempt to stop her. 'Don't *fuss*, I really am all right . . . What happened, exactly? . . . No, doctor, please . . . I want to know.'

Bruce looked questioningly at Dr Stoneleigh, who hesitated, then nodded. Bruce said: 'You went over to show us where you said there was a triangle on the floor . . .'

'I remember that, yes.'

'There wasn't one, of course, but you insisted there was. First you pointed at the place, with your sword, then you stood on it. And then you didn't seem to see or hear us any more – you just stared at the altar. We spoke to you but you went on staring – oh, ten or fifteen seconds, maybe . . . Then you just closed your eyes, sort of shuddered, and *flopped*. Ted caught you, or you'd have gone straight to the floor. That was when I tried your pulse, and couldn't find it . . .'

'I must teach you how,' Dr Stoneleigh put in. 'Amateurs often do miss it, if it's at all faint.'

'Yes, well . . . So I phoned the hospital while Ted wrapped you up warm and all that. We kept trying to wake you . . .'

'Where's Ted now?'

'In Reception. Nurse wouldn't let us crowd the place, so we've been watching you half an hour each.'

Jane was touched, and smiled at him apologetically. 'How long, for God's sake?'

He looked at his watch. 'Three and a half, four hours.'

'Oh, Bruce, I *am* sorry . . . Do go and fetch Ted. Tell him I'm fine.'

Bruce hurried out. Jane suddenly and inexplicably shy with the tall young doctor, commented to break the silence: 'A private ward, no less.'

He scratched his cheek, thoughtfully. 'It seemed advisable, in the circumstances.'

She pondered that for a moment, and was about to ask him to explain, when Bruce came back with Ted, who walked straight over and took her hand in both of his. 'Welcome back, love. Sure you're okay?'

'Fine, thanks, Ted. I'm sorry to have kept you all up.'

'We're nocturnal animals at the moment anyway, remember?'

'For watching your instruments. Not for nursemaiding me.'

'Makes a change,' he grinned. 'Anyway, the instruments are looking after themselves right now. Turning over nicely. If anything else happens, they'll record it.'

'Anything else,' Jane said, without a question mark.

'Well, it *would* be a bit of an anti-climax.'

She sensed that Bruce would have liked to shut him up; and suddenly Dr Stoneleigh's remark about 'in the circumstances' made sense.

She asked deliberately: 'After those first few minutes – was I delirious?'

Dr Stoneleigh said 'No' and Bruce said 'Yes', simultaneously. Ted just shrugged, smiling as though it didn't matter.

'Are you being the tactful physician, Dr Stoneleigh?' she challenged him.

He replied 'Anything but,' and stood for a moment scratching his cheek again. Then he pulled up a chair and sat down, announcing 'The name is Keith' as though to make it clear that the discussion now transcended medicine. 'Bruce and I aren't contradicting each other, really . . . Yes, you were talking while you were unconscious – clearly and coherently, even though the content might have surprised most people. As Bruce sees it, that was delirium. As I see it, it was *not* delirium in any ordinary sense. It was your recapitulation of a trance experience. And as I said – when I first examined you, in the chapel, your physical symptoms were exactly those of a medium in deep trance . . . Which is why I'm glad these two did *not* succeed in waking you up. Best of intentions, I know – don't get me wrong – but trance *is* a special state, and you can shock a medium severely if you try to force her out of it.' He smiled placatingly at Bruce and Ted; 'You weren't to know that. What you tried to do would have been sensible first aid – in ninety-nine per cent of cases. Quite frankly, most doctors or nurses would have done the same. I just happen to have had the specialised experience which enables me to recognise deep trance when I see it.'

At this point Nurse Monaghan came in, not with the single cup of tea the doctor had ordered, but with a tray of pots, cups, and biscuits so large that it only just cleared the doorway. Jane did not know if Keith would want to continue the discussion while she was there, so she waited till the tea was served and the nurse gone before she asked: 'What specialised experience?'

'I've worked a lot with spiritualists, and witches, and psychic healers, and so on.'

'I'd have thought they were anathema to you,' Bruce said.

Keith smiled. 'Only the ones to whom *I'm* anathema, and they're usually the phoneys. Most of the real ones are glad to cooperate with open-minded doctors. You'd be surprised how much we can complement each other.'

'So you think there are some "real" ones?'

'Considering what you're up to at Orley – don't *you?*'

'It's hardly the same thing. We're trying to track down objective phenomena – I mean, alleged phenomena, to see if they *are* objective. Witches, mediums – all that's *subjective*.'

'Rather an arbitrary distinction. I've seen their "subjective" activities produce some very objective results.'

'You'd have to convince me the causation was watertight, case by case . . .'

And then, of course, they were at it, hammer and tongs. Jane closed her eyes and rested her head back on the pillow. Bruce, released from his immediate anxiety about her, was back with his obsession . . . She was longing to ask the one important question: how much had she talked? – how much

84

of what she had lived through had she passed on in her 'delirium'? But that question, once put, would plunge her directly into the middle of the argument; and although she was physically well enough, she was too emotionally drained to face the inevitable buffeting, too overwhelmed with her experience to want to bandy it around, until she had absorbed and considered it herself. (So recent, so real, so vivid; her loins cringed involuntarily, her sword-hand clenched, as her memory flicked from altar to Triangle and veered away again.)

One other memory stayed with her, too – her last from the waking world before the Dream took her, and all the sharper for that: Ted's cry, 'Good God – the Battle Maid! Jane *is* the Battle Maid!'

Could it be true? And yet if it couldn't – weren't the implications just as mind-boggling? Either way . . .

Herself the Battle Maid, haunting the centuries, touching a procession of lives with the reverberations of her battle with Gadd . . . or Katherine's battle? *My sister, my self?*

Me, Jane Blair, B.A., Oxon.?

Or herself not the Battle Maid, yet drawn by a train of bizarre coincidences and mysterious compulsions to act her part, put on her armour (with an Oxford Street label!), grasp her sword, espouse her cause – and all so utterly unconsciously that no hint of it surfaced, till she stood face to face with the Battle Maid's enemy?

Even less believable.

She needed time to think – but not now.

Jane opened her eyes and picked up her cooling tea.

'But all that stuff about a Black Mass,' she realised Bruce was saying, 'and her giving names – Katherine, and Hal, and Father Gadd, and Basil . . .'

'She seemed puzzled by Basil,' Ted put in.

'. . . are you suggesting *that* was anything more than purely subjective?'

'The Grange library might substantiate the names,' Keith said.

'But she's been browsing in the library already. Does even *she* know what she's picked up there?'

Jane interrupted, raising her voice: 'Boys, do you mind? I think I'd like to sleep.'

It wasn't true, but she had had enough of them. Allies or sceptics, she had had enough of them all.

Keith, promptly the doctor again, hustled them all out; Nurse Monaghan came in and smoothed her bed, cleared away the cups, and dimmed the light. Jane answered the kindly young Irishwoman's goodnight with genuine warmth. It was nice to look on at least one face that was in no way involved.

Sleep was slow to come, but when it did, it was dreamless.

She woke about 5.0 a.m., restless with regained energy, unable to stay in bed. There was no sign of nurse or doctor, so she got up quietly, in case either of them should try to stop her. Nurse Monaghan (presumably) had dressed her in a hospital nightdress, but her clothes hung in the cupboard.

She felt a little incongruous, dressing up in gunmetal lamé – the Battle Maid's armour, as it would now always be for her – in the bright still dawn. Not exactly warm, either; but fortunately the boys had thought to bring her stand-by case from the Grange with her, so she had a cardigan, make-up, and cigarettes. The combination of lamé and cardigan seemed even more incongruous, but a new face and a cigarette improved her morale.

Nurse Monaghan looked in as she was giving her hair an extra brush. 'Good morning . . . Discharging yourself, then, are you? Oh dear. Well, I suppose there's no harm, but it's the doctor must say so.'

'Good morning, nurse. I feel fine now, honestly.'

'You look it, sure – though whether you're dressed for a ball or a round of golf I'd be hard put to it to say. May I lend you a coat, perhaps?'

'Oh, bless you! Have you got one to spare?'

'I think so. And we're much of a size.'

So when Keith came to check on her as she drank a cup of coffee in Nurse Monaghan's kitchen, she was wearing a powder blue tie-belted coat that was probably Nurse Monaghan's best and feeling much readier to face him and the world. Anne (as she had already become) had taken her pulse and temperature, so Keith had little to do but look at her.

'We don't usually discharge patients at cock-crow, but I've no excuse for keeping you . . . Can I run you back to the Green Man?'

'How far is it? I've no idea where this hospital is. Afraid I hadn't spotted it during my look-around.'

'Not surprised. We're a couple of miles from the village and round the hill. Finished your coffee?'

'Well, thanks, then . . . And you can bring back Anne's coat with you.'

'Och, there's no hurry,' Anne insisted. 'Keep it as long as you like, I've little use for it this weather. But then *I* don't run around dressed in three-quarters of nothing at all, with the sun hardly up.'

'Nor do I, usually . . .'

On the way back to the village, they passed the entrance to the Grange, and Jane asked Keith on an impulse: 'Can we look in the chapel? Have you time?'

Keith stopped the car. 'Do you think it's wise?'

'Oh, nothing'll happen this morning.'

'You know that?'

'Yes, but don't ask me how.'

'No, I believe you . . . But that wasn't what I meant. I meant, is it wise to plunge straight into a clash with Bruce? He's dead against your going back there at all . . . He was on about it for quite a while after we left you to sleep.'

'He has been, ever since he realised the place affected me.' She smiled wryly. 'I disturb the objectivity of the experiment.'

'So I gathered – though it depends on your definition of "objectivity".'

'Anyway, not to worry – they'll have packed up and gone to breakfast by now.'

'In that case . . .' He drove up to the Grange front door, which was locked and bolted; but Jane already knew of a side entrance where the key was kept under a stone, as casually as though the place were a cottage.

'Not like Charley Unsworth,' Keith remarked as she let them in. 'I'd have thought he'd be much too security-conscious.'

'He's probably always done it at home, and has the common blind faith that no burglar would think of it.'

They joked about it as they made their way to the chapel, and Jane knew she was fending off nervousness, for all the assurance she had expressed. But when they reached it, she found she had been right; the psychic charge of the place had stilled to the faintest undercurrent, offering memory but no menace.

Keith watched her curiously as she wandered around the silent chapel like a dog sniffing the air. She seemed hesitant to step into the invisible 'triangle', but she did so, drawing her breath, and letting it out slowly when nothing happened. Then she walked to the altar.

She stood in front of it for a moment, palms spread an inch or two above the stone before she lowered them on to it. She paused, as though listening, and stood up.

'Hold Anne's coat, will you? I don't want to get it dusty.' She slipped the coat off and handed it to him.

'Careful,' he warned her. 'Why not leave well alone for now?'

'I have to see.'

She lay back on the altar, feet dangling, hands clasped at her midriff. She stayed there for almost a minute, her eyes open, and then sat up with a faint sigh.

'Well?' he asked her.

'Through a glass·darkly.'

'Still there, though?'

'Yes. Oh, yes. We're still there.'

He echoed the 'we', thoughtfully, and she shook her head. 'Sorry, I'm not trying to be mysterious. This . . . merging of me and Katherine is . . . central to it. Didn't you get that from my "delirium"?'

'Don't call it that.'

'I don't know what else to call it. I can't say "involuntary vocal recapitulation of deep trance experience" every time, can I? Can't you accept "delirium" as shorthand?'

'All right – between you and me, but not in front of Bruce, especially . . . But to answer your question. Yes, I did get that feeling. In fact, half the time it wasn't clear whether it was you or Katherine talking.'

'How clear a picture *did* I give, in general?'

Keith smiled. 'Through a glass, darkly. Copious, but confusing . . . would you care to fill me out – or would it distress you?'

Jane stood up from the altar and went to the left of it. 'No, not at all. In daylight it's still clear but powerless, so to speak. Emotionally switched off . . . There was a triangle marked on the floor, here . . .'

'The Triangle of Evocation – yes, there would be.'

'That was the only thing I actually *saw* before it all started. I pointed it out to the boys, with my sword . . .' She frowned suddenly. 'My sword!'

She ran down the chapel to the door, and out into the corridor, reappearing at once looking relieved. 'It's all right. They put it back on the wall, in its scabbard.'

'You looked worried for a moment.'

'I was. That sword is the Battle Maid's. And it's *mine*. It's important.'

'Interesting . . . On the altar, you are yourself and Katherine. In the Triangle, you are yourself and the Battle Maid.'

'Yes.'

'Does that suggest anything to you?'

'Oh, yes. That when the Battle Maid steps out of the Triangle, sword in hand, Father Gadd will be in trouble.'

There was a glint in her eyes which made Keith hold back the question he had been going to ask.

'Tell me the rest of it,' he said instead.

They walked in on Bruce and Ted at breakfast, ordering breakfast for themselves at the kitchen on the way in. She was reminded again of how wrong she had been about Ted's sensitivity; he showed, subtly though without calculation, that he was concerned for her as a person, whereas Bruce was concerned about her as a problem. Not quite fair; at moments of crisis, Bruce's concern *had* been genuinely personal – but he was much more quickly convinced than Ted that the crisis was over.

Bruce's 'All fit now, love?' was friendly good manners, no more. It was Ted's worried eyes that kept watching her, surreptitiously, as they talked. She kept the talk light and cheerful till the worry seemed to have abated.

The crunch had to come, of course – which was why she had asked Keith to stay with her.

Bruce was building up for the confrontation, too; of that she was certain. She had a feeling that he was waiting to see if Keith would go; but when Keith's breakfast arrived with her own, and it became clear he intended to stay for at least another half hour, Bruce launched his attack without even apologising for changing the subject.

'Well, one thing's clear,' he said. 'No more chapel for Jane.'

She had been ready to be sweetly reasonable, but his dogmatic declaration needled her. 'Clear to whom?' she asked.

'Clear to all of us, I hope. If we carry on like this, the experiment's a farce.'

'So what I experienced was a farce, was it?'

'Not your experience – the experiment. God knows *what* your experience was, because nobody does, not even you really. One thing it wasn't, and that's scientific experiment, which is what we're here for. You're just a bull in a china shop.'

'Don't you mean a cow in a laboratory?' – icily.

'If you like to put it that way, yes. I'm sorry, love, but you are. Every time you come into that place, any hope of a methodical investigation flies out of the window.'

She knew that she was about to lose her temper, and that she would regret it; but Ted interrupted her unexpectedly, with the calm question 'Methodical investigation of what, Bruce?'

'Of the alleged psychic phenomena at Orley Grange.'

'Including the Battle Maid – the most recurrent phenomenon of all?'

'Well, yes, but . . .'

'And what if Jane *is* the Battle Maid? Because I think she is.'

'Oh, for Christ's sake . . .'

'And that's a phenomenon really worth investigating. Right in our lap. So it doesn't seem very scientific to run away from it.'

'But what do you *mean*, Jane's the Battle Maid? Just because she happened to put on that silvery trouser suit, and pick up a sword off the wall . . .'

'*And* trigger off what she did – Bruce, it wasn't just subjective, and you know it. God, man, go and look at those traces. Temperature *up* where she saw the Triangle, *down* by the altar, pressure going wild, I'm not sure about humidity till I check the mean, but it was certainly up – all those variations at once, returning to normal when we carried her out of the chapel . . .'

'Ted, you can't give an analysis like that, off the cuff! You'll have to examine that roll properly . . .'

'Of course I will, but I'm not daft. And I *can* tell you off the cuff and before a detailed analysis, that some marked objective fluctuations coincided with what happened to Jane. That's only an interim report but I'd bet money on it.'

91

'Even if you're right, that's the hell of a long way from saying Jane's the Battle Maid – playing fast and loose with time and coincidence . . .'

'Ever read Dunne on Time?'

'Or Jung on Synchronicity?' Keith put in.

'Yes to both, and I couldn't make head or tail of either. Obscurantist nonsense.'

Jane said: 'All I know is that I'm deeply involved in an experience – an *active* experience, a conflict – which is real to *me*. And apparently real to Ted's instruments too. So why won't you let us pursue it?'

'Hold on,' Bruce objected, 'you're jumping to conclusions. Even if Ted's right, his instruments didn't show a Black Mass, or people with names – they just showed that *something* was going on. That same something, whatever it was, could have triggered off your hallucinations – but their content could have been a fantasy rehash of subconsciously remembered facts. A few wiggles on Ted's traces don't prove you're the Battle Maid!'

'I never said they did,' Ted answered. 'For me, Jane being the Battle Maid is just a working hypothesis with so much pointing to it that it's got to be tested.'

'So much? A trouser suit and a sword off the wall . . .'

'And Jane herself. She wasn't wearing that thing when she visited Mrs Cannon. But Mrs Cannon's seen the Battle Maid three times – and one proper look at Jane knocked her for six.'

'Good God,' Jane said, 'I'd forgotten her. So that *was* why!'

'Once you start wanting to believe something,' Bruce said wearily, 'you'll soon find evidence to fit it.'

'And if you're determined *not* to believe something,' Jane countered, 'you'll find a hundred and one reasons for not looking at it.'

'You can say what you like, but there's one good reason for keeping you out of the chapel which you *can't* get round.'

'Oh?'

92

'It's too bloody dangerous for you, yourself. Do you want to land up in hospital after every session?'

Jane said: 'You're the doctor, Keith. *Is* it dangerous?'

'Medically? I doubt it. There was no actual need for you to be in hospital last night, as it turned out. Now that we know definitely it's a deep trance condition, you could just be carried to the camp bed in the corridor and kept warm till you came round of your own accord. Bruce and Ted could go on watching their instruments and keeping an eye on you. You're physically and emotionally strong enough, I've satisfied myself of that . . . And they could always call me if they were worried.'

'Well, then!' Jane cried, triumphantly.

'Wait a minute, I said it wasn't *medically* dangerous. Psychically, I just wouldn't know. Look, Jane – accepting your account as authentic for a moment, you've joined in a psychic battle. In fact, I'm sure you have anyway, whether or not the characters your stage is peopled with are histori- cally real – and I'll concede to Bruce that they *could* be projections. But either way, you're prepared to take on psychic forces that might be more than you can handle alone.'

It was Bruce's turn to be triumphant. 'Thank you, Keith! You see, Jane? Even on your own terms, I'm right – it's too bloody dangerous.'

'I didn't say that,' Keith corrected him. 'I said it might be too much for her *alone*. If she feels it's something she's got to go through with – a challenge she couldn't run away from even if she wanted . . .'

'It is, you know, Bruce.'

'Then she needs more expert help than I can give her, as a doctor – even as a doctor with some knowledge of the field.'

'What kind of help, for Christ's sake?' Bruce wanted to know.

Keith poured himself another cup of coffee, maddeningly unhurried.

'I told you I knew some witches,' he said.

93

CHAPTER X

Jane was glad to escape to the solitude of the library. She had been heartened to find that both Ted and Keith were on her side, but Bruce's continuing opposition was beginning to distress her. There was something obsessive about it, something at times almost hysterical, incompatible with the detachment upon which he insisted.

She was beginning to wonder if beneath Bruce's determinedly scientific exterior there did not lurk a superstitious primitive, which he suppressed with a vigour that verged on panic whenever it threatened to break out. Perhaps, deep inside himself, he was far more afraid of the Devil and his Legions than she was . . . She was afraid, yes, but with a warrior's fear that sharpened her awareness, her readiness for battle. Perhaps Bruce's fear was more atavistic, more blind, only kept in check by forcing it below the threshold of consciousness, by erecting a barricade of scientific formulae and polygraph recorders. And when that barricade was threatened . . .

Perhaps it was Bruce, and not she, who should stay away from the chapel.

She had not thought of Bruce in that light before; but she knew intuitively, as she brooded over it, that she had come to a deeper understanding of him. It gave her no feeling of triumph or superiority; on the contrary, it made her afraid for him.

She had to meet the challenge, pick up the gauntlet which had been flung so unexpectedly at her feet; that much was indisputable, the starting point of all her calculations. Whether she was the Battle Maid herself, or her representative in the here and now . . . No, that wouldn't do; 'here and now' wasn't enough; in her Battle Maid role, she had broken through the fabric of time, seeing and being seen. Somehow, God knew how, a bridge had been built . . .

Her mind shied away from trying to understand it. Back to Bruce.

What if her battle was a danger to *him*? What if a side-effect of it were the sweeping away of Bruce's defensive barricade – leaving him helpless against the shock-waves of the forces which that battle unleashed?

And she could not discuss the danger with him. Even to hint at her analysis of him would make him more frantically defensive than ever, more actively hostile as his gut told him his barricade was threatened.

Bruce must go.

The thought came to her unbidden, and it shocked and saddened her. Shocked her because it anticipated reason, jumped a stage or two ahead of conscious logic. Saddened her because she knew, suddenly, that she *was* attracted to him; that her sexual coat-trailing had not been a mere tactical move to get her own way over the chapel. She had liked him and desired him, wanting him to respond to her body and emotions, to engage in mutual arousal . . . She still liked and desired him, but it was over, it was still-born. Bruce must go. For his own safety, and her own conscience; she could not take the responsibility of letting him be a casualty of the battle; and if he stayed, he would be.

Whether Ted went or stayed was irrelevant. She liked him and was warmed by his support, and if he went she would miss a friend; but his instruments, elegantly responsive as they were, had no more effect on the conflict itself than a war correspondent's camera on the success or failure of an infantry assault.

And it was no longer a question of satisfying the scientific curiosity of the Midland Psychical Research Society. It was the urgent question of destroying an agent of evil, and of

95

saving two souls – Katherine's and Hal's – one of whom had cried out to her.

Urgent? In a century long dead?

The challenge was real, yet inconceivable. Her mind veered away, again, from the paradox. Meet the challenge; understand it afterwards – if ever.

She wondered, casually as yet, what help Keith's witch friends would be. She knew Keith had gone to ring them, and that their names were Bridget and George Blake. Bridget would certainly come, he had said; she would be unable to resist such a bait, and as a freelance writer on folklore she could move as she pleased. George, it seemed, was an electronics engineer working on something hush-hush at the National Physical Laboratory, but his programme was flexible, and he would come if he could; husband and wife liked to work together.

'But why *should* they come?' Jane had asked.

'Because it's their kind of thing.'

'A folklore writer and an electronics engineer – and both witches. An odd combination.'

Keith had smiled. 'Not if you know the Blakes.'

Oh well – time enough to assess them when, and if, they turned up.

Meanwhile, she had come to the library to work; in particular to track down Sir Henry and Lady Katherine Montgris. She knew she *would* find them – and that Bruce would be unimpressed, alleging subliminal knowledge from her earlier library browsing.

It did not take long; the family tree had been traced very fully by some Victorian genealogist called Wilfred Mitchell, and his main, collateral, and related trees were all together in a big japanned tin box. Fully, but for one gap; the Orley parish records (Mr Mitchell noted in his meticulous copperplate) from 1578 to 1622 had been destroyed by fire during the Civil War.

But there, just before the gap, were Jane's couple.

Sir Henry Montgris, born 1549; Katherine Courtfield,

96

born 1554; married 11th June 1576. And Henry had a younger brother, Basil, born 1565!

Subliminal, eh?

Unfortunately, there the certainty stopped. For the 44 years of missing parish records, the tree was full of dotted lines and question marks. Some names were there – in particular the successors to the title, and their ladies – but no birth or death dates, and some relationships were uncertain. Hal and Katherine must have been dead by 1622 (when he would have been 73 and she 68) because there was no parish record of their deaths thereafter – and a Sir Basil had been Lord of the Manor in between; and in 1623 the holder was already Sir Christopher, husband to the diarist Lady Clara. But was Sir Basil the young brother of Hal (implying that Hal had died young and childless) or the son of Hal and Katherine, named after his uncle? There was no way of telling.

Jane frowned, disappointed. It had been important to her; she needed to know.

As she had seen Katherine and Hal in the Dream (she still called it that in her mind, through habit, though she knew it was no longer anything of the kind) the girl had been 23 or 24 – in other words, just married, at most by a year or two. Did she and Hal survive the psychic battle, raise a son, and live to their fifties or sixties – a reasonably ripe age in the sixteenth century? Or did they succumb, destroyed by Gadd's evil, leaving the Manor of Orley to the stripling brother? For though the battle with Gadd had been psychic, yet Jane knew it had been a battle to the death. In such a conflict, not even the body could survive psychic defeat.

The paradox again. Historically, the battle was over – lost or won four centuries ago. Katherine and Hal's bodies, young or old at death, were dust in the Montgris vault – the dates of their deaths unmarked or long obliterated. And yet for Jane (and with a desperate reality) the battle was now, and Katherine and Hal's survival depended on her winning it.

97

Time is a spiral . . .

Again Jane shied away.

Had Katherine, like Clara, kept a diary?

If she had, at least it would be in English, and not in lawyers' Latin; so it should have been correctly place by the anonymous chronological arranger.

1570 household accounts . . . 1571 . . . Ah – 1576, *Diary of Lady Katherine Montgris, neé Courtfield* – boxed and labelled in Wilfred Mitchell's handwriting, as she could now recognise. Jane opened the box eagerly.

The diary was frustratingly slim; eighteen months in all, and cryptic. Katherine had none of Clara's verbosity. Most of it was less a diary than a consecutive accumulation of notes and jottings.

Item, xii Capons.
Item, iv Geese, lesse fayre than formerly; Grayson sh. speake w. Harry Drover.
Item, v Hayres . . .

Interesting, but unhelpful. Jane skimmed the pages for something more personal.

Father Gadd . . .

The name seemed to jump out at her as she turned a fresh page. She glanced quickly at the date; 27 September 1576, three and a half months after Katherine's marriage.

I reprove myself therefor, that having the inestimable Blessing of the true Religion, for wh. may the Blessed Virgin be prais'd, when the whole Lande lyeth deepe in Heresie . . .

Dangerous words, in Elizabethan England. Katherine must have trusted her Diary's hiding place, or the illiteracy of her servants.

. . . that I finde it not in Myself to love Father Gadd, Bearer of that Blessing. He doeth alle exactly, but no Ardoure therein. On his meager Lippes, the Masse lacketh all Nobilitie in the Telling; as it were an Inventorie of householde Provender. Yet

98

believe I verily withal, there is a Fyre burneth in that Priest,
tho' deep bury'd; on wh. Fuel it feedeth I know not, only that it
toucheth not the Holy Duties for wh. we depend on him, and for
the Observance of wh. we doe maintain him. But when I try'd,
w. much Caution and Circumspection in my Wordes, to convey
these my Thoughtes unto Hal, he much perplex'd thereat,
holding the good Father in great Respecte, and this grieveth me,
in that Hal and I are as one in our Heartes and Bodies, and I
greatly content w. our Marriage; in this only am I alone. Yet is
this I think the Burden we Women beare, that whereas our
Men, in the Commonwealth of Husbande and Wyfe, do have
the Sinews and Puissance for both, and withal the Nicetie of
Logick (or so they persuade us), yet do we oft see farther, having
the Eyes for both, inward and outward withal, and the Dis-
cernment in those Straits wherein Logick faileth; yet must we
for the most Part confess it not openlie, lest our Men be amaz'd
and fear for their Authoritie.

And then, without a break, straight back into domes-
ticity:

The Supper this Night barely to be stomach'd. And Jenny
have I warn'd in round Termes, that if she mend not her Wayes,
she shall finde herself Cooke no longer . . .

Oh, Katherine! Oh, Bruce! . . . Jane, in the dark drama of
the chapel, had already come to terms with her resonance
with Katherine; but this fading script, so touchingly
human, illuminated it with unexpected vividness. So
Katherine too – devout Catholic and loving bride as she was
– had sensed the wrongness in Gadd; and Hal, dedicated like
Bruce to the 'Nicetie of Logick', had pinned his faith
on surface appearances and discounted her intuition. She
had assessed Father Gadd before the terrible revelation,
whenever that had come, whereas Jane had become aware
of Gadd and of the total evil simultaneously; but she had a
feeling that if she had known Gadd first as Katherine had
done, as a member of the household expected to play a
certain role (a secret one, of course, in those Reformation

99

days), she would have reacted to him in the same way as Katherine – with disappointment and unease ahead of the horror.

She hurried on with the Diary. There was little reference to Gadd in the months which followed; that revealing passage seemed to be exceptional. Perhaps, in the vagaries of the political climate, the maintaining of a private priest had become more dangerous, and written comments on the fact, even in a secret diary, correspondingly more unwise. Jane, the historian, tried to remember just how things stood in 1576 to 1577, but the details escaped her memory – and in any case, local conditions would have entered into the picture, and those would be harder to check.

But for all the brevity of Katherine's notes, she did emerge as a personality. Her love for Hal (though sometimes expressed with almost motherly exasperation) was obviously the lodestar of her life. Jane had the feeling that Katherine, the daughter of a squire herself, had accepted as natural her betrothal to a neighbouring squire of suitable age, and had looked forward to the domestic fulfilment which marriage would bring; but that she had been taken delightedly by surprise at the emotional fulfilment – indeed, overwhelmed by it.

Dazzled by love she might be, but not blinded or paralysed. On the contrary, she had obviously flung herself into her new role as mistress of Orley with enthusiasm and efficiency. The fate of Jenny the cook was typical; there could have been little improvement after the 27 September warning, on 9 October Katherine wrote:

> *Jenny back to her Father, with my plaine Wordes pursuing her, and she muttering, with many blacke Lookes. Mary Yorke appoint'd in her Steade, who shd. doe better, she being bound to me by Gratitude for her Elevation, and eager therefor to hearken to my Instruction. And I taking Care this Daye to shew dutifull Respecte and Love to my Lady Helen, lest she remember that Jenny was her Creature, and take Offense at my Rashness.*

Sack the cook that mother-in-law trained, then be extra sweet to mother-in-law to sugar the pill. A tricky time for a twenty-two-year-old bride. But she seemed to have dealt with the Lady Helen tactfully, for Jane got the impression the widow was only too glad to hand over the reins and to withdraw in lazy dignity to the Dower House.

Katherine had apparently even found herself *in loco parentis* to Basil, her eleven-year-old brother-in-law, whom she described succinctly as:

> *. . . Fruite of my Lady's Autumn, and she I think much astonish'd thereby; he a fine Lad, but with sufficient Spirit for a Dozen such, and liking not Restrainte.*

It became clear that Katherine developed a great affection for her handful of a brother-in-law, and that she and Hal worried together, both about his upbringing and about his health, which for all his boisterousness was not, it seemed, always robust . . . Another fact fell into place in Jane's mind; in her 'Dream', Gadd had been evoking Marbas – and Marbas, she had picked up from Katherine's mind, was a demon who could inflict or cure diseases . . . Had that been the bait Gadd had used to embroil the young couple in his evil magic – their desperation over a sick Basil?

There must have been more to it than that; Katherine, at least, could never have been enlisted as altar for a Black Mass, by a priest about whom she already had reservations, just to cure a child, however much loved. She would have done her practical best for a sick or dying Basil, and devoutly placed his soul and body in the hands of God. It would have taken more – infinitely more – to bring her to that degrading blasphemy; only one power would have been strong enough – her adoration of her husband.

Yes, of course! Katherine's agonised prayer, felt and shared on the altar-stone, flooded back into Jane's memory: *But Thou, Holy Mother, Thou knowest I submitted only through love, to stand beside my husband even in the fires of Hell . . . be my sin as foul as night, my love is pure . . .*

So that was how it was. First, her naive beloved drawn into black magic by his admiration for the insidiously persuasive Gadd; discovering too late, perhaps, that their 'priest' was an unfrocked impostor; believing himself thus cut off from Mother Church, allowing himself to be persuaded to accept as compensation the power that could be bought by the sacrifice of scruple . . . little by little at first, then deeper . . .

And Katherine discovering, somehow, what was going on; rushing without thought to her beloved's side, sacrificing herself to blasphemy rather than leave him alone . . .

Yes, that would have been Katherine. In the same circumstances, Jane knew suddenly, it would have been herself.

All guesswork, all extrapolation, yet it rang true. Jane pushed ahead with the Diary, hoping for confirmatory hints; but there were fewer and fewer pages left, and no suggestion . . .

Ah, wait a minute . . .

I find it strange of late, and scarce true to my Husband's Nature, that he shd. be closetted for such long Houres with Father Gadd. And this, lightly and as if it were of lyttle Importe, have I charged him withal; and Hal, more roughly than is his Custome with me, hath answer'd, that the good Father doe but hear his Confession. And I feigning a laughing Surprise, have asked are his Sinnes so black, that to unburden Himselfe of them shd. keepe him from my Bed in the Night, often for an Houre and more by the Telling of the Clocke? And he with no responding Smyle, but seeming put oute, hath answer'd that it is but his Christian Duty, yet asketh my Pardon if I feel Myselfe ill used by him. Thou hast never us'd me ill, Hal, I vouchsafe him, and for that Reason doe I feel thine Absence the more keenly, so that a Minute seemeth an Houre. Whereat he laugheth at last, and falleth to wooing me, and I making the barest Shew of gainsaying him.

A loving outcome to an uneasy little exchange of verbal parries; yet clearly Katherine's question had not been answered. So it must have been in progress already, Gadd's subversion of Hal, even his instruction of the by now captive younger man. The stage was being set for Katherine's awful discovery.

Page after page, and no further hint. Nothing but domestic preoccupations, until the very last entry, for 22 December 1577 – written in haste, and with violent pressure splaying out the quill pen on the downstrokes:

> *Holy Mother of God, helpe me – I feare for our verie Soules, if in Trewth they be not damn'd already!*

And with that desperate cry, abrupt and unheralded, Katherine Montgris' Diary came to an end.

It was only just noon when Jane left the Grange for the Green Man. Professionally, she could bury herself in intricate research for hours on end, and had often done so; she did not easily become surfeited with facts. But *this* research, so personally significant, so emotionally charged – this was something different, and she could only absorb so much of it at a time. Apart from anything else, as a historian she found it eerily unnerving to explore a fragment of the sixteenth century, never knowing if the next corner hid a psychic link, a direct personal involvement. Eager though she was, the undertaking drained her.

At the end of the Long Walk she had discovered a path among the rhododendrons, leading through the woods behind the houses in the village street, from which she could reach a little gate at the bottom of the Green Man garden. Coming that way today, her tension relaxed by the bee-humming sunshine and the absence of people, she was nevertheless glad to see Trevor Cox sipping a lager all by himself on the terrace. He waved to her, and she joined him. He offered to fetch her a drink, but she gestured him back to his seat with a smile, and filched the second can he had ready

103

beside him. She pulled the tag and drank it straight from the can, stretching happily.

'Not very elegant, on your select terrace,' she apologised, 'but I've just realised I'm thirsty.'

'Be my guest. I doubt if it'll lower the tone too much.'

'I like you, Trevor. You're just the same as Nurse Monaghan.'

Trevor laughed. 'I'm afraid I don't see the resemblance.'

'I mean you're uninvolved. I'm surrounded by people with attitudes . . . You've heard about last night?'

'Yes, when Bruce and Ted came in for breakfast. Two versions, both partisan, and conflicting.'

'You'll see what I mean, then. When I woke up in hospital, everyone was at me, with an axe to grind one way or the other. Even the ones on my side – Ted and your doctor friend, Keith.'

'That can be wearing.'

'Yes. Except Nurse Monaghan; all she did was smile at me and give me tea. All *you* do is smile at me and give me your lager. That's why you both do me good. Uninvolved.'

'Oh dear. Now I feel blackmailed into perpetual silence.'

Jane laughed. 'Don't take me too seriously . . . Come to think of it, you did give me some unscrupulous advice the night before last.'

'Which you followed, successfully.'

'How did you . . .? Oh well, yes, I suppose it was obvious.'

Trevor seemed to hesitate, then asked: 'Will you accuse me of getting too involved if I ask for *your* version of last night?'

'Of course not. Please, I *didn't* mean that. I like you being interested – it's just the axe-grinders who've got me down a little . . . You make an excellent father confessor.'

'I don't mind the confessor bit, but I'm not sure about the father. I doubt if I'm a dozen years older than you.'

She looked at him, and estimated: 'Thirty-nine?'

'Thirty-seven.'

104

'It must be being a Councillor gives you a mature air.'

'I'll resign tomorrow.'

'Eleven years, actually, so I withdraw the "father". And don't you dare resign, or Orley would never forgive me.'

'Want to bet?'

She was enjoying this nonsense, undemanding and mildly flirtatious, but she felt she owed it him to answer his question, so she became serious. 'Actually, I can tell you more than the boys could. I've been in the Grange library, getting to know Katherine better . . . All the names were right, by the way – Katherine, Henry, Father Gadd, Basil. In the 1570's. Bruce won't like that.'

'Bruce will ignore it,' Trevor contradicted her. 'He's already told me he believes you had the names stored up subliminally, from your first visit to the library.'

'I didn't, you know. *I* know what material I looked at, that time, and I've got a job-trained memory. I had those names in the chapel, from Katherine's mind.' She could hear the challenge in her own voice, and she glanced sideways at Trevor. 'Do you find that quite unacceptable?'

'You forget, Jane – *I* was the first to call you the Battle Maid.'

'But what did you *mean*? All you said was that she and I had a lot in common.'

'In a village like this,' he answered obliquely, 'we live with the past. In our own ways, each of us here interacts with the past. I wouldn't like to be dogmatic about just how far that interaction can go.'

She knew her voice was rising. 'But you'd seriously accept the idea of the sixteenth and twentieth centuries haunting *each other*?'

'Is "haunting" the word, really?'

'God knows! And you're dodging the question.'

'My question was – what's your version of last night? . . . Did you know your knuckles were going white?'

Disconcerted, she looked down at her clenched hands and saw he was right; she was getting tense again. She spread

105

her hands deliberately, took a deep breath, and laughed. 'Damn you, Trevor – don't be *too* detached!'

'Aren't confessors supposed to be?'

'Sorry . . . I'm hedging, aren't I?'

'You've every right. Honestly, you needn't tell me if you don't want to.'

'But I *do* want to. I want to very much.'

So she did, trying to start at the beginning – except that she was no longer clear where or when the beginning was.

CHAPTER XI

There were too many people around, Jane decided, at the first meeting with Bridget and George Blake. It was not so much an introduction as a reception committee.

It took place the day after her talk with Trevor, and in the same corner of the Green Man terrace. Jane had taken things very easily in between. She had avoided all discussion at lunch with Bruce and Ted, had gone off by herself to explore the Grange woods in the afternoon, and at dinner had again guided the conversation, steering it firmly away from everything that really mattered.

Bruce's frustration had been apparent; he was dying to resume the argument, but faced with the tacit refusal not only of Jane but of Ted (who, bless him, had picked up her cue quickly and helped her to keep the talk neutral) he had got nowhere. She knew that her attitude had been not merely of neutrality, but of withdrawal from him, and that he sensed this too and was hurt by it. Sadly, the thought *Bruce must go* still lurked, unyielding, at the back of her mind. Even her dress for the evening had been almost pointedly unprovocative; her femaleness had become a danger to her purpose with him, and was sheathed, like the sword which hung on the Grange wall.

After dinner the boys had gone to the chapel for their night watch, and Jane had made no attempt to accompany them. She had gone to bed, sleeping only moderately well; dreaming, but not the 'Dream'. Katherine had figured in her dreaming, it was true; but so had Bruce, the two arguing together; they had been normal dream-figures, symbols of her anxieties and preoccupations, and in no way the people themselves.

She came down after the boys had had breakfast. Bruce had already gone to bed, but Ted was still around, and lingered for another coffee while she ate her bacon and eggs. Tactfully he made no mention of the night's watch until she herself asked about it.

'Not a thing,' he said. 'Dead quiet. Humidity and temperature a bit high, and only slow fluctuations . . . Boring, in fact. I dozed off most of the time, but I don't think Bruce did at all. He's very restless at the moment.'

'Yes, I know. And I'm not helping, am I – refusing to discuss it?'

'What's the point? He's closed his mind.'

'And how about mine, Ted?'

'Not the same, love. You know something real's happening to you – you're right *in* it. Either you can report back to us on it, or you can keep your mouth shut. Not your mind – your mouth.' He paused, then shook his head regretfully. 'I don't think he'll stick it out much longer. One of you'll have to go, and I don't see it being you.'

'It can't be me, Ted. I don't want to drive Bruce out, but . . .'

'I know.'

'And what will *you* do?'

He answered a little sadly: 'Well, all my "boxes and wires", as Bruce calls them – they've become pretty irrelevant, haven't they? It's *your* thing that matters. They just echo it.'

'Oh, Ted! It's such a shame. Your instruments are *good*. You know they are'

Ted shrugged, and added diffidently: 'But if *I* can be any help, just by hanging around, say so . . . At least I know what to do, now, if you go into trance.'

'Bruce is your friend,' Jane pointed out. 'He'd be very upset if he went and you refused to go with him.'

'I'd be sorry about that. But you're my friend, too.'

108

Jane could only say 'Thanks, Ted,' and mean it. He stood up to go, giving her a brotherly grin. As he reached the door, she called after him: 'Ted!'

'What then?'

'Angela Sowerby's a very lucky girl.'

He scratched his head, said, 'Well, anyway,' and disappeared.

Half an hour later she was called to the phone; it was Keith Stoneleigh, reporting that Bridget and George Blake would be arriving by car soon after lunch. So she lazed away the morning, wrote a few letters, lunched early with Trevor (another snub to Bruce, she was uneasily aware) . . . and now here they all were on the terrace: herself, Bruce, Ted, Keith, and the two newcomers. Trevor had merely seen them all seated and served, and had withdrawn quietly.

Jane liked the Blakes at once; Bruce, just as immediately, bristled with hostility. Keith introduced them like a public relations officer. Ted was amiably courteous.

Too many people.

She felt detached from the summing-up of the events in the chapel which Keith was giving. She knew, in a distant sort of way, that it was a well-balanced and reasonable account, but it was just words flowing past her, the emotional reality of the experience quite untouched. More real to her, at the moment, were the two listeners. Bridget, whose voice, figure, and pale yellow hair (braided now, but Jane guessed she could probably sit on it when it was down) proclaimed her unmistakably as a Highland Scot of Viking ancestry; George, who looked more like a farmer (Worcestershire, perhaps?) than a scientist; both middle or late thirties . . .

She was snapped out of her almost dreamlike detachment by Bridget asking her directly: 'Could you show me where to freshen up, Jane? We've been driving for hours.'

Jane, murmuring an apology, jumped to her feet and led Bridget indoors. 'Hasn't Trevor Cox shown you your room yet?' she asked as they climbed the stairs towards

Jane's own room. 'You shouldn't have let Keith plunge you straight into things like that.'

'Of course he has. I wanted to get you away from the reception committee, that's all.'

Jane laughed. 'That's just what I'd been calling it, in my own mind.'

'I knew it was getting you down.'

'Here, come and sit in my room . . . I felt a bit mean about it, though. Keith was explaining things very well, really.'

'The bare facts, yes. Very clinical. But not the *quality* of them. You're on your own with that . . . No, not quite true. I'd say that boy Ted's in tune with what you're going through, even though he doesn't say much . . . And the landlord – what did you say his name was?'

'Trevor Cox . . . But he went away – so how did you know?'

'He had the *sense* to go away, because he understood you. Am I right?'

'Yes – and about Ted. They're not the problem.'

'Obviously . . . Why don't you tell me about it?'

So for the third time Jane found herself relating the whole story; but this time it was different. Partly, maybe, because she was talking to a woman. But Bridget asked quite different questions from the kind that Keith and Trevor had asked. Keith's questions had been (as Bridget had said) clinical, like those of a good detective. Trevor's had been sensitive, sympathetic. But Bridget's were *empathetic*; she seemed to be joining Jane in the Triangle, and Jane and Katherine on the altar; to be hearing Jane's answers with the antennae of her mind as well as with her ears.

Jane found herself relaxing, gratefully. For the first time since it all began, she was feeling less isolated, and therefore less defensive.

'Do you find all this . . . well, believable?' she asked Bridget wonderingly after a while.

'I find *you* believable,' Bridget told her. 'That's what matters.'

110

'But all this muddling-up of time . . .'

Bridget shook her head. 'Jane – I'm a hereditary witch; my grandmother and mother brought me up to it. I've been a High Priestess with my own coven since I was twenty-two, which is fifteen years ago . . . Witch law says "Never boast, never threaten" – but I'll be forgiven for saying I'm more experienced in these things than most people. I've lived and worked with psychic phenomena all my life, and I know a thing or two by now. And I'll admit there's one thing I still do *not* understand – and that's the nature of time.'

Jane smiled. 'You could say I'm a hereditary historian. My father still teaches history at a Newcastle comprehensive. And I thought if there was one thing I *did* understand, it was time. The one constant of our profession . . . Not any more, I don't.'

'I've only known two people who I think really did have an understanding of it,' Bridget said. 'They were both Adepts, and very gifted teachers. But even they couldn't explain it to me . . . Perhaps, with all this, *you'll* be helping me to grasp it better.'

'I thought *you* were coming to help *me*!'

'I hope so, yes . . .'

'Everyone keeps telling me this thing's dangerous for me,' Jane said. 'Is it?'

'Do you feel it is?'

'Oh, yes, *I* do. But I thought, maybe I was just being scared by the eeriness of it. I'm no judge of whether it's really dangerous.'

'Don't underestimate yourself. You're a very good judge. You're a true sensitive, a natural – but you're only just discovering the fact. And learning to trust yourself is how you discover it.'

'But how can you *know* I am?'

'Do you think I can't recognise one, by now? I knew it as soon as we walked into that garden.'

'So you're telling me I'm right to be scared.'

'Not scared – careful. Take the proper precautions – or call up help, as you've done. Because you've got to go ahead, haven't you?'

'You think so too?'

'Heavens, lass, *I* wouldn't dictate to you. That's what *you've* decided.'

'How did you . . .' Jane broke off, laughing. 'Okay, okay, I won't even ask how. But you're right . . . I'm afraid it's just one of those things. I've *got* to, and that's all there is to it . . . Bruce thinks I'm only being pig-headed. But then he's being pretty pig-headed himself. And you know what? *I* think his obsession with scientific ghost-hunting is really a defence. He's cutting the ghosts down to size, because in his gut he's terrified of them.'

Bridget nodded. 'I got that feeling, too . . . I hate to say it, but he'll have to go, you know. If you go ahead, he'll be a danger to himself and to you.'

'I know. But how am I going to fix it? On paper, he's in charge of the exercise. He's a Committee member of the Society, and he's the one who arranged for us to come to Orley Grange in the first place. We can't just say "Thanks and goodbye, Bruce, we'll take it from here".'

Bridget pondered for a moment, then asked: 'When do you want to try again – in the chapel, I mean?'

'Tonight. I keep feeling it's – well, urgent, though that sounds . . . You know? As though whatever's happening in the sixteenth century is moving in parallel with now, and I haven't much time. Is that silly?'

'If *you* feel it's urgent, then it's urgent . . . Right. The immediate thing is to keep Bruce out of the chapel for tonight anyway . . . Leave it to George and me.'

Jane found the Blakes' behaviour over the next couple of hours a little puzzling. They asked Bruce, Ted, and Jane to show them around; first the chapel, where Bridget said nothing – just looked, and seemed to be listening – while George, in his soft unhurried voice, talked equipment with

112

Bruce and Ted. Ted, chattering away with him like a long-lost friend, was quite unresentful about George's much greater knowledge of electronics and instrumentation, pleased with his clearly genuine approval of the polygraph, and delighted when he suggested a neat solution to a response-lag problem on the humidity channel.

Even Bruce's hostility thawed a little as the talk remained purely technical. George handled him very tactfully, and Bridget kept away from him; so far, Jane could see what they were up to. But after twenty minutes of that, George and Bridget started sniffing along the corridor outside – almost literally sniffing, like dogs following a scent. Bruce and Ted followed them, apparently taking it all seriously; but Jane could not escape the feeling that the Blakes, for some reason, were putting on an act. The 'scent' seemed to lead them on, down the staircase at the end of the corridor, and into a lobby by the small side door through which Jane had brought in Keith the morning before.

In this lobby Bridget halted, a little dramatically Jane thought, and closed her eyes for about fifteen seconds. Then she said, 'Yes, George; this room.'

George nodded. 'You could set up in here, couldn't you, Ted? I presume that 13-amp socket's live . . .' He produced a small screwdriver from his pocket, and holding the insulated handle, probed the socket. A neon tell-tale in the handle glowed briefly, and George nodded. 'Fine. And there's space enough. Okay?'

'Sure,' Ted said. 'But why? Why here? We've been getting results in the chapel.'

'Certainly you have. And that's why I think readings in here would be helpful. If you got significant results here while the phenomenon was being observed humanly – psychically, if you prefer – in the chapel, this would help to orient it.'

Bruce interrupted: 'But . . . No, I'm not with you.'

George launched into a dissertation on lines of psychic force, with passing references to ley lines, the movement of astral shells, Akashic records, and other things most of which Jane had never heard of. Bruce asked occasional questions, and seemed impressed; but Jane felt increasingly uneasy. Somehow she *knew* that George was talking nonsense – cleverly convincing nonsense, but . . . She caught Bridget's eye behind Bruce's back, and Bridget winked.

Of course. Jane smothered a smile.

In remarkably little time, the night's experiment was agreed upon. Bruce and Ted would operate the polygraph in the lobby, while Jane, Bridget and George would 'observe' in the chapel. (The chapel being, Jane noticed, a good minute's walk away.) With synchronised watches, it would be possible to compare and coordinate the two sets of results – polygraphic and psychic – at the end of the session. 'If there *are* any results, of course,' George added cautiously.

When it became clear that the plan included Jane being in the chapel, Bruce was ready to plunge back into the old argument; but somehow – obliquely yet effectively – the point was made that in that way the polygraph sensors would be safely out of reach of Jane's disruptive effects on them; no noises, no sudden air movements. Bruce came out of it looking as though he had won a victory.

Jane and Bridget left the three men to their technicalities, and strolled in the sunshine down the Long Walk. As soon as they were well out of earshot, Jane began to laugh helplessly. 'You conned him,' she spluttered. 'You conned him rotten.'

'It was the simplest way,' Bridget replied, unabashed. 'And it worked . . . Don't feel too badly about it. It's for his own protection, as much as anything else.'

'I know . . . I'm sorry you had to fool Ted, too, though. He doesn't deserve it.'

Bridget halted, looking at her with raised eyebrows. 'Jane, lass – you don't really imagine that Ted was fooled for a moment, do you? He caught on right from the start, and played along beautifully. If he hadn't, it would have been much harder work.'

Jane sighed. 'I'll believe you. I know I've been making that mistake from the start – underestimating Ted . . . Trouble is, I began with the idea that he was nice but thick, except over electronics. And it's not true – he keeps catching me out, and *I* keep making the same mistake. . . .'

They started walking again, and Jane continued: 'I suppose I've found it hard to acknowledge his sensitivity properly, because *he* didn't pick up any of the things that I did, in the chapel. He believed me, and he supported me against Bruce – but he was blind to the thing itself.'

'There's different kinds of sensitivity, you know,' Bridget said, 'You're a medium . . .'

'I've never been aware of it, before.'

'Or let's put it this way – you have the latent abilities of a medium, and they've suddenly manifested now because you're involved, you're part of this situation yourself. Whatever it is.'

'You mean I *am* the Battle Maid, I suppose.'

'You are *now*, effectively. And don't ask me what "now" means . . . But to get back to Ted. I don't want to oversimplify, but his is a characteristically male kind of sensitivity. The best of them tend more to emotional and psychological awareness than psychic – and that's true even of the witches.'

'Even George?'

'Ah now, George – he's something special . . .' For a moment Bridget looked several years younger; then she laughed at herself, almost shyly. 'Don't listen to me, I'm daft about the man. But leaning over *backwards* to be honest, I'd say yes, even George. He *is* psychically aware, very, but he still has to rely on me for the subtleties and the details . . . And I rely on him for strength – well, obviously . . .'

'"*The Sinews and Puissance for both, and withal the Nicetie of Logick*",' Jane quoted, smiling.

'Eh?'

'Katherine's Diary, on the roles of men and women. She also said that women had "*the Discernment in those Straits wherein Logick faileth*", but had to be diplomatic about it.'

'Wise girl, your Katherine. But with the best men, you don't have to hide it . . . I rely on George for optimism, too, believe it or not. Sometimes I can be overwhelmed by an immediate psychic impact, so that my long-term perspective is swamped. Because he's rather less vulnerable, he balances that danger. Psychic sensitives can be a bit manic-depressive, without someone who speaks their language to hold their hand . . . Oh, don't get me wrong. It's not a question of watertight compartments – men this, women that – but of emphasis, of the centre of gravity of the psyche. . . .'

Jane listened happily, finding herself more and more in tune with this flaxen Scot whose views on men and women, though expressed in different words, were so like her own. As they made their way slowly down the Long Walk, Jane was soon talking as well as listening, becoming more and more absorbed . . .

Then suddenly she halted in her tracks. Bridget, reacting, broke off in mid-sentence. Both of them were staring at the stone seat, and for a moment they stood motionless.

'Break free,' Bridget breathed. 'Don't let him touch you. He's probing, but this isn't the time. Break free.'

'Can you *see* him? I can't, but I know he's there . . .'

'No, I can't, but I can feel him. It's your Father Gadd, isn't it?'

'He's trying to . . .'

'Don't let him!'

Bridget stepped in front of Jane, blocking her view of the seat, and made a quick gesture in the air, with short vigorous movements of her right hand.

The tension evaporated as quickly as it had arisen. Jane breathed with relief.

'What did you do?'

'The Banishing Pentagram of Fire.'

116

'Why Fire?'

'Because it's his element. Inflamed pride, and hatred . . . I caught him unawares. It mightn't be so easy, another time.'

'Katherine said that, too.'

'What?'

'"*There is a Fire burneth in that Priest, though deep buried; on what Fuel it feedeth, I know not.*"'

'She soon found out, poor lass,' Bridget said grimly.

Bridget, Jane discovered had a gift for taking charge of things. She was not bossy, but the developments that mattered seemed to go the way she wanted them to go. The evening, before the five of them went up to the Grange, divided itself clearly into two stages – social and preparatory.

Keith turned up for a pre-dinner drink before his night duty at the hospital, and all of them joined him on the Green Man terrace. He was told what was planned, of course, but Bridget and George between them managed to explain it in a way that drew in Bruce and made it seem non-controversial. Jane wondered if they had briefed Keith beforehand, but decided not.

Dinner was certainly social. Bridget had dressed up, baring her excellent shoulders and softening the arrangement of her hair from compact braids into heavy loops (letting it down completely would have been *too* spectacular, Jane guessed), and had urged Jane to dress up too. Jane, almost reluctantly, had done so, in classic black; she was still unwilling to provoke Bruce – and in any case, her mind was increasingly drawn to the night ahead; her battle-nerves were beginning to tighten. But as to the one, Bridget and George were deliberately holding Bruce's attention; and as to the other, Jane could not quite define what they were doing but every time the coming ordeal threatened to dominate her thoughts, she could feel them pulling her back. Not with words – the talk continued, unruffled – but with something else, with a gentle, friendly pressure on some other level, in the eddy-and-flow of some undercurrent of knowledge they were inviting her to share. It could not work entirely – the foreboding was too strong for that – but it helped her to control the tension, to push it into the background, and to turn the spotlight of her thoughts back to the dinner table and the people around it.

But when dinner was over, and Bruce and Ted had left to set up their equipment in the lobby, Bridget shepherded Jane upstairs and started preparing her for battle. George had gone to help the boys, at Bruce's invitation – a victory in itself, that – so the two women were alone.

It really was before-battle atmosphere, with Bridget the seasoned warrior, watchfully ensuring that the younger, untried friend was as ready for the assault – as well-armed, as well-counselled, as the Gods of War might allow. They went to the Blakes' room first, where Bridget changed into blue slacks and sweater and collected an attaché case.

'George will be coming to the chapel too, won't he?' Jane asked as they crossed the landing to her room. 'He won't be staying with the boys in the lobby?'

'Oh, no, he'll be with us . . . You find that reassuring, eh?'

'Yes – I need you both . . . .' She smiled, nervously. 'You must have done a good job of convincing me how you two complement each other.'

'That's witchcraft for you – at any rate, our kind. Very much based on polarity . . . Actually, it's too bad you haven't got a husband or a lover . . . .' Bridget laughed, and went on, 'That's not as trite as it sounds. I mean there's something he could do for you right now. Never mind, you can do it yourself. You've got the willpower, and the psychic charge – and they're the main ingredients.'

She shut Jane's door behind them, laid the attaché case on the bed, and took out a black-handled knife, two silver bowls, and a jar of salt. 'Go and have a shower, lass. Hot or cold, whichever you feel like. And while you're doing it, tell yourself that any hostile or negative influences that have attached themselves to you are being washed away.'

118

'That sounds good psychology,' Jane said, pulling off her dress.

'It is also, believe it or not, good magic. These things do have a real existence on one particular plane – most people call it the astral – and confidently-directed willpower can manipulate them. In this case, send them away. Literally down the drain.'

'Do you *mean* literally? That by willpower I can actually make the water carry away my astral infections?'

'Well, while you're trying,' Bridget replied blandly, 'it would be sound psychology to believe you can – don't you think?'

Jane laughed, obeyed Bridget's instructions as she showered herself, and had to admit she felt better for it – psychology or magic or whatever. She returned to the bedroom, towelling herself dry.

'Don't get dressed just yet.' Bridget said. 'It's my turn for a little willpower.' She had put water into one silver bowl and a little salt in the other, on the dressing-table, and now she dipped the tip of the knife into the water.

Holding it there, she intoned, with a quiet intensity: '*I exorcise thee, O Creature of Water, that thou cast out from thee all impurity and uncleanliness of the spirits of the world of phantasm; in the names of Kernunnos and Aradia.*'

Transferring the knife-blade to the salt, she went on: '*Blessings be upon this Creature of Salt; let all malignity and hindrance be cast forth hencefrom, and let all good enter herein; wherefore do I bless thee, that thou mayest aid me, in the names of Kernunnos and Aradia.*'

She then tipped the salt into the water, and held out the water-bowl to Jane. 'Here, take it.'

Some impulse of awe made Jane drop her towel and stand naked to take the bowl in her two hands, so that there was nothing but herself, the bowl, and the consecrated water.

Bridget nodded. 'Good. Now dip your right forefinger in the water, and touch each of the openings of your body in turn, starting with the eyes. Nipples and navel too – regard

119

them as openings. Thirteen openings in all. A man has twelve. And while you do it, *know* that you're making it impossible for any hostile influence to break in.'

Somehow, the ritual made sense to Jane, and she carried it out with all the concentration she could muster, gaining extra confidence from the charge she really could believe Bridget had put into the water. When it was done, instinctively she took several seconds to relax her concentration without haste, as though giving the protection time to mould itself to her.

'You're a natural.' Bridget told her. 'You know what to do.'

'Was that what my husband or lover would have done for me, did you mean?'

'If he was your magical partner, yes. If a pair are really in harmony, polarised effort is more magically effective than solo. But don't worry, you did splendidly . . . Now, Battle Maid – your armour!'

So Jane put on the gunmetal lamé suit once more, with care, feeling the tension mounting again, but now a tension of excitement, of eagerness, a tension she welcomed. Bridget brushed her hair for her till it gleamed brighter than the lamé; then she slipped a silver talisman – a shining pentagram in a ring of twelve smaller stars – round Jane's neck, and a necklace of amber and jet round her own.

Jane stood up and faced Bridget, trembling a little, but smiling gravely. 'I think I hear the sound of trumpets,' she said.

George was waiting for them at the entrance to the chapel, a quiet welcoming presence. He watched Jane take the sword from its sheath on the wall, and nodded, as though assessing and approving her readiness. The three of them entered the chapel together. It was lit, but softly; George must have removed all but one or two of the bulbs, and the result was calmer, more acceptable.

Bridget stood in front of her husband, turning her back

120

on him and gesturing with her hands, backwards. It was obviously a familiar signal, because George at once removed the pins from her hair, letting it cascade down her back, a full flaxen yard of it. The effect was dramatic, a magical arming in itself, a banner unfurled, warning the enemy of the power it represented.

The only words spoken came from Bridget: 'We're with you, Battle Maid. Hold that thought.'

George turned out the lights. Jane found herself bathed in moonlight, but the moonlight was fitful, for broken clouds were gathering above Orley, and the rumble of thunder could be heard in the distance.

Bridget and George were dimly visible, side by side and not too far away from Jane. She saluted them with her sword.

Then she stepped into the Triangle.

For an instant there was no movement, no sound but the muted thunder; nothing to feel but a mounting invisible pressure, a tightening of the screws of reality . . .

In that instant, time stood still; then it burst its shackles and spun free.

CHAPTER XII

Robin Fulbright, man-at-arms, rode a pace behind the Lady Katherine, his eyes darting watchfully from side to side of the forest path. Everything depended on those eyes, he knew; for Stephen, the second guard who followed him, was an eager lad who would fight bravely if need arose but who lacked the experience to smell out ambush.

Robin had carried his sword for young Sir Henry Montgris, and for his father before him, since the boy Edward was king – and Edward had died twenty-four years ago. But Robin's eye was still keen and his muscles were still hard, and men half his age would think twice about crossing him. No harm had come to a Montgris with Robin at hand; and no harm would come to his young mistress either, except it be over Robin's dead body – and he would not be easy to kill. Many had tried, and few had lived to wonder over their failure.

That, he knew without false modesty, was why his master had charged him with the safety of my lady's person. She was not to ride out of the Grange without Robin in attendance; even when Sir Henry himself was escorting her, Robin was to be within call. Sir Henry was not a dictatorial husband – the year and a half since their wedding had shown that his treatment of Katherine as an equal was no mere flattery – but on this one point he had laid down the law to Katherine herself as well as to Robin, in a tone that had invited no questions.

Not that Katherine would have questioned it, for she knew as well as he that the danger was real enough. Even in these fertile and prosperous Midlands, manor demesnes

were still clearings in the primordial forest, which surrounded and interlaced them like the sea embracing a host
of islands. The land was more peaceful than it had ever been,
but vagabonds and outlaws still lurked in those sprawling
woodlands; and a fine-clothed lady, her jewel-encrusted
garments proclaiming her station and her husband's wealth
as custom decreed, offered tempting booty. A temptation
enhanced, Robin was well aware, by the comely young
body within those garments, which could expect no mercy
at the hands of any successful ambusher – or band of
ambushers.

For my lady Katherine was certainly comely; the high
round breasts, the narrow waist, the small elegant hands,
the sparkling eyes, the red lips, the fine brow and the
gleaming chestnut hair that winged out from it – all this was
not only pleasing in itself to any man's gaze, it was also well
in accord with the fashion of the time, so that she carried
gracefully the tight pointed bodice, the puffed sleeves, the
convoluted ruffs at neck and wrists, and the wide-skirted
farthingale with the padded hips, into which less fortunate
ladies must cram themselves unbecomingly.

Robin could use his eyes for other purposes besides
watching for flashes of movement behind the thick pine-
branches; and he strongly but silently approved of the
young mistress of Orley. There was no envy in his approval; such treasures were not for the likes of him; but he was a
Montgris man, body and heart, and the brighter the jewel
that was entrusted to his care, the greater his pride in that
charge.

He approved, too, of her lively spirit, though it added to
his problems. The Lady Helen, he remembered, had always
visited the village by way of the safe track between well-
tilled fields. Not so Lady Katherine. She delighted in the
mere activity of riding, and in the variety of the land over
which she rode. If she fancied a gallop across the common,
or a detour through the sun-dappled forest – that was the
way she would ride, with Robin ever-watchful at her heels.

123

He never remonstrated with her. Such a falcon, he told himself with rueful admiration, was not for him or anyone else to cage. All he did, once he had realised her adventurous nature, was to make a habit of taking a second man with him for extra safety.

Today, as ever, he breathed more easily when she left the forest path for the wide Orley fields. His relief was all the greater because he had sensed, of late, a new restlessness in her, an unwonted quickness of temper which could lead to a rashness that even Robin might have to check. Something, he was sure, troubled her. Was she with child, perhaps? Robin thought not; his wife Bess was my lady's chambermaid, and Robin would have been one of the first to know such news.

But there was something; and if my lady Katherine was troubled, then Robin, her watchdog, was troubled.

They approached the village by a small path Katherine had not ridden along before; in summer it had been too overgrown with nettles and cow-parsley to be even visible as a path, but in this surprisingly mild and dry December weather it had caught her eye between the trees, and she had wheeled into it on impulse, looking around her with her usual inquisitiveness. This was *her* land, hers and Hal's, and she meant to become intimate with every inch of it. She knew, by orienting herself with familiar landmarks, that the fields to her right were in the tenancy of Harry Drover, father of the intractable Jenny, and she reminded herself that she must create an opportunity to be gracious to him, in the hope of softening the blow to the family pride of Jenny's dismissal . . .

A small cottage on the other side of the path – which was widening now into a lane – attracted her attention. Almost all the villagers' homes were clustered around the central green, and she wondered casually at this one's isolation. It stood back from the lane, with perhaps half a dozen rods of herbs and vegetable patch in front of it. As she looked, she saw something which puzzled her; a little girl, four or five years old at most, approaching the front gate almost fearfully and laying a skinny pullet beside it.

Katherine reined in, and watched.

She was still a hundred paces from the child, who ignored her, peering over the gate and calling out something which Katherine did not catch. Then she turned and ran back towards the village as fact as her small legs would carry her.

Katherine turned to Robin, who had halted alongside her. 'Who liveth there, Robin?'

'Old Bella Withecombe, my lady. She hath been blind these many years.'

'So the villagers send her victuals?' There were other things beside the pullet, she could see; a winter vegetable or two, a few eggs, a flask probably of ale. 'That is Christian of them . . . Hath she no family?'

'A son at sea, gone to the Indies, and dead for all any man knoweth. None other. She was widowed young.'

Katherine started to walk her horse on. 'What did the child cry out? I could not hear.'

'Her family's name, my lady. She's Hetty Danvers, the blacksmith's youngest.'

'So that the old woman should know from whom the gift cometh?' She laughed. 'That is less Christian, to proclaim thy charity . . . And then to run away!'

Robin seemed to hesitate, then he said: 'My lady, the people fear her – or fear her ill-will, rather. That is why they bring her gifts, and why they make certain she knoweth who giveth them.'

'She is a witch, I suppose,' Katherine said, crossing herself.

Robin copied the gesture automatically. 'I cannot say.'

'Cannot, or will not?'

'In plain truth, my lady, I know not. But if you ask my thoughts . . .'

'I do, Robin.'

'I think, my lady, that she is an old blind widow of ill-favoured countenance, and that **ignorant** folk are too

125

quick to call such unfortunate wretches by evil names . . . She hath the Sight, that I know; but for myself, I have found no wickedness in her.'

They had reached the gate, and Katherine reined in again, looking down on the small heap of offerings. 'And *I* think, Robin, that there is more Christian charity in thee than in those who placate what they fear with a few cabbages.'

'My lady is kind.' The villagers' attitude to Bella Withecombe was something Robin seemed to feel strongly about, for he went on: 'An honest man needeth no learning to understand that the Sight may be a gift of God. She who hath it is only a witch if she useth it ill.'

'I see I am guarded by a theologian,' Katherine told him, making the joke into a compliment by her smile. 'And since I would not have thee believe that I, too, am ignorant – I think I will call upon Mistress Withecombe.'

Robin seemed to approve, for he was out of the saddle at once and ready to help her dismount.

He and Stephen remained politely at the gate as Katherine walked up the path. She noted that the herbs were tended, but clumsily and raggedly, as a blind person might.

She was still a pace or two from the door when it opened, and Bella appeared in it; shrunken, with thin grey hair straggling from under her cap, and – as Robin had said – of ill-favoured countenance. But the voice which came from the withered lips was surprisingly musical.

'Thou art welcome, Mistress of Orley.'

Katherine was taken aback, both at the strangely oracular form of address, with the familiar 'thou', and at having been recognised before she spoke. Her immediate thought was that old Bella must have at least the remains of her eyesight; but the two milk-white cataracts which stared past her shoulder put paid to that idea. She pulled herself together and remembered her manners.

'Good day to you, Mistress Withecombe.'

Bella laughed. 'There are Mistresses and Mistresses.

126

Thou'rt the Lady Katherine, and I am old Bella, who all say is a witch. Dost thou not smell brimstone?'

'I smell naught but a well-made broth – if my nose doth not deceive me.'

'It doth not. And if thou fearest not to enter – my cottage is small but it is clean. I have only a stool, but it will not soil thy fine velvet.'

She stepped aside, almost challengingly. Trying not to betray any hesitation, Katherine went in. Bella was right; the cottage was astonishingly clean. Even the straw on the earth floor was fresh, and mixed with dried rosemary and lavender kept from the summer. There was indeed a pot of broth simmering on the hob. Other dried herbs hung in bunches everywhere, but there was little furniture; a rough table, two stools, and a truckle bed. Katherine seated herself on one of the stools, and asked directly; 'How didst thou know who I was?'

'Did they not tell thee that old Bella hath the Sight? . . . I watched thee riding through the forest's edge, with Robin and the young one behind thee. And Robin much concerned for thy safety, till thou wert under God's sky again.'

Despite her front of composure, Katherine felt a shiver of superstitious awe. The old woman was so eerily confident . . .

'Thou dost fear me, after all,' Bella went on, as though answering her thought.

'Thou hast given me no cause to fear thee, Bella.' She was relieved to find that her voice was steady enough.

'A courteous lie, so let it pass. Yet in truth, Katherine Montgris, thou hast nothing to fear – from *me*.'

'Whom then should I fear?'

'The Devil – who is not my master, whatever the ignorant may whisper.'

'I believe thee, Bella . . . But surely, no Christian who fears God, and honours the blessed Trinity and God's loving Mother, need fear the Devil?'

'Unless what thou believest to be thy pathway to God be a trap, signposted by the Devil.'

Katherine could make no sense of that – till a suspicion struck her. 'Art thou a Puritan?'

'Thou thinkest I mock thy Popery? Not I, child.'

'Then what is thy meaning?'

Bella was silent for a long time. Then she said: 'Yes, I have been blessed with the Sight – and a bitter blessing it can be. There are bounds set around what I may tell . . .' The strange music of her voice had become a lament. 'I can weep for thee, Katherine of Orley, and weep I shall. But a sea of my tears could not wash away what thou must discover for thyself – face to face with the Evil One.'

Katherine cried out, crossing herself: 'Mother of God, what art thou saying?'

'Aye, call on Her from the Abyss – She may hear, for two things cut thee off from Her Son. The false signposts – and the purity of thine own love . . .' Her voice broke. 'Now go. I can help thee no further.'

Katherine was on her feet. 'But Bella, for the love of God . . .'

Bella had not moved, but tears had begun gathering in the corners of her blind eyes. 'No more!' And then, seeming to wrench it out of herself: 'Only this – ask thyself, Katherine of Orley, and tremble at the answer. Who is it that shriveth thee?'

'*Oh, no!*'

'Go, now!'

Katherine needed no second bidding. She ran sobbing out of the cottage and down the path between the ragged herbs which caught at her skirts. Robin and Stephen stared at her, wide-eyed, their hands going instinctively to their sword-hilts. She scrambled into the saddle almost faster than Robin could help her, and rode like the wind in a straight line across the fields for home.

As though the Devil himself were after her, Robin thought, as he spurred in pursuit.

By the time Katherine's horse reached the Grange door, and

stood steaming and blowing while Robin helped her dismount, the Mistress of Orley was a great deal calmer. Though she had a keen mind, Katherine was a very direct young woman, in whom mind and body reacted immediately upon one another. Violent physical exertion, like the mad three-mile ride from old Bella's cottage, always released her tension and left her thoughts clear and poised.

'Is it well with you, my lady?' Robin's face was full of concern.

She let her gloved hand rest briefly on his arm. 'It is well, Robin. The old woman touched on a dream that hath troubled me of late, that is all.'

'The fault is mine. I should not have . . .'

'The fault is *not* thine, nor hers. She is clever; she hath made me face my dream bravely, which is better than to fly from it. If thou sayest otherwise, thou callest me coward.'

Robin smiled, relieved. 'Never that, my lady. I have known men – soldiers – with less spirit.'

'That spirit failed me for a space; think not too ill of me for it.'

She accepted his vigorous denial, making light of the matter, and went on up to the great bedchamber, glad that she met no one on the way. She had spoken more bravely than she felt. The 'dream' had been all too real – no fantasy of sleep, but a waking unease; and Bella had hit upon it unerringly. Eighteen months of dissatisfaction and irritation over Father Jonathan Gadd, the family priest of whom, as a new bride, she had hoped so much – were brought terrifyingly into focus by that one question: *Who is it that shriveth thee?*

In her parents' more modest manor, a few miles away, the most memorable events of her childhood and adolescence had been the half-dozen occasions when a travelling priest, referred to the Courtfields by like-minded friends, had reached their door in careful anonymity to hear their undramatic confessions, decree undemanding penances, and administer to them the Blood and Body of Christ. Each of these visits had sustained them until the next.

The Montgris, however, were different. They were wealthy, they were locally much respected, and they had high connections, being distant cousins of the Cecils. The pretence was that the Grange chapel, with its Romish furnishings, had remained unused since Queen Mary died; everybody in Orley said so, and nobody in Orley believed it. Just as everybody was quite well aware that Dr Jonathan Gadd, the studious poor relation of Sir Henry's mother who enjoyed the family's permanent hospitality, regularly donned his vestments within the privacy of the Grange walls, and that within those walls he was addressed by his true title of Father. Discretion there still had to be, in Elizabeth's England; but discretion could embrace wider freedom for the Montgris than it could for their less powerful neighbours.

So as the Mistress of Orley, Katherine (unless times became a good deal harsher, and who could ever read the future?) had looked forward to enjoying the consolation of the True Church in the safety of her own home. And that meant a great deal to her. But from the start, she could have wished that the True Church's representative who was the means of that consolation had been a less forbidding figure. Unsmiling, gaunt, and keen-eyed, he made her ill at ease, and he knew it; though as a lady and a believer, she always addressed him with fitting dignity.

With the unease had gone disappointment. Accustomed to the quiet fervour, the spiritual devotion, of the handful of priests who had visited the Courtfield home (for none but the devoted would have risked such a perilous way of life) she had found Father Gadd's celebration of the Mass cold and perfunctory. The services in the chapel were regular, if less frequent than Katherine had expected; but the priest hurried through them almost as though his thoughts were elsewhere. She told herself that her disappointment was presumptuous; God had blessed her with the solace of the

Mass in a land where the Mass was forbidden, and that should be enough. The attitude of the priest was not her concern; judgement on that lay between him and his Maker, and it would be impious of her to trespass on it, even in her thoughts. But the feeling would not quite be banished. Nor could her resentment of his almost casual indifference, in confession, to what she regarded as her shortcomings.

When she knew, for example, that her quick tongue (a useful but sometimes dangerous asset) had been unfair to one of the servants, not only did she find some way to make amends, she also meticulously recounted her fault next time she came to the priest for absolution; and in truth her busy but innocent life gave her little else to confess. But the Father either brushed these peccadilloes aside or imposed almost derisory penances. And yet she knew he was neither indifferent to her nor contemptuous of her. He always seemed to be watching her. His face remained set, but in his eyes there lurked something that chilled her; an appraisal, even a secret excitement. At first she had thought: *Mother of God, a lustful cleric?* – but her woman's instinct soon told her that this was not the motive for his unnerving watchfulness.

Gradually, over the months, habit had blunted her concern; she had become used to Father Gadd, if only because she was too busy to waste time over insoluble mysteries. Or she had believed she had become used to him . . . until Bella's deadly question: *Who is it that shriveth thee?*

As she stood by the leaded window, gazing unseeingly out on to the Long Walk, her brooding was suddenly interrupted.

'Ah – thou'rt returned, Kate!'

Hal always burst through doors noisily – usually driven by sheer cheerfulness and surplus energy; Katherine was quite used to it, finding it lovable rather than annoying. But today there was something in his bearing which suggested urgency of another kind, and his habitually smiling face was grim and anxious. She ran to him.

'Hal? Is aught amiss?'

131

'Basil . . . The fever is worse, of a sudden. Kate – I fear for the lad. Wilt thou come?'

A practical emergency was all that Katherine needed to banish her spiritual preoccupation. She hurried with Hal to young Basil's bedroom, asking questions as she went, and as soon as they reached it she took charge, sending maids scurrying for cold compresses while she sat on the bed and held the boy's hands. He looked dreadful, and was muttering incomprehensibly; he seemed to be trying to clutch at her hands, but there was no strength in his fingers. Katherine waited till the servants were out of earshot, then whispered to Hal: 'I would not alarm thee, Hal – but Father Gadd should be here. I like this not.'

'God's blood, nor I. But dost thou truly think . . .'

'I think only that there is danger. Let it not be danger to his soul. Pray God I am wrong. But it can do no harm to call the Father.'

Hal hesitated. 'The boy hath a strange aversion to him. I would not distress him, while he is thus weak.'

Katherine thought she knew her young brother-in-law well, for they had become very close; but this prejudice – if it were a fact – was news to her. (Food for later thought, a corner of her mind noted.) 'Let him be nearby, then, where Basil cannot see him, but where he can be summoned quickly . . . I beg thee, Hal.'

Hal nodded and went out, for the plea in his wife's eyes was real. Basil's sudden deterioration had shocked her, and she had a dread of anyone dying unabsolved. (*Who is it that shriveth thee?* – no, drive away the doubt!) She would fight, by all the practical knowledge and skill at her disposal, to save the body and to ward off death; and indeed, in this close-knit family, young Basil was as dear to her as he was to Hal. All the more reason to run no risks with his soul, if her own efforts should fail . . .

Her dread of physical failure grew as the afternoon wore on. There was no surgeon within a day's ride of Orley; young Stephen, Robin's assistant, had been sent for one, but

132

meanwhile, as always, the burden fell on the mistress of the household. The Lady Helen, who after all was Basil's mother, was worse than useless, fluttering and moaning and getting in the way without managing to help in the simplest task; fortunately Katherine's maid Bess had the gift of handling her, and kept her quiet most of the time.

Father Gadd had arrived quickly, and he and Hal stayed talking together in the next chamber – Hal fidgeting and nervous, the priest calm as ever.

It was only gradually, as her own tasks became less demanding and there was little she could do but wait and watch, that Katherine began to notice something disquieting about the Father's calm. Whenever she went to Hal (knowing instinctively that he needed the comfort of an occasional word from her, even if she had nothing encouraging to report) she had the feeling that she was interrupting, not merely a discussion, nor (as one might reasonably expect) the priest's attempts to give spiritual solace to a worried man – but something else . . . She could not put her finger on it, but it was as though Father Gadd was trying to persuade Hal, to win him over to some course of action relentlessly, remorselessly – and as though while hope for his brother's recovery faded, so Hal's resistance weakened . . .

She could not understand why; but Katherine found herself beginning to be afraid for more than Basil. (And always, pushed underground, fled from, there was Bella's question: *Who is it that shriveth thee?*)

There came a point, towards evening, when sheer exhaustion defeated Katherine. Basil was quite unconscious, oblivious to her presence, and Bess was capable enough of keeping watch over him and calling her if there was any change. So Katherine went to her bedchamber to lie down and rest.

She told Hal she was going, and he walked with her, one arm around her shoulders. She leaned against him gratefully, to tired even to talk.

133

Hal picked her up and laid her on the great high bed. 'Rest now, dear one,' he said, kissing her brow.

'Oh, Hal – what are we to do?' She felt she was near to tears.

He was silent for a moment, then replied: 'Desperate straits call for desperate measures. It may hap . . . There could be a way.

'A way? We have attempted all ways. He is in the care of God's mercy now.'

'Our priest,' he said slowly, 'is a man of many talents.'

Tired as she was, she could hear the edge of bitterness in her own voice. 'Let him apply them, then. Till now I have not even seen him pray. Do a priest's prayers count for so little?'

'Prayer is not all.'

She knew, suddenly, that Hal was trying – but not daring – to tell her something. A tremor of ill-defined alarm made her sit up.

'I understand thee not, Hal. Be plain, I beg thee!'

He shook his head. 'Our priest is not all thou thinkest, Kate. Oh, there has been so much . . . No, I cannot tell thee. Thine innocence . . .' Now he was the one who seemed near to tears. 'Thine innocence, Kate, is a pledge for us both – if even that can still avail us. And without grace, what remains but power? The price of it is already paid. Only a fool would pay the price, and forgo the treasure . . .'

Now she was really afraid. She stared at him, uncomprehending. 'Price? Treasure? What is this, Hal?'

He seized her hands, gripping them till she thought the bones would crack. 'Kate, I have been so besieged by fear – and yet entranced . . . And now, with Basil's very life at hazard – and since, for me, there is no turning back . . .' He dropped her hands again, and jumped up. 'Gadd is right. His Lord will protect us!'

He was halfway to the door. Katherine cried after him: '*His* Lord?'

'Ask no questions, Kate. Hold to thine innocence.'

134

'Hal!' The words came to her throat unbidden, almost uttering themselves. *'Hal – who is it that shriveth us?'*

He turned in the doorway, and his eyes were alight with a kind of terrified joy. 'No priest, Kate – *that* he forfeited years since. But the knowledge – the power!'

The gates of Hell seemed to open before Katherine. She fell back on to the pillow as though she had been stunned. She made one supreme effort to harness her chaotic thoughts into some kind of order, but body, mind, and spirit could bear no more.

The room around her faded, and she slept.

Katherine awoke to the sound of thunder; and her first thought as she drifted back to consciousness was: *Thunder in December? It is against nature!* Then the memory of Hal's words came back to her, in full clarity, and she sat up, gasping.

Two or three hours must have passed, for someone – presumably Bess – had drawn the curtains and replenished the fire. Katherine jumped from the bed, automatically tidying her clothes and her hair while her mind raced.

That mind, sharp and unevasive for all the horror with which it had to cope, had no doubt of the nature of Hal's disaster. *No priest . . . but the knowledge, the power . . .* It could mean only one thing. An unfrocked cleric, probably excommunicate, perverting that knowledge and power to black heresy and worse – to necromancy, to sorcery, to the service of God's Adversary – and dragging her beloved husband with him! Hal, the credulous, the generous-hearted – Hal who would face any man with muscle or sword, unflinching, but who would have been defenceless, a babe in arms, against the serpent tongue of corrupt learning . . . Why, she herself could out-manoeuvre Hal any day with words, with the cut-and-thrust of ideas and imaginings; it was a joke between them, something he acknowledged with a laugh. So what could Gadd, the scholar, the skilled disputer, have done with him? And Hal, if the truth were told, loved power; loved it as a child loved toys. Well enough, when power meant the command of men, the ordering of his own acres, success in valour. That was the power of light. But the power of darkness, offered to him almost unnoticed at first, drawing him step by step into deeper sin – and Gadd revealing to him slowly that there was no going back, because the earlier sins – more mortal with each step – were unshriven, unabsolved?

Unabsolved! And so was she, Katherine! *Who is it that shriveth thee?* Blind Bella had seen, and wept for her . . .

But it was worse than that – far worse. Her own sins had been venial – and even though Hal's were mortal, a true priest might yet cleanse him of them, heavy though the penance would be. But they had both accepted a defiled Host from hands that had forfeited the right to administer it – hands steeped in evil . . . From the implications of that supreme blasphemy, Katherine's imagination reeled.

Characteristically, it did not cross her mind that all Orley – the Lady Helen, Basil, all the servants who followed the Montgris' lead in the True Faith – were in the same case. She could think of nothing but Hal – not even of herself (after the first shock) except in terms of her ability to save him.

Could she still save him? Hal's position was far more perilous than her own, as yet; for he had partaken of the mockery of the Mass knowingly, while she had partaken in ignorance . . .

The purity of thine own love.

Bella's other warning, meaningless at the time, sprang again to her mind, and she understood. Even to save her own soul, she could not cut herself off from Hal. She must stand beside her beloved, even in the Pit.

She did not even argue with herself about it. It was a fact of her existence, as real and inescapable as her own bones and flesh. Where Hal went, she went; snatch him back from Hell if she could – *Mother of God, help us* – but together, only together.

Katherine drew herself up, taking deep breaths to steady herself; became aware again of the room around her, of the thunder that rumbled and threatened outside; opened the door, and went in search of her husband.

Basil's room, first.

On her way she was accosted by John Grayson, the manor steward; a conscientious but unimaginative man.

'My lady – what news of the boy?'

Basil was 'the boy' to all Orley; it was almost a title, affectionately bestowed. Katherine replied: 'Come with me, Master Grayson. I have been sleeping, so we will assure ourselves together . . . He can be no worse, or I should have been wakened.'

'Pray God he may recover.' Grayson crossed himself as he fell into step beside her. 'It were a sad day for Orley if he should die.'

Good blunt John, she thought, That greying head slept at night with no worse dreams than the ailments of cattle or the idleness of grooms. She hurried with him to the boy's room, where Bess sat apparently tireless at the bedside. The maid rose as they entered; Katherine waved her back to her stool and leaned over Basil.

'I fear he is no better, my lady.'

It was true. If anything the small face was greyer, more deathlike already. Katherine realised she had been hoping that here, at least, there would be an improvement to hearten her – but no. She sighed.

'Where is Sir Henry?'

'I know not, my lady. He hath looked in upon the boy a little time since, the Father with him. They departed together. It may be they went to the chapel to pray. Naught else will aid the lad, God knoweth.'

The chapel . . .

Katherine asked: 'Hast thou supped, Bess?'

Bess shook her head, as though food were unimportant. Katherine turned to the steward. 'Master Grayson, wilt thou find someone to take Bess's place, while I seek my

137

husband? This watch may be long, and I will have no one go hungry through diligence.'

'Assuredly, my lady. And neglect not thine own stomach, in thy care for others.'

Katherine promised him, and hurried away. She knew, with a sudden certainty, what Hal would be doing; *Desperate straits call for desperate measures* . . . Some dreadful sorcery, in the hope of saving Basil's life. But where? In Gadd's study? No – sacrilege mocked at limitations. It would demand the chapel itself.

Mother of God, help me.

She met no one. When she reached the chapel door, it was closed.

And bolted, she found.

She stood there for a moment, listening. There were sounds inside, but faint, indistinguishable.

And a scent. Faint too, seeping through the door-cracks; incense-smoke on the cold air, but not the incense of sanctity – a foul miasma, nameless . . .

Katherine cried out, loudly and firmly: 'Hal!'

There was a moment's pause. Then the door swung open, and Gadd himself confronted her.

At first she could make out nothing but his outline, tall, thin, robed and hooded in black, framed in a red diabolic light which came from behind him. She trembled, but stood her ground. Then as warmth drifted out to envelope her – bringing with it more of the evil incense – she realised; a brazier glowed in the middle of the stone floor. And Hal was there, to one side, robed like Gadd, looking uncertainly towards her.

'So my lady has come,' Gadd said. His voice was mocking, triumphant.

She was surprised at the steadiness of her own voice. 'Yes, I have come, Master Gadd. To see for myself what blasphemy thou workest in God's holy place.'

'Very well, then. See, Katherine.'

He stepped aside, and she saw. Spreadeagled on God's

altar – naked, voluptuous, outrageous, flanked by the obscene black candles; unmoving, yet seeming to move, as firelight and candlelight flickered, and smoke drifted across the white limbs.

Incredulous, Katherine walked to the altar in a daze of shock. For a moment she did not know who the girl was; then, as she came near, she recognised her. Amy Tanner, the most pert and shameless of the Orley kitchenmaids, notoriously free with her favours to any village lad who caught her eye.

Katherine's control broke. She rushed at the altar, grabbing at Amy's thick yellow hair, and dragged her by it sideways on to the floor. Amy screamed with the pain while Katherine yelled 'Blasphemous whore!' and kicked again and again at the bare flesh.

Hal cried out, once, and stepped forward as though to intervene. But Gadd barred his way, and stood watching.

The sobbing Amy scrambled to her feet and ran, snatching up a gown that lay by the door and struggling into it head-first. Then she was gone. Unhurried, Gadd closed and re-bolted the door behind her, and returned to the altar to set upright, and relight, one of the black candles that had been knocked over in the brief struggle.

He turned to face Katherine, and asked: 'Well?'

Panting to get her breath back, Katherine hissed at him: 'Thou excommunicate cur! God be thanked I've prevented thee!'

Gadd laughed. 'Prevented? *O sancta simplicitas!* . . . And yet for all thy simplicity, not so holy withal. For if I am excommunicate, art thou not damned? My so virtuous lady, hast thou not received Mass at my hands? And thy husband?'

'God is merciful . . .'

'God is not here. He hath left this place to His Enemy. Call on the Prince of Darkness, if call thou must. For only He will hear thee . . .'

Katherine opened her mouth to interrupt, but Gadd came

139

a pace closer and something in his eyes seemed to paralyse her. His voice went on, remorselessly: 'I am pledged to Him, thy husband is pledged to Him – and thou, Katherine, thou art helpless, without allies, for all unknowing thou hast severed thyself from thy God's grace . . . Thou hast the choice, Katherine of Orley. Either thou canst stay, summon the wench back to the altar, and put thy trust in the only One who will listen to thee now. That way lieth power, and riches – and the life of the boy Basil, for that hath been placed in His mighty hands. And if Basil dieth, God will not help him – for remember, Basil too is unabsolved . . . Or else, Katherine of Orley, thou canst walk through that door, leaving us to finish our work – for finished it must be, or Basil dieth, be sure of that. Thou canst go, Katherine, for I will not stop thee – go to call in the darkness upon thy deaf God, and to hope without hope.'

He stepped back, smiling. Katherine, released from his hypnotic hold, took a pace towards the door, involuntarily.

'And leave Hal to whatever awaiteth him,' Gadd added in a voice almost too soft to hear.

And with that, he had her. He knew, with a surgeon's exactness, where to cut.

Katherine's shoulders slumped. Gadd smiled again, and turned to nod to Hal.

'Call the wench back.'

'No!' Katherine's cry halted Hal in his tracks. She was unfastening her gown, her bodice, her underskirt – flinging away to right and left the farthingale, the padded hip-rolls, all the splendid armour of an Elizabethan lady. 'I'll not have that strumpet a part of this!' she was sobbing. 'And if souls are to be damned, I'll not have hers, too, on the ruins of my conscience! . . . Thy Master demandeth woman-flesh for His altar, doth he? Then woman-flesh He shall have – but *mine*! If my husband danceth to Hell, he'll have no kitchen-whore for a partner . . .' She stormed on and on, not pausing for breath till she stood naked, dark hair falling free,

140

the tears bright on her cheeks. Then, in silence, she walked to the altar and lay back on it, as Amy had lain.

She would not look at Gadd, and dared not look at Hal. In the roof above her, a carved angel gazed down unemotionally. She fixed her gaze on him, and waited.

Gadd placed a chalice in her hands, between breasts and navel. She gripped it, trying not to let her hands shake; but they did shake, for she felt spilled wine on her skin.

'We summon Marbas,' Gadd told her, almost conversationally. 'He is one of Satan's legions, a mighty Prince who hath command over all maladies and fevers. Play thy part, and he will come; and Basil will be saved. Fail, and Basil dieth.'

Then he stepped back, and his voice became sonorous as bronze. At first Katherine listened to the words, to the dreadful evocations; but when the English became inverted Latin, and she recognised the mockery of the Mass, disgust screened her mind and his voice seemed to come from a distance. There was nothing distant, however, about the hands that took hold of her knees and spread them apart – nor about the anointing . . .

It dawned on Katherine, at last, how she was to be used. Her body was no mere table, however sacrilegious that was in itself. It was to be a vessel, a receptacle for the defiling of the Host . . .

In that terrible instant of realisation, when she thought all hope and all help was dead, it was as though Bella prompted her memory: *Aye, call on Her from the Abyss – She may hear . . .*

Gadd's fingers were probing her.

Ave Maria, gratia plena, Dominus tecum, benedicta tu in mulieribus . . . Holy Mother of God, blessed helper of women, save us . . .

'Suproc tse coh . . .'

Mary, Queen of Heaven, Thou knowest of love and sacrifice – Thou knowest I submitted only through love, to stand beside my husband even in the fires of Hell – be my sin as foul as night, my love is pure, my love for him . . . If this much grace is left me, hear me, Queen of Heaven . . .

Her outraged flesh, cringing but helpless, fed the flames of her prayer as the Black Mass rolled forward. She was divided in two now, her body supine before Satan, her soul prostrate before the Friend of Women. She could hear everything, every blasphemous phrase – even hear the thunder which still mocked December above Orley's rooftops . . .

'Marbas, I summon thee . . .'

No, Mother of God, prevent him – send Thy messenger – all power is Thine, no wickedness can withstand Thy radiance – send Thy messenger . . .

'Marbas, Prince of Plagues . . .'

Queen of Heaven – Thy messenger . . .

Lightning blinded the chapel; and without pause between, an earthquake of thunder that must surely shatter all . . . Katherine's head jerked to the right, as though forced by an invisible hand.

Gadd cried out loud.

They all three saw her: the shining maid, the silver close-fitting armour that looked like chain-mail, the straight fair hair; saw her erect in the Triangle of Evocation, the sword in her left hand starting to move . . .

Then all was blackness. It seemed an age before their dazzled eyes could again see by the red glow of the brazier. The candles were out, every one.

Hal's voice, almost comical in its bewilderment, broke the spell. 'Was *that* Marbas?'

Katherine knew better, and laughed aloud, in joy and relief. *Mother of God, Thou hast heard me! We may yet be saved!*

Gadd, after a stunned pause, looked as though he might go berserk; then he seemed to control himself with a mighty effort, and barked at them: 'The rite is finished for this night. Clothe thyself, woman. And both of you – go!'

Katherine had never dressed herself with such speed. Hal,

142

uncomprehending and speechless, threw off his robe and then helped his wife.

Within minutes they were outside, clinging to each other. Then Katherine stiffened.

'Basil!'

They could hardly believe their eyes. It was Basil, true enough; night-robed, tousle-haired, but full of energy and life, bouncing along the gallery with Bess in anxious protesting pursuit.

'Basil – what in God's name? . . .'

He grinned at her, slightly puzzled. 'I thought I heard thee call me – so I came.'

It was not until they had chivvied him back to bed, all of them babbling cheerful nonsense in their incredulous delight, that they were sobered by the grim face of Robin Fullbright, waiting respectfully in the shadows.

'What is it, Robin?'

'Sir – my lady – I would not tell you till the boy was abed. He is too newly recovered to learn of tragedy – and he loved Master Grayson well . . .'

'Master Grayson? Why, what ails him?'

'He is dead, sir. The lightning hath struck him as he walked in the courtyard. God rest his soul – he was a good man.'

They looked at each other in silence; then Hal said, 'Amen to that . . . I must go see to him.'

Is that how it must be? Katherine wondered – a life for a life?

143

CHAPTER XIII

'Exactly the same as last time,' Jane said, her voice puzzled. 'It wasn't another Black Mass – it was *the same* Black Mass. A complete recapitulation . . . I don't understand.'

'Don't try,' Bridget told her. 'Accept that it was the same. Just ask yourself if there was anything you were more aware of, that you hadn't been last time.'

'Only the very end. It was as though . . . after they saw me in the Triangle, it lasted a second or two longer. I know, because I'd begun to raise my sword. And last time, I hadn't.'

'That's good,' George said, and Bridget nodded.

Jane had recovered consciousness almost immediately. She had only been in trance for about five minutes, they told her, standing motionless in the Triangle (they spoke of it as real) and unaffected by the thunderstorm which had suddenly intensified. They had stood close, ready to catch her if she fell; but there had been one last tremendous explosion of lightning and thunder, immediately overhead – and as its echo died, Jane had simply walked out of the Triangle, breathless and pale, but fully herself.

Now the lights were on, and they sat in the folding chairs, Jane with a rug round her shoulders and a mug of coffee from the thermos in her hands. George – careful to ask her permission first – had put the sword back in its sheath on the gallery wall. After that final burst, the air outside was still, and the storm might never have been.

'Did I win?' Jane asked suddenly, wondering at her own question.

'What do *you* feel?' Bridget wanted to know.

Jane frowned, searching for words. 'In a way . . .' Then she heard herself say: 'Basil's all right, at least.'

'You say he *is* all right. Not "was". That's interesting.'

'It came to me just then. And it *felt* like the present. I know it's true, though . . .' She frowned again. 'But there's something else . . . I don't know . . .'

Bridget said: 'Yes. Try to get it yourself. It will be better if you can.'

'It's . . . vague . . .'

'If you can't get the facts of it, get the feeling.'

'As though . . . Well, as though I, or the Battle Maid or Katherine's prayers – or all three, I don't know . . . As though Gadd wasn't *defeated* – I mean, the thing he was summoning – so much as *deflected* . . . And I don't like it . . . Does that sound terribly muddled?'

George and Bridget said 'No' together, and Bridget went on: 'I got that too. George?'

'Yes. The thunderstorm – it was part of it . . . Look at it this way, Jane. Accept for a moment that there's some kind of breakthrough in time – that in some way, right now, there's a situation in the sixteenth century and a situation in the twentieth that have got locked on to each other. Don't ask me to explain it, because I can't – but it's happened, hasn't it?'

'I've got to accept that. I'm right *in* it.'

'Then let me ask you something. Was there a thunderstorm going on there, too? In Katherine's time?'

'My God, yes – there was! I hadn't thought of it – I suppose because it was going on here, before it all started, I just accepted it without noticing. But Katherine could hear it, too. It was going on all the time . . . And yes, at the last moment, that tremendous flash – it happened in *both* times.'

'I thought so . . . It was a manifestation of the power that was building up, across that bridge in time.' He paused, and then told her gently: 'You'll have to be prepared for it, Jane. When someone as powerful as Gadd raises something as powerful as Marbas, all Hell can be let loose. You stopped it reaching its target . . .'

'*Was* it me?'

'Not of your own strength entirely – no. Katherine called on the Goddess – Mary to her, but it's the same thing, in our terms – and in a sense you did too. Between you, you provided a channel for Her. You must be in tune with each other *and* with Her, whatever each of you calls Her. And it was *that* which stopped Marbas . . .'

'Is Marbas real, too?'

'Again, the evil *force* Gadd's a channel for is real, whatever he chooses to call it. The two forces met head-on – and the evil was, as you say, deflected. But it may have spent itself on a substitute.'

'You mean – we may have saved Basil at the cost of someone else?'

'Jane, you didn't start this war. You can only fight it. But in this kind of war, innocent bystanders can get hurt.'

Jane was silent for a while. Then she said, reluctantly: 'I hate to admit it, but that makes sense . . . My God, what a responsibility.'

'The responsibility's with Gadd, not you. As I say, you *can* only fight the war he started. When he's finally defeated, the innocent casualties will stop. As with Hitler.'

'And that's why I must go on.'

'It's up to you, lass,' Bridget said. 'No one's forcing you. Don't try to exceed your own strength.'

Jane smiled, wryly. 'I thought you said it wasn't *my* strength.'

'I said not *entirely*', George corrected her. 'It's still a tremendous drain on you. Channels have to be strong, too, you know – or they burst.'

'I stood it better this time than last, didn't I? *And* I – or we, or it – won a round . . . That's why next time I don't think it'll be a recapitulation. It'll be Round Two . . .' She hesitated. 'Will it always be a question of deflection? Of other people getting hurt? Or is complete victory possible? Neutralising Gadd once and for all, for instance?'

Bridget laughed. 'Oh, yes. When the crunch comes, one

side finally wins, and the other channel is blocked off . . . But you have to watch it. It's easy to kid yourself the enemy's dead, when he's only crawled off to lick his wounds. I've been caught that way myself – though not for a long time, I'm getting wily in my old age.' She shook her head. 'There I go again. Never boast, never threaten. You should keep me in order, George.'

George just grinned and said: 'Yes, Grandma.'

Jane had more questions, but she sensed that the mutual teasing into which George and Bridget dropped was deliberate, so she relaxed, merely adding as an afterthought: 'I don't *feel* drained.'

'You see?' Bridget answered, 'I told you you were the Battle Maid.'

After a while, when Jane had finished her coffee, they put away the chairs and prepared to join Bruce and Ted. Nothing more would happen tonight. It was as though the chapel needed time, after each encounter, to rebuild the bridge, Jane thought . . . No, not altogether, because there had been other instants of contact – at the seat in the Long Walk. But the chapel itself – that was no instant, but a profound involvement. It *must* take time to recharge itself . . . Time? What *was* time?

No, she must rest a while – not only from battle, but from impossible paradoxes. They were right to lower the tension, the Blakes – this humorous, gentle couple who dealt with incredibilities in such a matter-of-fact way . . . Gentle? Jane realised she could envisage situations in which Bridget could be a holy terror and George a bull elephant – but never wantonly, never without cause.

She was glad they were on her side.

They walked downstairs to the lobby.

Bruce and Ted were kneeling over the polygraph, fiddling with it. Ted looked up and said: 'Oh, hullo . . . That thunderstorm's sent everything haywire.'

'Mains voltage fluctuations?' George asked.

'Quite big ones – on top of wild temperature and pressure

147

changes, and of course the sound being swamped. It's mucked up all our zero lines.'

'No damage, though?'

'Doesn't look like it . . . Checking now . . . Hey, hold that steady, Bruce!'

'Sorry . . . George, would you take over from me? I'm all thumbs.'

George complied, and he and Ted were soon exchanging technicalities barely comprehensible to the rest of them. Bruce straightened up, and came across to Jane and Bridget.

'That's incredible hair you've got, when you let it down,' he told Bridget. 'Like Lady Godiva's.'

'I always wear it up when I'm riding. Otherwise it tickles the horse.'

'Lucky horse . . .' He kept up his would-be casual gallantry for another sentence or two, Bridget answering him easily, but he was becoming a little laboured, and it was obvious that he was dodging the question he really wanted to ask. So Jane intervened and came to point.

'We've finished for tonight, Bruce. I had the same experience, all over again, in the Triangle. Only this time I came out of it at once. No fainting or anything.'

She could sense his hackles rising, but he seemed to want to avoid a direct clash. And I know why, she realised suddenly. He's scared stiff of Bridget. Well, well.

Bruce jerked a thumb towards the polygraph. 'If you can unscramble anything psychic out of that lot, you'll be lucky. The traces are a real cat's cradle.'

'Even if we could,' Bridget said, 'it'd only be confirmation.'

So. She's not going to let him avoid it.

'Made up your minds, have you?' The hostility was back in Bruce's voice.

'Haven't *you*?' – sweetly.

For a moment Jane thought Bruce was going to lose his temper, which was perhaps what Bridget intended. But the

148

clash was postponed by the arrival of Keith Stoneleigh, letting himself in through the side door from the garden.

'Hullo, everybody. Quiet night at the hospital, so I thought I'd drop in to see how things were going . . . Aren't you in the chapel this time?'

Everyone turned to welcoming and explaining, except Bruce, who withdrew further into his shell of hostility. Jane told herself that she had been considerate towards him (well, mostly) and tolerant of his rigidity, but as she watched him sulking now, she decided she was beginning to lose patience. She made herself charming to Keith, knowing that this would upset Bruce even more, and not caring.

Bruce edged towards the outer door, as though he wanted a walk in the fresh air. He paused with his hand on the latch, waiting to catch Jane's eye, to invite her to walk with him. Jane was well aware of it; she awaited her moment, looked directly at him, answered the invitation of his eyes with a bright, empty smile, and turned back to Keith.

'Are you *always* on duty at night?' she asked him, loud and clear.

She heard the door slam.

'That,' Bridget said, 'was naughty but necessary . . .' and putting an arm round Jane, continued the discussion in the suddenly relaxed atmosphere. Keith, the only one unaware of the overtones, looked briefly puzzled, but was soon swept away by his interest in the subject.

The relaxation did not last.

'*Doctor! Doctor!*'

Bruce's cry, his running feet in the courtyard, froze them all for an instant; then Keith jumped at the door, pulling it open just as Bruce appeared in it, breathless and white-faced.

'Doctor – out there . . .'

'What, man?'

'Charley Unsworth. The Curator – out there in the court-yard. The lightning must have hit him . . . Doc, I think he's dead.'

CHAPTER XIV

Jane could never remember, afterwards, quite how she lived through the next twenty-four hours. She knew with her brain that she was not responsible for Charley Unsworth's death; but in the first shock, her stomach crawled with the conviction of guilt.

It must have been plain in her face, the moment Bruce's words hit her; for as they all moved forward to follow Keith out of the door, Bridget looked at her, and checked. Then she caught her arm and said 'Stay here'. She murmured something to George, who nodded and followed the others. Jane was still half-straining to go too, blind and unthinking, but Bridget stopped her firmly and made her sit down.

'I know what your guts are telling you, Jane – but don't let yourself think it, because it isn't true.'

Jane shook her head, more in bewilderment than denial. 'Poor man, it was nothing to *do* with him,' she cried. 'He was stupid and harmless and nice, and he loved this place, and he thought ghosts were all nonsense, and he's dead, and it's my fault . . .'

'It is *not* your fault, and you dam' well know it. It was the thing you're fighting against – the evil that Gadd's let loose.'

'Gadd's been dead three hundred years . . .'

'Has he?'

'. . . and I'm alive *now*, and so was Charley Unsworth . . .' She jumped up. 'Suppose he isn't dead? Perhaps Bruce was wrong!'

'Sit down, lass. I've told George to come straight back and tell us what Keith says . . . And listen to me. You can't have it both ways. Either this battle is real, and Gadd's causing it – never mind those three hundred years – in which case *he's* responsible for Unsworth's death. Or else it's all hallucination, in which case Unsworth got killed by lightning and nothing more. And if that's so, no one's responsible.'

'Or I let loose something that's been bottled up for three hundred years – something which Gadd caused *then* – and it would've stayed bottled up, and hurt no one, if I hadn't meddled.'

'For God's sake, Jane – you didn't "meddle". You were dragged in. You *had* to react as you did.'

'Preordained?' Jane asked, with an attempt at sarcasm she didn't feel.

'If you like to call it that. Let's say you were as much part of what happened *then* as Gadd is part of what's happening *now*. You're the only free soul on the side of the angels, lass. Without you, Katherine and her Hal are helpless, and Basil would have been, too. If it weren't so – why have you been haunting Orley Grange for three centuries, waiting for the final battle?'

'Me?'

'Or the Battle Maid – what's the difference? I think it's you – in that lamé trouser suit, which they all saw as armour, and carrying the sword in your *left* hand – it's *you* everyone's recognised, from Katherine through Lady Clara to Trevor Cox's grandfather and old Mrs Cannon.'

Jane paused, a little calmer. 'My common sense denies it, but my guts say it's true. Just as my common sense tells me I had nothing to do with Charley getting killed, but my guts say it's my fault.'

'Then your guts are contradicting themselves, aren't they? If you're the Battle Maid, then Gadd killed Charley . . . If he *is* dead, that's to say.'

The Curator was dead enough; George came back just then to confirm it. 'Direct and instantaneous, Keith says, so he won't have felt anything . . . He also says he was a bachelor with no family. He knew the old boy quite well.'

151

Jane realised these mitigations were for her benefit, and was grateful.

'Thanks, darling,' Bridget told him. 'I expect the boys could use your help packing up the equipment – why don't you ask them? Obviously they won't do anything more tonight. I'll see Jane back to the Green Man.'

'Right,' George said, and disappeared again.

The bar was closed and the evening drinkers gone by the time they reached the hotel. When Bridget told Trevor what had happened, he looked badly shaken, but he was in control at once, shepherding them into his private sitting-room and producing brandy.

'Here, get this inside you.' He looked at Jane, his intelligent face concerned. 'I hope you haven't got any daft idea that it's your fault?'

'The thunderstorm?' He's being kind and I'm being sarcastic again, Jane thought unhappily.

'You know I don't mean that. But it's a by-product of the thing you're fighting against, is my guess. And since you're fighting *against* it, whoever or whatever's to blame, it isn't you.'

'I know. That's what Bridget's been saying. But I still feel dreadful.'

'Natural battle reaction. Every soldier knows it. The chap next to you gets shot, and your first reaction is relief that it wasn't you. You smother the thought, before you're even conscious of it – but it breaks through as guilt.'

'You mean I'm *glad* Charley caught it instead of me? . . . That'd be dreadful.'

'No – human. Be honest, love. A perfectly natural survival reflex.'

Jane rested her head against the chair-back, closing her eyes. 'I'm too tired to go analysing myself.'

'You've got to, or you'll be even tireder, because you won't be able to rest.'

She opened her eyes again, glaring at him. For that instant she thought she hated him, but she knew at once that she

152

was wrong, and she managed a genuine smile. 'Thanks, Trevor. I'm sorry.'

Trevor sighed. 'Remind me to analyse myself, too.'

Bridget looked at him thoughtfully, but Jane was too drained to wonder about it, then.

She slept, and she dreamed – tangled, unresolving dreams that refused to be recalled when she woke, even though the change from sleeping to waking was protracted and restless. When the bedroom finally became solid around her, she lay for a while trying to pin down the dreams, but they had already disintegrated.

She looked at the clock; it was nearly half-past eight. The boys would have had breakfast and gone to bed already . . . Oh, no, of course. They'd called it off and gone to bed last night, after . . .

Charley Unsworth was dead.

She took the thought out and looked at it. It still numbed her.

So the chap next to me was shot. Relief, guilt, natural chain of reflexes. Mustn't let it undermine me . . . All very well, but Charley *is* dead, and . . .

She sat up in bed, angry with herself for her apparent lack of progress in coping with the situation, and tried to turn her thoughts back to the others. They'd probably be sleeping in late, too; they had still been milling around, when Bridget and Trevor between them had practically ordered her to bed. She remembered that she and Bruce had tended to avoid each other, though the details of the last half hour before she came upstairs were somewhat confused.

At least now she was hungry; that was a good sign. She had a quick bath and dressed, and went down feeling a little better.

In the dining-room, immediately, she was faced with a decision. Bruce and Ted were breakfasting at one table, the Blakes at another some feet away. Whether that had been deliberate (and if so, who had snubbed whom), or whether

153

the room had simply been crowded when they started, was impossible to say; Bridget and George's table for four had had one place cleared away, so perhaps Trevor had been eating with them when the boys came down, and there had not been space for five. Whatever the reason, there it was; and Jane must choose, even though she did not really want to make any apparent gestures with the day hardly begun.

She greeted Bruce and Ted friendlily enough, and then went and sat with the Blakes, who were after all (or so she told herself, though she knew it was not her real reason) in a sense their guests.

'Good morning,' Bridget said. 'Did you get some proper sleep?'

'More or less, I suppose. Did you?'

'I'm afraid so. Sounds unfair, doesn't it? But then, we usually do sleep like babies. And if the astral's a bit turbulent, we cast a Circle round the bed. We did last night.'

'Give the girl a chance,' George told her. 'Blinding her with technicalities at this time in the morning . . . Try the mushrooms on toast, Jane, they're good. Gathered this morning, Trevor says, and I'll believe him.'

'I like this husband of yours, Bridget,' Jane said, feeling easier already. 'He's very relaxing.'

'I know. So calm I could hit him, sometimes. But he's right about the mushrooms.'

Trevor served and poured her coffee, in person; another morning gesture, Jane thought, but a nice one this time. She noticed that he knew without asking that she liked very little milk but two sugars. She had been thinking of bacon, but she felt obliged, in the circumstances, to order his mushrooms. They were talking about them, pleasantly, when she realised that Bruce was standing at her other elbow.

Well-disposed for the moment, she said: 'Oh, there you are. Did you have the mushrooms, too?'

'No . . . Jane, I've asked Trevor to have our three bills made out, up to and including lunch. That'll give us the

154

morning to pack, and we can leave about two. Can you be ready?'

Her goodwill towards him vanished like a switched-off light. If he had merely reopened the argument, merely set out to persuade her that they should call off the experiment and leave, she would have been prepared for that, and she had intended to put her own viewpoint as one friend to another. But this arrogance, this unilateral decision, was too much.

'Make that *two* bills, please, Trevor,' she said calmly. 'I'm staying, of course.'

Bruce protested to her still-turned back: 'But Jane! After last night, we've *got* to call it off . . .'

She turned deliberately to face him. 'You can do exactly what you like, Bruce. I make my own decisions, thank you, and I don't like them anticipated. For a start, I want to be at the Curator's funeral.' That was meant to embarrass him, and it did. He was about to stammer something, but she went on: 'And I still have a commitment in the chapel.'

Trevor said 'Two bills, then' in an expressionless maître-d'hôtel voice, and withdrew. Bridget and George watched, saying nothing.

'But Jane . . .'

Jane smiled at him, icily. 'But Jane what?'

He stared at her for a moment, his colour rising, and then turned on his heel and walked out.

She was glad that Ted had already gone, and that only the three of them were left in the room, because as soon as the confrontation was over her icy composure deserted her. 'That was *horrible*,' she found herself saying tearfully. 'I *like* Bruce, I don't *want* to be a bitch to him. But can't he *see*?'

'You know he can't, lass,' Bridget soothed her. 'You know why, too. There wasn't anything else you could do. It's not your fault.'

'You keep telling me things aren't my fault.'

'If they were, I'd say so. I can be a bitch, too, when I have to – can't I George?'

155

'That's why I married you,' he grinned. 'I feel safer on the same side.'

'How can I persuade this girl I'm serious if *you* won't be?'

They went on, teasing each other and her, pulling her gently out of her misery. She was more or less herself when Ted came in, diffidently.

'Do you want me to stay, Jane?'

She took his hand as he stood over her. 'Bless you, Ted – it'd be good to have you around, but you'd better go with Bruce. I've had to be – well, rough with him.'

Ted shook his head. 'Don't see what else you could have done. Not to worry, I'll calm him down . . . If I were you, love, I'd skip lunch. You both might try to make it up with each other, and then *he* might decide to stay after all. And that wouldn't work . . . . It's a bugger, isn't it?'

Bridget said: 'Good idea, Ted. We'll take her out for lunch.'

Ted said his shy goodbyes; Jane stood up and kissed him. So, unexpectedly, did Bridget, and wished him good luck.

'I think you're the ones who'll need that,' Ted told her.

Jane's guilt over Bruce probably helped to push her guilt about Charley farther into the background. Her brain, if not yet her emotions, had already accepted Bridget's arguments about Charley; but she was by no means convinced that her harsh treatment of Bruce had been necessary. Surely she could have stuck to her decision, and still handled him like a friend? . . . Because he *was* a friend. Apart from his one blind spot – the reasons for which she felt she understood – she respected his mind, and had enjoyed communicating with him. And in retrospect, her sexual manoeuvres towards him seemed to her to have been less and less tactical, and more genuine, more prompted by real attraction, to the point where she began to wonder whether the tactical reasons she had given herself – the need to overcome his resistance to her returning to the chapel – had not been rationalisations. She had desired him, and had excused her

156

own blatant behaviour with irrelevancies – because after all he couldn't have *stopped* her going to the chapel . . . No, that was nonsense. She wasn't a coy adolescent. If she wanted a man, she used the time-honoured manoeuvres without hypocrisy.

Jane felt confused.

Maddeningly, as the morning wore by and she knew he really was leaving, he grew more desirable as a man, in her imagination. She avoided seeing him, and he made no further attempt to see her; he simply vanished, leaving Ted to do most of the packing of the equipment. Bridget and George took her away about noon and drove her to another village for a pub lunch; she found herself talking compulsively and at random, and quite unable afterwards to remember what she had talked about, except that she had only once touched on the things she was really thinking.

That was when she had said suddenly: 'Ted was dam' right. If I'd seen Bruce again, I'd just have thrown my arms round his neck and bawled.' They had been sympathetic, but Jane could tell that they agreed with Ted. So did she, come to that. Reconciliation now would be disastrous, and she knew it. But she returned with them to the Green Man in the afternoon restless and, as she told herself bitterly in her own mind, as randy as a bitch in heat. Pull yourself together, Jane Blair. Try a cold shower . . .

The cold shower came, but metaphorically, and it was Trevor who administered it. 'I've had quite a morning,' he told them when they got back 'Bruce went to Orley R.D.C. and got hold of Chadwick, the chairman of the Grange Trustee Committee. Tried to get him to withdraw permission for the experiments . . . It was touch and go, because Morry Chadwick was in a state about Charley's death, of course – and after all, Bruce is the official representative of the Midland Psychical Research Society, and as far as the Council's concerned he's in charge of the experiments they gave permission for. Fortunately Morry's a stickler for procedure, and since I'd moved the original resolution, he rang me up for my agreement to have the permission withdrawn. I persuaded him the whole thing was a private row, and that Jane was not only in the right, but was a highly qualified historian and a very responsible person. But I had to go down there myself and spend an hour fighting it out, with Morry shuffling backwards and forwards between me and Bruce – he wouldn't see us both together; said it would be incorrect procedure. So I was arguing with Bruce at second hand all the time. In the end I took personal responsibility for you three, so if you wreck the place, I'm on the carpet . . . I was dreading meeting Bruce when he came to pay the bill, I'll admit – it's not easy being a Councillor one minute and a publican the next. Cowardly, I suppose, but there it is. Bruce must have felt the same, though, because he sent Ted to settle up. Ted told me, off the record, that he was glad I'd won.'

So was Jane, and she said so; the possibility of the Council stopping them had never occurred to her, and she was so committed to her battle that she dared not think what the consequences would have been if Bruce had succeeded. She was so furious with him for having used such tactics, for having tried to bring an outside veto to bear on her personal decision – a decision she had every right to make – that all her sympathy and desire for him went cold.

'I wish I *had* stayed, just to kick his car door shut on him,' she spat.

'That's the spirit, girl,' Bridget approved. 'Write him off. Never look back.'

So Jane wrote him off, and rolled up her psychic sleeves.

By the evening, the tide of strength was flowing in her direction again. She found herself wanting to dress for dinner, and mentioned the fact to Bridget as evidence that she was feeling better. She was delighted to learn that it was Bridget's habit, too.

'Even when it's just you and George?'

'Quite often, yes . . . Sometimes he asks me to.'

158

'I like that. I wonder how many husbands would bother?'

'A lot more would if their wives made it clear they dressed up for *them*, top of the list . . . What are you going to wear tonight, then?'

'A green Empire style thing, I think.'

'Yes, Empire'd suit you. Right, then, I'll go all stately – my turn for black, with some silver. Lucky George – tonight he's got a High Priestess and a Maiden. And in the Goddess colours, too.'

Jane laughed. 'It doesn't sound outlandish, coming from you, somehow. Witches' jargon, I mean. You make it seem natural.'

'I should hope so. An artificial witch is a contradiction in terms.'

'As though it were an everyday thing for a man to have a High Priestess.'

'Every *happy* man has – even if she's an abstraction. But most men prefer them incarnate. Including George, I'm glad to say . . . Come on, lass. Tarting-up time.'

Later, when Jane joined Bridget in her room for the nail-varnish stage, she asked: 'What did you mean by the Goddess colours?'

'Well, there are several, for different aspects. Light blue – sky blue – copper . . . But black and green are very much the two fundamental aspects – Binah and Netzach, if you know your Qabalah . . .'

'I don't.'

'There, you see – even I can overdo the jargon. You should study it sometime, it should be very illuminating for a historian. Anyway . . . Stand up. Come and look.'

Bridget led her to the long mirror, and stood at her side.

Jane's first reaction was: She's right, George *is* lucky. We're quite a pair for a man to escort. The High Priestess, severely lovely, hair braided into the crown of an absolute monarch. The lines of her near-perfect body seemed stern in the loose black, yet completely feminine; seemed to give

159

out a dark powerful radiance, shot through with the touches of silver that only accentuated the mystery.

And herself? A Nature being, poised midway between spring and summer, slenderly sensual, fecund and joy-giving and bright with the complementary radiance . . .

'We frighten me, a little,' she said.

'No need.' Bridget went back to her dressing-table. 'Only if it were unbalanced. But each contains the other and can become the other. The Dark Mother is at the core of the Bright Mother, and the Bright Mother at the core of the Dark Mother. I am both, and so are you. Every High Priestess has to be.'

Jane said: 'You've got me confused. I'm not a High Priestess. And neither of us is a Goddess, which is what we were talking about.'

Bridget smiled, and answered obliquely. 'You remember George said that when Katherine called on the Goddess – Mary, to her – you were doing the same thing, in your own way? You let it pass, but you thought you didn't believe him. Really, though, you knew what he meant.'

'I'm not sure that I did . . . How *does* one call on the Goddess – if one isn't even sure that She exists?'

'*As we have of old been taught that the point within the centre is the origin of all things, therefore should we adore it; therefore whom we adore we also invoke. O Circle of Stars . . .*' Bridget broke off; she was still smiling.

'What's that?'

'Just a quote . . . Jane, when you're alone tonight, before you go to sleep, try this . . .'

It had been a lovely evening, Jane decided as she undressed. An evening to exorcise the clouds that had surrounded her since the night before, Satisfactorily, the dining room had been well filled, and Bridget and she had been the focus of interest, from unabashed to surreptitious; just what she needed, she admitted without shame, to restore her morale. And George had been the ideal third – his blend of humour, seriousness, and quiet courtesy appealed to her; he never seemed to lose it, whether he was coping with a crisis like last night's, or enlivening a dinner.

She had pushed Bridget's suggestion to the back of her mind, but now she wanted to try it.

When she had finished preparing for bed, she turned out the light and opened the curtains, and the window as well, for the night was still warm. The moon, which had been full when she and Bruce and Ted had first arrived, was now near to the last quarter, so although the sky was cloudless it had not risen yet. The soft glow from Orley's few lights was not enough to obliterate the stars, and Jane sat naked and cross-legged on the bed where she could see a scattering of constellations above the black treetops.

She and the Blakes had been the last to go to bed, and everything was quiet.

Now . . .

Jane tried to be fully aware of herself as part of the universe, merging with it, inseparable from it. It took a little time, because her attention kept jumping back and forth between herself, solid and small on the bed, and the universe, starry, vast, and impersonal; it was all very well to talk of merging the two, but . . . But – but – gradually the merging seemed less impossible, more natural; she tried to describe the strange feeling to herself in words, but that began to drive it back, so she contented herself with experiencing it, and like a shy animal, it came out to play once she herself was still, observing it, identifying with it . . .

Now carefully . . .

She started focusing her attention inward, inward, inward, to what must surely be the vanishing-point at the centre of her universe-self. Once or twice the sound of a passing car, or the bark of a fox in the woods, broke her concentration and she had to retrace her steps; but with each attempt, her surroundings became more remote, less disturbing, till she was no longer aware of them at all, till she and the universe were shrinking together towards that

161

inconceivable Centre, that dimensionless point where all must surely cease to exist . . . She was conscious of a moment of muted terror, which flared briefly but hardly seemed part of her, and then for a mere diamond-point of time only the Centre was real.

But the point was infinity! The Centre was the Circumference . . . Frontierless, the Goddess touched her . . .

But she was Jane Blair, naked and cross-legged on a hotel bed, gazing at the stars through an open window.

Wondering, she climbed between the sheets and lay on her back, feeling as though a flood had swept through her. *What* had she experienced? Had she truly experienced anything, or . . .

All she knew was that she felt clean, and content, and wonderfully powerful.

Jane turned on to her side and slept like a baby.

CHAPTER XV

It was nearly midnight before Hal realised that Katherine was missing.

Master Grayson's death had triggered off confusion throughout the big manor house. There were things to be done, of course; the steward's body to be lifted on to a hurdle and carried indoors; his stunned and weeping daughter Doll (a twelve-year-old orphan now, poor brat, for Grayson was a widower) to be handed over to the motherly Bess for comforting; Grayson's mare to be caught, for he had apparently been leading her at the time (why, Hal could not imagine) and she had bolted; other horses to be quietened, because the thunderstorm had panicked them, and one or two seemed in danger of kicking their stalls down; some burning straw to be quenched, for the same lightning that had killed Grayson had set fire to it – and why had there been no rain? – it was not natural, when the storm had been so ferocious . . .

Hal hurried to and fro, giving orders and trying, as he did so, to instil some calm; for the confusion seemed greater than the practical tasks warranted. It was as though the storm, and its fatal climax, had conjured up a hysteria that would not easily be brought under control. As Robin Fullbright, giving a hand in the chaotic stables, growled to Ned the head groom; 'Death by sword or sickness I've seen a-plenty, and felt no more than sorrow; but by lightning . . . There's something weird about it that seizeth my stomach. 'Tis like the wrath of God.'

'Or the Devil,' his friend replied, crossing himself as he dodged a flailing hoof. 'Easy, thou fool beast, easy . . .'

When Hal realised that the men with the hurdle were making their way, naturally enough, to the chapel, he remembered with horror the black candles and the smell of unholy incense that might still be there. He hurried off, knowing that he would at least have time to replace the candles. But when he reached the chapel, Gadd had fore-stalled him; the white candles were back on the altar, the altar cloth had been relaid, the cool aroma of frankincense had practically banished the earlier scent, and the refuelled brazier, off to one side, looked as though it had just been brought in to warm those who would keep vigil. Even the Triangle of Evocation, which had been formed with black cord laid on the floor, had been whisked away.

Hal leaned against the chapel doorpost, gasping his relief. Gadd, standing by the altar in his normal garments, smiled at him ironically.

'Didst thou think I'd be so easily discovered, Hal? Those who serve the Master dare not fumble.'

'They are fetching John Grayson hither. I feared . . .'

'Fear is for children . . . Let them come. All is ready for their ignorant eyes. And ears — I shall chant and mutter fittingly, and they shall be satisfied.'

'I did not doubt thee, i' faith,' Hal said hastily, anxious to placate Gadd, whom in his heart he feared more than he feared discovery. 'So much hath happened in so short a space, my wits are awry.'

'Then gather them again, boy,' Gadd ordered him sharply.

The pathetic little cortège arrived, with the steward's corpse draped in a horse-blanket, hastily snatched up; for the lightning had stripped and charred him. Most of the Grange servants trailed behind, the women weeping (except Bess, whose whole concern was for the stumbling Doll) and the men white-faced, for Robin had not been alone in his reaction to the manner of Master Grayson's death.

Hal, as befitted the master of the house, moved to the head of the rough bier in the role of chief mourner; and indeed his sorrow was real, for John had been a tower of strength to him when his father's death had made him Lord of the Manor as a mere stripling of fifteen. If he now governed his little kingdom with passable success, he knew it was John who had taught him its management, as soundly as Robin had taught him to handle a sword. He had loved the man, and now God had taken him. *Or the Other?*

He pushed the thought aside, uneasily. Hal was no philosopher; for all Gadd's spiritual seduction, and for all the frightened eagerness with which he had followed the sorcerer-priest's tuition in pursuit of the dream of power, his instinctive reactions to any situation were still those of his Christian upbringing, and his uncomplicated mind, with no gift for theological hair-splitting, was unaware of the inconsistency. *God hath taken Master John* was the thought that sprang naturally to his grieving mind. But though he was simple, he was not a fool; and his memory of the Black Mass, right here in the now innocent-looking chapel, was too fresh to be ignored. Katherine had been the altar (traumatic enough in itself, that, and still unabsorbed), *something* had been evoked, while Hell had broken loose in the sky above . . . And Master John was dead. *Could* it be that Gadd's Master, forestalled in the Triangle of Evocation by that strange bright warrior-maid Hal had seen with his own eyes, had turned aside in anger and taken an innocent sacrifice?

Father Gadd, beside Hal, was chanting and muttering as he had promised; Hal did not listen. He had long stopped listening to Gadd when he was pretending to be a Christian priest; it was meaningless, and distasteful in its falsity, so better ignored. Looking down on his old dead friend, Hal was divided between his genuine grief and a growing bewilderment. *What* hand, divine or diabolic, had flung that lightning-bolt? And who, or what, was the slim Amazon that had flashed so briefly into their vision?

He wanted to talk to Katherine. He dreaded her wrath at the sacrilege in which she had discovered him, and into

165

which she herself had been dragged by her love and loyalty to him – for he realised that too, with a deep shame. But he would rather face that wrath than forgo the help of her keen mind, among the dark riddles that besieged him . . .

Where *was* Katherine? She should be here, with him, to lead the vigil . . .

He was suddenly anxious, but reminded himself that there might be other demands on the Mistress of Orley in this time of crisis. Basil, for instance – in spite of his miraculous recovery, he must still be watched, and kept to his bed. And the stables – she might be helping there, for she had a way with horses that even the grooms respected.

Reassured by these second thoughts, he turned his attention back to the dead.

It was a good half an hour later when he moved aside to let others pay their respects in his place.

He slipped quietly out of the chapel and roamed through the half-empty house in search of his wife.

No one had seen her. A young maid looked after Basil, who was now asleep. The maid whispered to Hal that he had not yet been told of the steward's death, and Hal approved; let the boy get his strength back first, if only by one night's sleep.

He could not believe that Katherine was asleep herself. But he had looked everywhere else inside the house, so he went to the bedchamber, his anxiety mounting.

Fire and candles had burned low, and the only sign of Katherine was the gown she had been wearing, laid apparently hurriedly on the bed.

Why in God's name should she have changed?

Perhaps into something more fitting to help in the stables – yes, she must be there. He almost ran out of the house, and found Robin mopping his brow wearily by the great stable door.

'All quiet now, sir, but God willing I'll never see such another night. The Devil himself must've entered the poor brutes. We may lose Blackberry – he'th kicked himself sorely, and cannot rise. Ned's with him now, but to little avail, I fear.'

'Hast thou seen my lady? I'd thought she was with thee.'

'No, Sir Henry. Is she not with the mourners – or with young Master Basil?'

'With neither, nor elsewhere in the house – I have searched every corner . . . Robin, can aught have befallen her?'

'Mother of God, no . . .'

Hal's anxiety awoke Robin's own, and they hurried about, calling others to help, spreading the search outwards through the Grange grounds with a growing urgency as everyone denied having seen my lady anywhere, since the time when Master Grayson's body had been discovered. Soon only old women were left to watch in the chapel – even from there the able-bodied were called out. Even Gadd himself, his face dark as though with some private anxiety alien to the others, searched with them. No horses were missing, so she could not have ridden away – and why should she?

Candles within, and lanterns and torches without, lit every nook and cranny of Grange, gardens, and orchards. My lady was not to be found.

The crisis seemed to bring out the soldier in Hal, as though he were at his best with terror threatening his heart.

'So be it,' he said at last. 'Fetch every horse in the stables, lame or sound – every jade that can stand. Robin, thou'lt take the northern woods. Ned, the village. Father Gadd, by the river. I'll take the eastern forest. How many else can we mount? . . . Eighteen? Five, then, with me, and five with Robin; among the trees, we'll have most need of numbers. Four each with the Father and with Ned. Go to't. And the first to find my lady, or even a breath of tidings of her – let him seek me out in all haste, though his jade die under him.'

With a clatter of hooves, the torches fanned outwards into the night.

167

My lady Katherine had an hour and a half's start on the searchers. No one would have recognised her, dressed in a kitchen-wench's clothes which she had taken unseen from the laundry-room while the house was in its first turmoil after Master Grayson's death. She met no one, in any case. Till she was clear of the Grange gardens, heading for the nearest edge of the forest, she was preoccupied with remaining hidden. But once among the dark trees, her heart was in her mouth. Country-bred, she was unperturbed by country sounds; the scuffle of a badger, the eerie yelp of a fox, the clatter of a disturbed bird, the nameless sounds of even smaller life, held no terrors for her at all. It was the footfall, the snapped twig of a lurker, the stifled breathing, which her ears strained for with every tiptoed yard. Lady or servant, she was a girl, young, and alone – as any forest rogue would soon discover, if he had not knifed her first; and the discovery once made, he might of course still knife her afterwards.

She moved as fast as she could without making noise that could be heard more than a few yards away. She wished she had remembered to bring a knife herself; it would at least have given her a chance in the dark, if she were waylaid. But she had run away too quickly, too much on the spur of the moment, to have thought of it.

It seemed an age, the forest path seemed interminable, before she saw the end of the lane through the trees, the hedges dimly outstanding in the starlight; now she could move faster. So it was a breathless girl who ran up the path towards the window where the firelight glowed, and stumbled in at Bella's door.

'I was awaiting thee, Katherine of Orley,' blind Bella said from her stool beside the hearth. 'Shut the door, child. There is more without than Death.'

'Thou speakest truth,' Katherine panted, doing as Bella said.

''Tis all I *can* speak – that is the burden I have borne since I was of thine age, and younger. Truth is a harsh mistress.

Her slaves earn little love, and much fear. But she permitteth them one easing of her burden; they may bide silent.'

Katherine took the other stool and huddled close to the fire. 'Be not silent now, Bella, I pray thee. I have dire need of thy counsel.'

'Thou hast faced Truth naked.'

Katherine laughed bitterly, 'Thou'rt free to make sport with words and double Truth's meaning, I see . . .'

'Thine own nakedness? That was a trifle.'

'Bare like a tavern whore on God's altar? Thou callest that a trifle? My body used, to defile God's Body and summon a fiend from Hell?'

'God hath seen thee naked before tonight.'

'Bella, thou veilest truth to ease mine anguish. The time is past for that.'

Bella sighed. 'When thou camest to me a few hours since, I spoke of naught but doom, and thou hast fled from me weeping. Now, when thou hast lain naked and helpless before the doom of which I spake, and hast looked into its face, thou demandest of me that I spare thee not.'

'What canst thou say to me that could worsen it? There is nothing.'

'Then why art thou here?'

Katherine was silent for a long time. Then she said slowly: 'I have cut myself off from God's grace, and the voices around me are evil or ignorant – or enchanted, as Hal. It may be that I yearn to hear a voice that is none of these.'

'Even if I can bring thee no comfort?'

'Even so. Thou'rt a hand in the darkness, though the hand be empty.'

'Oh, child . . .' Bella's voice was once again the solemn music Katherine had heard that afternoon, 'I have sat here, by my hearth, and seen much, this night. I have seen Marbas . . .' (Katherine caught her breath; was there nothing this strange creature did not know?) '. . . striding around Orley like a wrathful tiger, summoned yet baulked, *quaerens quem*

169

devoret, a black flame taller than the trees, circling, ever circling, powerless to enter the Triangle . . . And I have heard thee, Katherine of Orley, a sacrifice to thine own love, crying out to *Her* from the Abyss . . . And I have seen the Helper, sword in hand – and in the moment of her coming, I have heard Marbas' roar of anger, seen him turn aside and rend the innocent – God in his mercy receive the man's soul, for what befell was naught of his doing . . . And then I have slept, for the wind of it hath buffeted me also. Slept till I felt thee coming.'

A log collapsed on itself in the fire, making Katherine jump. She leaned forward and put another on the red glow.

'And if I have dealt with thee more gently than I did before,' Bella said, her voice more ordinary now, ''twas because thou hast met the first challenge, and not failed . . . Mistake me not, child – thou standest on the brink of Hell itself, and thy peril is great; all my Sight cannot tell thee if thou wilt conquer, or be destroyed. But even as the Host entered thy womanhood, and black clouds covered the face of God, thou hast found strength to cry out to the Queen of Heaven. And the Helper hath held the Triangle.'

'Who *was* she?' Katherine asked in a whisper.

Bella shook her blind head. 'That is hidden from me, as it is from thee; that answer thou must seek thyself . . . I see but dimly when I look at her; words come to me, and I discern not their meaning.'

'Tell me the words, natheless.'

'That she is thy sister from the womb of Time.'

They brooded on that together as the flames ate their way up the fresh log, but no enlightenment came. At last Bella rose up and walked over to a rough chest that stood in a corner, and took something from it, bringing it back and handing it to Katherine.

Katherine looked at it, curiously. It was a small silver amulet on a chain, also of silver; it was no symbol that Katherine knew – like a slender pillar with a pedestal foot and a crescent head, the points upwards cupping a disc. The

170

workmanship was barbaric yet delicate, and it gave her a feeling of immeasurable age. She wanted to ask what it was, but the question would not come.

'Wear it, Katherine of Orley,' Bella said. 'And if thou shalt conquer in the end, restore it to me when the battle is won.'

'And if I do not conquer?'

'Then shalt thou be beyond its help, or mine. But it shall return to me, whatever the outcome.'

'I do not care to conquer, if Hal be lost,' Katherine said. 'Thou talkest of trifles; without Hal, my soul is a trifle indeed.'

'Have no fear, child. Whither thou goest, he goeth, to darkness or light. That is *thy* burden – that thy love is stronger than thee, and thou art stronger than the one thou lovest. Thou'rt not the first. When the gate closed on the Garden of Eden, I doubt not it was Eve led the way in the wilderness.'

Katherine slipped the chain over her head; and as the strange amulet hung between her breasts, it seemed to glow with a warmth that had not come from Bella's hands or her own.

Robin knew the forest around Orley as well as he knew his wife's face; and in daylight, he could have read any signs of Katherine's passing – even alone, still more if she had been abducted – like the words in a book. Better, indeed, for he had had little schooling. But tonight, by the flicker of dim lanterns which revealed little, and two torches which burned badly, frightening the already nervous horses even worse as they flared and spat, the going was hard and the progress slow. And three of his five helpers, though willing enough, would have been clumsy even in daylight.

He kept them close together, for even a few yards apart they could have missed a fallen Katherine if she were unconscious or dead, huddled in a dark cloak as she would probably be. They had to lead the horses, for they were searching,

171

too, for anything she might have dropped, and any such clue could only be seen on foot. But their close-order advance meant they covered a narrow front, and quartering the woods even a mile in, on the area that had been allotted to them, might take till dawn.

Robin would rather have faced battle than this. My lady Katherine was his responsibility, and in his heart he did not qualify that responsibility. He knew he could not watch her day and night, and this evening everyone, including Sir Henry, had believed she was in the house – had no reason indeed to suspect otherwise. But that did not make Robin feel any better. If my lady had come to any harm – if (God and His angels forbid) she were dead – Robin would blame himself, whether reasonably or unreasonably.

If the bright jewel he guarded were lost . . .

She *must* not be lost. Only this afternoon she had ridden these very woods, aglow with life – and he behind her, admiring but anxious. So bright a jewel . . .

This afternoon . . .

Robin halted, suddenly, and the men to his right and left checked, wondering why. He was puzzled himself; why had this strange thought come to him – this one possibility, less likely than so many others? It was absurd, but . . . He had to know.

'Close in, Jack, Dickon – and keep the pace. Eyes open, miss nothing – and if you find aught while I'm away, bide where you are, and send one for Sir Henry. I'll not be long gone.'

He leaped into his saddle and rode, head-down under the low branches. The lane could not be far – a mile, perhaps. After a while the sound of his men faded behind him, and he was alone; then he saw the gap in the forest-edge and wheeled into it.

In the lane, with no trees to clutch at him, he broke into a canter, for there was enough starlight for the horse to feel confident. Soon the cottage loomed up; and yes, there was light in the window.

172

He jumped to the ground at the gate, and would have run up the path – but found that, for some reason, he could not bring himself to enter the garden. He stood there, uncertain, frowning.

This was absurd. He did not fear Bella; he had always spoken fairly to her, and she to him. And he had come here to find if my lady was with her, and if she was not, to go. He was needed back with the others. He was wasting time – time that might be precious . . .

Robin forced himself up the path.

He was halfway to the cottage when the door opened and my lady Katherine walked out towards him. He felt no surprise, either that she was there, or that she was clad in the rough clothes of a servant girl. But he did not wonder at his lack of surprise until much later. Now, at this moment, his pent-up anxiety, the dread that had been growing in him since he had known she was missing, burst out in brief anger.

He spoke to her with the rough directness of a privileged servant twice her age.

'My lady, this was ill done. It was ill done indeed. Had you no thought for Sir Henry's distress – and ours? He deserveth better of you, and your servants withal!'

She lifted her face and looked up at him. It was a small and perfect face, magical in the starlight, unsmiling, but more beautiful than he had ever seen it. He was filled with a strange awe, and his anger dissolved.

'Forgive me, Robin. Thou'rt right to chastise me. But I had a need to speak with Bella Withecombe.'

He stood aside for her to lead the way to the gate. Then he swung her up on to the horse in front of him, and she leaned in his arms like a trusting daughter as they rode to find Hal.

CHAPTER XVI

'Why don't you go and see Geoffrey Withecombe?' Trevor asked.

He had joined them at breakfast, to find a fully recovered Jane eagerly discussing what they might do to fill the day and to add, if possible, to their factual knowledge of Orley in Katherine's time. She did not want to bury herself in the library, because she wanted to work with Bridget and George; and besides, it was a glorious day, and she was restless with energy.

'Who's Geoffrey Withecombe?' George asked.

'The eye-witness I haven't met yet,' Jane told him. 'Trevor says he and old Mrs Cannon are the most sensible people in Orley who claim to have seen the Battle Maid. I was going to interview him on the same day as Mrs Cannon, but he was off in Manchester, so I missed him . . . Yes, Trevor, good idea. Will he be in today, do you think?'

Trevor telephoned to find out, and came back to say Mr Withecombe would be delighted to see them any time that morning.

'He's a writer,' Trevor went on. 'He does rather twee romances under two or three different female pen-names. I read one, just to be neighbourly, and if he *hadn't* been a neighbour I'd never have stuck it past Chapter Two. God knows who reads them, but he's doing very nicely, thank you.'

'Is *he* rather twee, too?' Bridget asked.

'Not in the least. Chequered marital career, three grown-up children and one grandchild, finally settled down with a lovely creature younger than all but one of his children. They adore each other – it's almost funny to

174

watch. She gets on like a house on fire with her step-children, too, *and* with one of the ex-wives . . . No, anything but twee. Restrained Rabelaisean, I'd say. You'll like Geoffrey and Claire. They glow with sexuality, and they're interesting to talk to.'

'And you can't,' Bridget said, 'ask more than that, can you?'

When they met the Withecombes, they had to agree with Trevor. The house stood isolated in a side lane leading to a wood, and had been extended and modernised, successfully, from a thatched cottage that must have been sixteenth century or earlier. It stood back from the lane at the end of a long lawn, on which, as they opened the gate, they could see the 'lovely creature' Trevor had told them about, sweeping up lawn-clippings, and wearing a bikini and a large yellow openwork sun-hat that dappled her brown skin. She was no more than five foot two, and slim as a willow, except for the breasts with which her bikini fought a losing battle. She smiled and waved at them vigorously, an action which popped her right nipple out into the sun like an astonished brown eye. She thrust it unconcernedly back into place as she came towards them.

'Hullo, are you Jane and the Witches? Come and have a drink. Only Guinness or Lucozade, I'm afraid. I've tried mixing them, but it doesn't really work. The old man's inside.' She called piercingly at the house: 'Hey, Snaggle!'

Geoffrey Withecombe came out carrying glasses. 'I heard your car. Have some Guinness . . . My God, Trevor was right!'

He stood gazing at Jane, who gazed back questioningly. He was not only at least twice his wife's age, he was also a good foot taller and probably twice her weight, but reasonably well proportioned. Baggy corduroys, huge sandals, and bare sunburned chest, topped by a large-nosed face and a lion's mane of grey hair. The gazing had continued almost to the point of embarrassment when he suddenly seemed to realise it, and laughed apologetically.

175

'I'm sorry, I'm being rude. But you see, I've met you before, twice. Just as well Trevor warned me . . . You *are* the Battle Maid, by Christ you are . . . Here!'

He held out a glass to her, and she took it without thinking. Geoffrey nodded, 'Left-handed, too, like her. Incredible . . . Sorry, everybody. Sit down somewhere. The grass do, or shall I get chairs? Sling us the opener, darling. First things first.'

He refused to discuss the Battle Maid further till they all had drinks in their hands; then there was more postponement when Claire decided their guests must be far too hot to sit in the sun dressed as they were. Jane could get into another of her bikinis, while Bridget's more Viking figure 'would look smashing in that playsuit thing of Holly's, darling – it's in your pants drawer, I think'. It was not clear whether Holly was a daughter or an ex-wife, but look smashing in it Bridget certainly did; and Jane was not sorry to have the sun on her skin. George contented himself with taking his shirt off.

'Well,' Geoffrey said, some twenty minutes later when they were finally settled and another round of bottles had been opened. 'Shall I explain myself?'

'Yes, please,' Jane said.

'I feel a little diffident about it, actually,' he admitted, seeming much too large to be diffident. 'People look at me sideways, in Orley, when I say I've seen the Battle Maid out here, because no one else has ever seen her outside the Grange house and garden. They know I'm not a liar, but they know all writers are a bit touched anyway, so they reckon I've just fallen for one of my own fantasies. But I know fantasy when I see it – hell, I churn it out all day. (Dreadful stuff, by the way, don't ever buy it.) And my professional fantasies do *not* materialise, except on paper. But the Battle Maid did. And the first time was before either you, Jane, or this luscious elf who's been fool enough to marry me, were even born.'

As he remembered, the flippancy dropped away and he

became serious. 'I was sitting by the fire in there – I was twenty-three, just down from university, and feeling low because no one seemed to want to employ me in spite of my brand-new Eng. Litt. degree . . . I should explain that the house was half the size then – just the original cottage plus a kitchen my father had built on himself. The Withecombes have been here since God knows when – the first parish-register mention was a marriage in 1497 – and until my grandfather, they were all farm labourers and so on. Then my father made a few quid inventing some improvement to a reaper and binder, and spent it on my education, God bless him. Which has added up in the end to fifteen paperbacks, three extra bedrooms, a sun-lounge, and central heating . . . Anyway, in *those* days the place must have looked much as it always did, and if you like to think I *was* deluded, you could say sitting by the open fire with no other light, in the old square living-room, created the ideal atmosphere . . . As I say, I was brooding unhappily about the ungrateful world, when suddenly there she was, standing opposite me.'

He paused; and Jane could not tell whether it was the instinctive timing of the professional storyteller, or the vividness of the memory overtaking him. She was inclined to think it was the latter.

'What did she look like?' she prompted him.

'You.' He shook his head. 'No, that's not right. She wasn't *like* you. She *was* you. Wearing the silvery thing they all describe – though I could never see it as armour; I think people merely inferred that, from the sword she carried. I saw it as a trouser suit of some material with metallic threads in it. Wrapover blouse and flared slacks . . . And the sword . . . I've never told anyone but Claire this, but I've seen that sword, at the Grange. It hangs just outside the chapel door. I recognised it a few years ago, suddenly, and when no one was looking I pulled it out of its scabbard . . . That was the sword, all right – or its twin by the same maker.'

Jane had been prepared for recognition of herself; after all

177

that had happened, she had come to accept the visual likeness as established; and perhaps a corner of her mind still held to the possibility of coincidence. But this man's unexpected remark about the sword caught her unawares, almost frightening her. She listened to him even more intently.

'She was only there for a few seconds, but I never forgot her . . . I suppose they all say that. And if that had been the only time, maybe I wouldn't be so certain, now, about you and her. But the next time, only about five years ago . . . Jane, just now you were kneeling to get a cigarette out of your bag – remember? You had your back to me, bending over on one knee; then you rose and turned. Well, the second time I saw the Battle Maid she was doing just that. There was an old chest in the corner of the room – quite a valuable antique, early sixteenth-century village carpenter's work, I've got it upstairs now – and she was bending over it as though she were looking for something. On one knee, as you did. And then she rose, and she turned. And when you made the same movement just now – *exactly* the same, and you know how individual a movement can be, like a fingerprint . . . It turned my stomach over. Don't ask me how, or why. But if you're not the Battle Maid, as I saw her . . . Then I *am* suffering from delusions. Or rather, one delusion – a very vivid, detailed, and consistent one, spanning nearly forty years.'

Bridget asked: 'Do *you* think it's a delusion?'

He seemed distressed, and Claire laid a hand gently on his knee. It was as though the touch freed and strengthened him, for he smiled across at Bridget and said firmly: 'No, I don't.'

'If it helps you any,' Bridget said, 'I'm quite certain it isn't. And I think Jane is, too.'

Jane inclined her head, finding it somehow difficult to speak.

Claire's hand was still on her husband's knee. She said: 'Why don't you give it to her, darling?'

178

'Yes, I'll have to, won't I? . . . After all, it's hers . . . Strange, that we've always kept it in that chest.'

He left the room, and nobody spoke till he came back. Then he held up in front of Jane, letting it hang by its chain, a small silver amulet.

Jane took it in her hand, and a little gasp escaped her. 'It feels alive! . . . What is it?' He did not answer, so she examined it, cradling it in the palm of her hand. 'It's like a long-stemmed flower – or a tree with just one fruit, a disc cradled in a crescent . . . and another smaller disc in the stem. There's something familiar about it – I can't quite . . .' She heard Bridget exclaim, and passed it to her. 'Does it mean anything to you?'

'It does indeed – and look, George, it's *old*, for God's sake – could even be original!' She turned to Geoffrey. 'Where on earth did you get it?'

'Nobody knows. It's been in the family since the year dot. The tradition is that one day the Battle Maid will come to claim it, and that when she comes it must be given to her . . . My great-grandmother lived to be over a hundred, and she died when I was seven – and I can clearly remember her telling me that *her* grandmother said we'd had it for generations before *she* was born. And always the same tradition. It's passed on almost compulsively, as though it were something important which mustn't be forgotten – not just quaint . . .' He looked down at his hands, overcome. 'It's . . . strange, to have it come to a climax like this, without warning, in *my* time.'

Jane glanced at Claire, instinctively seeking guidance; Claire smiled at her secretly and warmly. So Jane asked him: 'You really believe I ought to take it?'

'It's not a question of belief, somehow. I know that you *must* . . . It's a relief, really. Like discharging a duty that's been on your mind for a long, long time.'

'Then I will. And . . . it may sound silly, but thank you for looking after it for me.'

'It doesn't sound in the least silly.'

179

Bridget came forward and slipped the chain over Jane's neck.

'Tell us what it is, Bridget. You said you knew.'

'It's an Assyrian Moon Tree. At least several centuries old – and if I'm right and it's genuine Assyrian, then it's three or four thousand years. The Moon Tree is one of the oldest and most sacred symbols of the Goddess.'

Bridget and George had some unspecified work to do after lunch, so Jane wandered by herself up to the Grange. She rested awhile on the seat in the Long Walk, almost as a challenge. Let Gadd accost her there if he wanted to. In her present mood, she was itching to get at him.

But nothing happened, and the garden continued to doze undramatically in the sunshine; so after a time she began to feel a little ashamed of herself. Her bravado had been childish – this was not the place of battle, and the thing had gone beyond diversionary skirmishes. She rose from the seat and walked round to the front of the Grange, admiring again the black-and-white intricacy of its half-timbered façade.

Half a dozen people stood indecisively outside the great door; two middle-aged couples who seemed to be together, and a pair of obvious girl students. Poor things, she thought, it's three o'clock and they're expecting the conducted tour. Surely someone's had the sense to put up a 'Closed' notice?

She went over to them, intending to explain. She could see as she drew near that there was indeed a notice; but it merely said that – 'Closed'. Not very enlightening, she realised; and one of the men confirmed her reaction by asking her – 'Do you know – does that mean closed altogether, or just that we have to wait till the next tour starts?'

Jane was about to answer when she suddenly remembered that she had the team's key in her pocket. And they looked so hopeful, so anxious not to be disappointed . . .

'It's not very clear, is it?' she found herself saying. 'Sorry

180

about that – we're a bit short-staffed at the moment. Come along in – it's just three, now.'

Jane Blair, you're crazy, she told herself as she collected twenty pence from each of them and issued each with a blue ticket, torn off the roll which was kept in the drawer of the table which stood just inside the door. Also in the drawer were the illustrated booklets, and she spread a handful of them on the table; the man who had addressed her, and one of the students, bought a copy. Two pounds altogether – she must remember.

Crazy – but so what?

'This is the Great Hall. It's the oldest part of the Grange, and it dates from 1362. Orley was one of four manors granted to the Montgris family by William the Conqueror, and they settled on this one as the family home in the fourteenth century. Sir John Montgris, who was the first to live here, built this Great Hall . . .'

Thank heaven for her memory – and for her absorbing interest in the subject. She felt a little nervous at first – especially when she found out that the two students were reading history at Manchester University, and were bright as well as inquisitive – but as she answered question after question her confidence grew. Perhaps, she joked to herself, the Moon Tree is helping – and she was immediately by no means sure that she was joking.

In the Great Bedchamber, she showed them the four-poster bed and explained that it was Jacobean – which she knew both from the guide-book and from its design. One of the older women, who had shown a housewifely enthusiasm for all the domestic details, asked: 'What did they sleep in before that, I wonder?'

'A slightly smaller four-poster,' Jane told her promptly, 'of unstained oak, carved with vine-leaves and grapes. It was local work, but rather beautiful. The hangings were French brocade; the ladies of the family were very proud of them. Unfortunately there's no record of what happened to it.'

And there's no record, either, of the bed itself. No record except . . . Thank you, Katherine.

Was she fooling herself, or did the Moon Tree between her breasts pulsate gently?'

She felt a little breathless as she led the way out of the Bedchamber.

She wondered if the chapel would be an ordeal; but it was not. From the moment she stepped in, she knew, triumphantly, that she was in command of it. She led her little flock from feature to feature, unperturbed. In the gallery outside she quoted Lady Clara: *The Gallerie where many such Curiosities are kept, to the ill Use of needful Room, and the Tyme of Servants in the Cleaning thereof, if alle be not to rust away.* That delighted the housewifely visitor, who wanted to know more about Lady Clara. On an impulse, since they had to pass the library, Jane left them outside it while she ran for the key, and then showed them a titbit or two from Lady Clara's diary.

The tour, she knew, had been a great success. They were talking with her like old friends by the time they had completed the circuit and returned to the Great Hall. She saw through the window that there were more people outside, and realised with astonishment that it was almost four o'clock. Oh, well – the four o'clock tour was the last of the day, and it was too late to turn them away now.

As the first party were leaving, one of the students asked: 'Isn't the Grange supposed to be haunted?'

Forgive me, Charley Unsworth. 'You mean the Battle Maid. A girl in silver chain-mail, she's usually described, with a sword in her hand. Quite a few people have seen her, over the centuries – Lady Clara, for one. And I know two people in the village today who are certain they've seen her more than once.'

'Have *you* seen her, yourself?'

Jane smiled, 'I have never,' she said, 'actually met her face to face.'

182

'Five pounds thirty pence,' Jane said proudly. 'I'd better give it to you, Trevor, hadn't I, as representative of the Grange Trustee Committee and the Council?'

'God knows how I'll explain it to Morry Chadwick,' Trevor said, pocketing the money and noting the amount on the back of a beer-mat which he pocketed too. 'But I wish I'd been there!'

'Come on my next tour.'

'No more tours, Jane, please – or Morry *will* start asking questions!'

She had found Trevor and the Blakes on the terrace, and had almost run across the lawn to tell them, she was so pleased with herself. She had even told them of her sudden certainty about the earlier four-poster, and of the echo of Katherine's pride in it which had come to her – told it gaily and without apology, either to Trevor or to her own professional conscience. They shared her infectious pleasure, and even Trevor's doubts were half-joking.

'I felt,' she said finally, 'as if I owned the place. As if I were showing friends round *my* home.' She jumped up. 'I'm going to have a bath and change for dinner. And when I come down again, Trevor – I don't care how busy you are, you owe me a drink, Councillor Cox.'

When she had gone, Trevor sighed and began: 'I wish . . .'

Bridget waited for him to go on, and when he did not, she said 'I know what you wish.'

'Do you?'

'Yes.'

'You witches see too much.'

'Good God, man,' Bridget said, but gently, 'one doesn't have to be a clairvoyant. Just to watch you watching her.'

Trevor coloured. 'Don't say anything to *her*, for Christ's sake!'

'*I* won't,' Bridget promised him. 'But why shouldn't *you*?'

'If the time comes.'

'Time,' Bridget said, 'is a pretty unstable medium around here. Don't lean on it too much.'

CHAPTER XVII

'Will you be going up to the chapel tonight?' Trevor asked over the promised before-dinner drink.

'Not tonight, no. Things aren't ready yet.'

Trevor had noticed in the first day of knowing Jane that she was a stander. She would stand, even if others were sitting, for two extremes of mood; if she were tense, or if she felt overflowing with confidence and strength. She was certainly not tense this evening. She was bright-eyed and mentally alert, and she held her glass lightly but steadily – and Trevor, who had grown up in the Green Man, could read a great deal from the way drinkers held their glasses.

This evening she stood, but companionably close, and Trevor – who was five foot eleven and disliked talking over people's heads – half-sat on the low terrace wall, looking up at her. She was wearing a slight, backless dress in a flowery mixture of orange and tan, and her skin glowed in harmony with it.

'You've caught the sun today,' he commented.

'I'm not surprised. Claire Withecombe lent me a bikini and Bridget a playsuit, and we just basked. It was lovely.'

'You liked them?'

'You knew we would. They're *alive*, aren't they? . . . He gave me this."

She lifted the Moon Tree amulet from her cleavage and held it out for him, obviously intending him to feel it. He rested it gently on his upturned fingers.

'Ah . . . Nice of you to let me touch it.' He nodded and let it drop back into place.

'Why do you say that?'

'Because I know about it, Battle Maid. And the family tradition that goes with it . . . So Geoffrey hadn't any doubts, either.'

'Either?'

'*I've* had none since the night they took you to Keith's hospital . . . Why do you say "things aren't ready"? What things have you got to do?'

'Oh, not me. I'm ready when the chapel is. But it's as though . . . I don't know, it sounds odd I expect, but it's as though Charley Unsworth were resting there for a day or two. I think he'll be gone by tomorrow, but if we tried to confront Gadd there again before then, it'd be . . . an intrusion.'

'Strange.'

'You think I'm being fanciful?'

'I shouldn't think so. You haven't been, so far.'

She laid a hand on his arm and said: 'Thank you, Trevor.'

He wished he had the courage to put his own hand over hers; but before he could summon it, Bridget and George came out on to the terrace, and Jane turned to greet them.

Waking early next morning, Jane found herself in a mood which she could not easily describe to herself. Her sense of power was unabated, but tinged, not exactly with apprehension – rather with an awareness that if confidence became arrogance, she would be in danger. And yet confident she must remain, or the danger would be far greater . . .

If I were my mother with her simple Christian faith, she thought, this is where I would pray, for guidance and the right kind of strength. In a way it's a pity I can't.

Or can I? That deliberate seeking of the Centre which was also the infinite Circumference – wasn't *that* a form of prayer? . . . I asked Bridget how I could invoke the Goddess when I wasn't even sure I believed in Her – and that's what she told me to do, and it worked – or at least, I think it did . . .

Jane tried it again, crosslegged and naked on the bed as before, facing the treetops and the morning sky.

It was the same, yet different; as though the moment in the Earth's wheeling had an effect greater than a mere difference of darkness and light; as though the Goddess, like the Earth, while Herself unchanging, offered a different face. The universe with which Jane strove to merge herself was the same, yet its heart and hers was not this time a dark mystery but a bright, still, crystalline one, and the instant when the Point became infinite left her dazzled and gasping.

Was that the Goddess? It seemed so impersonal . . .

But even as she formulated it, the thought, like the Point, was transformed into its opposite. For all its transcendent vastness, nothing could have been more living and real, more responsive, more aware of *her*, Jane. The mystery was She, not It.

Jane knew in that moment the answer to her question. Yes, the Goddess existed. And the more truly she, Jane, was a woman – warm, intelligent, intuitive, sexual, maternal, beautiful, compassionate, relentless, sensuous, discerning, shameless, tender, provocative, regal, unstinting – the more she was all these things to the limit of her human power and with all of her inner integrity, the more the Goddess shone through her. As above, so below. *And in this way truly are erected the holy twin pillars; in beauty and in strength were they erected, to the wonder and glory of all men.* The words came to Jane from within herself, and yet from elsewhere; she wondered at them briefly, but accepted them.

She realised also that her unease about the distinction between confidence and arrogance had evaporated. A balance (which she did not even have to examine) had been achieved, freeing her for action.

She jumped off the bed, pirouetting with a joyous little dance step towards her clothes.

What to wear? . . . She decided on white slacks, a wide-necked sleeveless white blouse, and a broad gold belt. At first she thought the belt would not go with the Moon Tree, but oddly, it did.

The Battle Maid in white, saluting the sun, she thought.

The Blakes, too, were down early, so as the dining-room was still empty, Trevor was able to join them for his own habitually lighter breakfast. Jane, effervescent, pulled his leg about the Grange guided tours, threatening to open the doors to visitors herself every hour and to take them round whatever the Council said.

'Sorry to disappoint you,' Trevor said, 'but you wouldn't find any visitors. I've put a notice on the main gate telling 'em the guided tours are suspended till further notice.'

'Spoiling my fun, eh? Bureaucrat!'

'As far as I'm concerned, you could be acting-Curator, and welcome. You'd do it very well, God knows. But it wouldn't be Correct Procedure; Morry would have kittens. It's not me who's the bureaucrat. I hate to see people being turned away.'

'Perhaps I'd better go and ooze charm and professional competence at your friend Morry.'

'That I'd like to see. He's a right Holy Willie. Wears pince-nez.'

'I didn't think they made those any more.'

'They probably don't. Morry's came out of the Ark.'

'If you really want to conduct a tour,' George said, 'why not conduct us? We haven't seen over the Grange yet. Only the chapel and the armour gallery, and that lobby place.'

'I wish you would, Jane,' Bridget agreed. 'And Trevor can come too. The Green Man won't fall down without him, for an hour or two.'

'Trevor knows the place backwards.'

'I know it, yes,' Trevor said, 'but I've never been taken round by a real historian. I'm sure you can tell me things I *don't* know.'

In the end Jane had an audience of four to lecture to, because Keith Stoneleigh dropped in at the Green Man just as they were leaving, and was invited to join them.

Jane enjoyed herself thoroughly, all the more so because they asked her intelligent questions, stretching both her knowledge of Orley Grange and her general historical learning. George, she found, had a lively interest in the technical problems of building and architecture; Trevor and Keith both knew a good deal of local history, but were a little vague on the national background and glad to have it filled in; while Bridget flashed bright unexpected questions across her narrative like a kingfisher traversing a stream.

She found herself wondering how Charley Unsworth would have coped with them, and blushed at her own unfairness.

When they reached the Great Bedchamber, Jane was aware of an unspoken tightening and concentration of interest; for they all knew of her flash of clairvoyance about the earlier four-poster, and of her complete confidence in it. The awareness embarrassed her a little, as though they were expecting her to repeat and amplify the clairvoyance for their benefit. She doubted if this were actually true, of Bridget and George at least, for those two never forced her pace; so perhaps it was she herself who was feeling she had a reputation to live up to. A subversive feeling, if so, and one to be resisted firmly; that way lay self-delusion.

So she was very matter-of-fact about the bedchamber, drawing attention to the star-painted ceiling, pointing out the maiden armorial bearings of many Montgris brides on their lozenges in the window-panes . . .

'Is Katherine's there?' Bridget asked.

'Yes, over here, look . . . Courtfield: Vert, a mermaid proper, holding a sword erect argent. In other words, a green background – the sea, I suppose – with the mermaid in natural colours, carrying a silver sword . . . Good Lord! Do you notice something?'

They all hesitated, and then George said; 'She's holding the sword in her left hand.'

Jane nodded, feeling her matter-of-factness wavering.

Keith laughed. 'Something else, too. Now that *is* uncanny. Look at the motto – "Temporis gratia superabo".'

'Translation?' Bridget asked. 'I never did Latin.'

'"By the grace of Time, I will overcome . . ." It would

have a perfectly ordinary meaning to them, of course – "If I'm patient, I'll win". It's a nice coincidence, Jane, all the same – the idea of help coming to Katherine *out of* time.'

Jane found that she was gripping the Moon Tree in her fingers. She caught Bridget's eye; Bridget gave her a smile which took the edge off Keith's brashness.

'Yes, isn't it?' Jane said, relaxing her grip on the Moon Tree. If only the mermaid didn't look so *like* her . . . She tried to mistrust the impression, telling herself she was in a suggestible state. But she knew that Bridget had seen it, too.

She moved over to the bed, and laid her hand on the fluted Jacobean column . . .

She held her breath, and kept quite still, closing her eyes and moving her fingers carefully. But there was no mistaking it; her fingers were tracing the outline of grapes, of vine-leaves . . .

'Dost thou fear Gadd so much, that Hell seemeth pale beside him?' Katherine was near to collapse, the argument had gone on so long; she held on to the bedpost for support. 'Doth it, Hal?'

'We have no choice, Kate. We are bound thither already! We are beyond hope!'

'I'll never believe it, while Our Blessed Lady is still in heaven . . .'

'What's wrong, Jane?' Keith asked.

Bridget whispered 'Quiet', with a restraining hand on his arm.

But Jane, her eyes now wide open and fixed on the other side of the bed, said calmly: 'Nothing's wrong. They're here, that's all. Can you see them, Bridget?'

'No, but I can feel them.'

'Come with me, Hal. Come and outface the wretch. Thou'lt see he's nought but flesh and blood. Tell him, my beloved! Tell him thou'lt serve him no longer!'

'Kate, I dare not! What powers may he not unloose . . .'

Katherine drew herself upright; if she could not persuade him to lead the way, now was the time to throw all to the hazard. 'If thou'lt not tell him, then shall I tell him for thee. Montgris no

189

*longer serveth him, and Orley speweth him out. We shall give him
a horse and a few groats for his journey, and Robin shall drive him
out of the gate at sword-point if he disputeth the matter. He is now
in the chapel which he hath defiled and disgraced. I go to accost
him; and if thou'lt not accompany me, then send Robin, or I accost
him alone.'*

*She walked to the door, fighting to hide the dread which she felt;
for she, too, in spite of her brave words, was in fearful awe of the
nameless powers Gadd might be able to unleash upon them. But
she must dare all now, or they were truly lost.*

*Katherine held firmly on to the amulet which Bella had given
her, and felt its strange warmth against her palm.*

*Ave Maria, gratia plena; Blessed Mother of God, friend of
women, be with me now . . . Praise be, Hal is following after –
though he stumbleth in terror and babbleth like a child . . .*

They all followed Jane in silence as she walked out of the
door, Keith and Trevor stepping aside instinctively to allow
Bridget and George to be closest to her. Keith was puzzled;
this was like no trance he had ever seen. Jane seemed utterly
confident of whatever it was she saw (and, by the tilting of
her head, heard), yet she was to all appearances still in full
normal consciousness, gesturing them to slow down or to
hurry their pace to match the quarry they could not see.

'She'll get him there,' Jane told them quietly but clearly at
one point. 'He's terrified, but even more afraid of letting her
out of his sight. She'll get him there.'

'Where?' Keith asked before he could stop himself.

'To the chapel, of course, Come on.'

*Mother of God, Thou hast sent Thy Helper before, Send her
now. Dominus tecum, benedicta tu in mulieribus . . .*

*The door, at last. Katherine pulled away from Hal's almost
hysterical effort to stop her, and pushed hard at the door of the
chapel.*

It was locked, and she beat upon it with her fists.

Jane stepped forward, carefully to one side, and pushed
the chapel door open.

The door gave way suddenly, swinging wide. Katherine

*grasped Hal's hand, and dragged him inside, just as Gadd ripped
open the sacrifice with his knife. It was a hare, and its body still
twitched in his hands as he turned his terrible eyes towards them;
the blood poured, poured, poured on to Amy Tanner's white
breathing flesh, supine upon the altar.*

Gadd roared: 'Ye fools!'

Jane reached up to the wall and slid the sword from its
scabbard; armed, she moved in behind Katherine, no longer
wondering if the others followed.

*Gadd swung himself round to face them, flinging the desem-
bowelled hare down on to Amy's belly. He raised his hands, one
still holding the knife, high and wide like a beast about to attack,
towering over Katherine and Hal from the altar steps. 'Ye fools —
what have ye done! Prince of Darkness, consume them!'*

*Fainting with terror, Hal slipped to the floor, but Katherine,
though she was shaking uncontrollably, stood her ground, and
cried out aloud: 'Queen of Heaven, save us! Thy messenger, dear
Mother of God!'*

Jane stepped forward beside Katherine, and her challenge
echoed through the chapel: 'Jonathan Gadd!'

Then they saw her. For a frozen instant, she was aware of
Gadd's enraged glare, Katherine's exultant recognition,
Hal's glazed bewilderment. She cried out again: 'Jonathan
Gadd, return to your evil Master!'

She saw Gadd's knife-hand begin to move, and she
lunged with the sword, straight at his heart, feeling the
shock of impact, the grating against bone, then the comple-
tion of the lunge as the point slid in between rib and rib.

And then the chapel was empty; except for Bridget and
George, Trevor and Keith.

She turned to face them, sword in hand, breathing fast.

It's over,' she said. 'It's over.'

Keith came to her and looked in her face. 'How do you
feel?'

'I feel magnificent. Don't be a doctor at me — there's no
need.'

He nodded. 'No, I don't think there is. But after a psychic

191

experience like the one you've obviously been through, one likes to be certain.'

'I'm not sure that "psychic" is quite an adequate word. I've just killed a man, with this sword.'

'You really have that feeling?' Keith frowned.

'I have that *knowledge*.'

Keith was beginning to look professional again. 'Jane, I'm sure your experience was real, and that you were picking up something genuine. But for your own sake, you ought to get it in proportion . . .'

Bridget interrupted him: 'Look at the sword.'

Jane lifted up the blade, and they all stared at it. It was red, from the point halfway to the hilt.

Trevor muttered 'Christ!'

Keith put out an incredulous finger and wiped it along the steel. He examined his hand, and looked up, his face pale with the shock.

'If that's not fresh human blood,' he told them in a shaking voice, 'I should go back to school.'

CHAPTER XVIII

'Pull up, darling,' Bridget said, 'I want to take a last look.'

George was used to acting on his wife's sudden impulses, and he parked the Volkswagen caravan at the top of the hill without comment. They both got out, and he followed her on to the grass.

Orley lay below them, looking ageless and peaceful in the sun. The roof of the Grange, a harmonious medley of slopes, was a dark heart to the park and gardens; below this again, the little river curved along the edge of the woodland, after a while turning right and disappearing into it. More trees interlaced with the village between their hill and the Grange; the Green Man brooded over its clutch of houses. Beyond and to the left, fields fanned out, elbowing the woods aside, spreading onwards to other parishes, other loves and hates.

Bridget stood still, looking.

George said at last: 'You're not happy, are you?'

'Are *you*?'

'As far as I can see.' The answer was not a metaphor; George meant it literally – 'to the limit of my psychic vision'. He was yielding to her sensitivity, recognising from long experience the moments when it reached out farther than his own. She was not always the one; at certain states of the psychic tide, it was he who took the lead; each of them had learned when to look to the other. 'I felt she really had won.'

'Oh, yes, she's won; but the battle – or the war?'

'At least,' George said, 'she saved her friends, I think.'

'So do I. She insisted that Katherine and Hal were safe

now, and I believe she knows what she's talking about – because she and Katherine are so in tune . . . No, what I'm afraid of is the sting in Gadd's tail. That man was a Scorpio, my hackles tell me.'

'Would it have been right to warn her?'

Bridget shook her head. 'With that blood only just cleaned off her sword? No, darling – she's too triumphant to listen, right now. And quite right too, in a way. She's learned so much in the past few days, gained so much power. I just hope that when the backlash comes, and we're not around to help her, she'll go on learning and understanding.'

'There's Trevor and Keith. They're not stupid, either of them.'

'Her little court?' Bridget laughed. 'Having a ball, wasn't she, with them both dancing around her?'

'Basking in it.'

'Well, good luck to her, That's part of the triumph. Let her enjoy it for a while. She's not the sort to go on playing them off against each other indefinitely. But for now, it's all in the game.'

George said 'Women!' with a pretence of scorn which they both knew was alien to him, but which was a part of *their* game. Bridget hugged his arm, and led him back to the caravan. They drove in silence for a mile or two.

'All I hope,' Bridget said at last, 'is that if things do go wrong, someone has the sense to send us a Mayday call.'

CHAPTER XIX

Katherine rode beside her husband, deeply content, knowing that he was himself again. The first primroses in the
hedge, the almost inaudible tune Robin was humming
behind them (Robin, that weathercock of his lord and lady's
wellbeing), the lambs that bounced and tottered in Harry
Drover's top field, the joyous and still undeclared secret of
her own womb – all seemed tokens of the new dawn in her
life.

She laughed, picking up Robin's song in her clear young
voice, so that he coughed with embarrassment and Hal
smiled across at her.

> *'Roundelay, roundelay,*
> *Blossom and berry,*
> *Spring bringeth summer,*
> *So let us be merry!*
> *Hawthorn and elder-flower –*
> *Winter is dead!*
> *Come to me, sweeting –*
> *The meadow's our bed!'*

By the end of it, Hal was singing with her; and even
Robin rumbled diffidently in tune with the gentlefolk.

A bright dawn indeed, Katherine thought, after so black a
night. She could remember without pain, now, for the
weeks had softened the horror; and in any case, at the heart
of the horror there shone that figure of deliverance – *thy
sister from the womb of Time*, Bella had called her. and
although Katherine could not say why, the description
appealed to her. She had no name for her but the Helper;

whence or how she came, Katherine had given up wondering. From Heaven, she had thought at first, for of one thing Katherine was convinced – the Helper had been there at the command of the Queen of Heaven (*benedicta tu in mulieribus*) who had answered her own call. But if the Helper's home was so exalted, so distant, why that feeling of sisterhood? Why, as the slim white-clad apparition with the fair streaming hair had lunged at Gadd, straight to his black heart, had her own hand moved with the Helper's, like the hand of a comrade-in-arms in the heat of battle?

She had only been present for the twinkling of an eye, but of her reality there could be no doubt; Gadd's bleeding corpse remained as proof. Almost harder to believe, now, was that she, Katherine, had found the strength to rally her stunned husband enough for the pair of them to carry the body unseen down to the river-bank and there, in a hidden place among the bushes, to bury him with their own four hands.

Strange, how little Orley had questioned his sudden disappearance. But then he was after all, in their eyes, a Catholic priest in a Protestant land, living always in fear of the Queen's heresy-hounds; and if he seemed to have found it wise to vanish without trace, it was equally wise for them to hold their tongues. Only Katherine and Hal knew of his river-bank grave, unhallowed as he so richly deserved.

The only other witness, Amy the living altar for that last fatal Black Mass, was silent – the silence of madness, poor child. Forgetting her in the haste of disposing of Gadd's body had been Katherine's only slip; and when she had remembered, as she trod the last turf back into place, she had turned cold with apprehension. She had hurried Hal away, back to the chapel, not knowing what to expect. But Amy had still lain there, alone, naked, and shivering, her blank eyes windows on to her blasted mind. Katherine had gathered her up like a baby, covering her with her cloak and carrying her to the warmth of their own bedchamber. In her body, Amy had recovered quickly, and was kept busy with simple automatic tasks in the kitchen – protected from mockery or persecution by my lady's fierce tenderness towards her, which the other servants quickly learned to respect. But her mind had never healed; dumb she had remained, following Katherine with her dog-like eyes whenever she was near. One stable-lad, doubtless remembering past favours, had tried to force her; her screams – the only sounds she had uttered since that day in the chapel – had brought Katherine running, and she had thrashed the boy with a snatched-up broom-handle till he had cried for mercy. Since then no one had dared lay a finger on Amy.

But poor mad Amy was the only cloud in the sky; and even that was alleviated by the warmth of her silent devotion.

As for Hal – for many days Katherine had kept him to his room, fevered and incoherent. The servants feared he had caught the ailment which young Basil had escaped; but Katherine knew better. He had recovered, slowly; the final cure had been brought about by the arrival of Father Randall, a remarkably sensible young priest discovered by Katherine's parents in response to her urgent appeal. So now, quietly and discreetly, Orley could again practise the True Faith. Katherine had not told Father Randall everything – merely that Gadd had been unveiled as an excommunicate impostor, and had been sent packing. The servants, she had said, knew only that he had gone; not of their own unabsolved state, nor that the chapel had suffered sacrilege. Father Randall had eyed her shrewdly, and had suddenly interrupted her story with: 'Tell me no more, my child. Let the past keep its secrets, for dead secrets have little power, and the grace of God is infinite.' Then he had absolved her and Hal, closeted himself in the chapel for an hour or two, emerged to tell her briskly it was fit for use again, and set about hearing the confessions of the entire household, taking great care to leave no one unshriven. Even Amy, as best he could; and he was the only one Amy looked at as she did at Katherine.

197

His absolution of Hal had been, to say the least, unusual. For one thing, Katherine had been present. Hal had been up, sitting by the bedchamber window, physically better but still pale and frightened-looking. Father Randall had said to him: 'Thou art deeply troubled, my son, that is plain to see . . . No, my lady Katherine, bide with us . . . My son, I have prayed long to our Lord, and sought enlightenment from His Blessed Mother, and in all humility I believe they have answered my pleas. Heaven's guidance to me is this; that thou hast suffered greatly from thine own weakness and folly; and that suffering, which hath brought thee to the very gates of Hell, hath been its own penance. Therefore let no more be said, save this: *Absolve te in nomine Patris, et Filii, et Spiritus Sancti . . .*' The astonished and delighted Katherine had watched and wondered; but from that day Hal had become steadily more like his own ebullient self, and her respect for Father Randall had deepened.

'Thou'rt pensive, Kate.'

Hal's voice snatched her from her reverie, and she smiled across at him, loving him as he sat so handsomely, so easily, astride his horse. 'Forgive me, Hal. I neglect thee.'

He laughed. 'That, never. My lady hath loved me, berated me, embraced me, scolded me, laughed with me and wept with me. But never, as God is my witness, neglected me.'

'Thou'rt too large and full of noise to neglect, i' faith.'

'But loving withal, Kate.'

'But loving withal, my Hal. And beloved.'

They rode on contentedly for a while, and then Katherine turned her horse into a narrow lane.

'Whither now?' Hal asked, turning with her.

'I have a goose and a cheese for Mistress Withecombe.'

'Old blind Bella? Thou'rt kind, my lady. For myself, I cannot be at ease with her.'

'Dost thou judge men by their countenances?'

'An I did, I'd have few servants. No – I judge them by heart and stomach.'

198

'Grant the same favour to Bella, then. I owe her much, and thou through me.'

'How, Kate?'

'That secret is privy to me and her.'

Hal shrugged good-naturedly, and stayed by the gate with Robin when Katherine dismounted to visit Bella. As always Bella was at the door to meet her.

'Good day to thee, Katherine of Orley. What bringeth thee here?'

'Good day, Bella. Why dost thou ask? It is thy custom to tell me why I come, ere I open my mouth.'

Bella smiled. It was the first time Katherine had seen her smile, except bitterly, and for an instant she caught the faintest echo of a beauty that must once have been the young Bella's. 'Be it so, Katherine child. Thou bringest gifts, for which I thank thee. But thou bringest also thy restored happiness, and a quickened womb, of which thou hast still not spoken to thy husband. And for these, I thank God.'

'And I . . . I bring one other thing, Bella.' She put the little silver amulet in the old woman's hand. 'I do not understand it, but it hath helped me greatly . . . Bella, I would ask thee something strange; and in truth, I do not understand this either. But I feel it within me, as I feel the quickened womb of which thou spakest . . . The Queen of Heaven hath sent me a Helper in my hour of need . . .'

'This I know.'

'This thou knowest, yes. I think I shall not see her again; her work for me is done. Ask me not how I know it is, for I cannot answer thee. But this I know – that she will come again, to this house, to thy seed, in God's good time. She will come laughing, in her own flesh, young and comely, a woman as thou and I are women . . . Tell thy son this, Bella, when he shall come home, that he may tell his son and his son's son; that when my Helper cometh, the Warrior Maiden thou hast called my sister from the womb of Time – when she cometh, she is to be given this amulet; for it is hers.'

199

'So thou, too, hast the Sight.'

'Not as thou hast it, Bella. It cometh and goeth as the wind. But of this I am sure.'

'It shall be done as thou sayest.'

'God bless thee, Bella. Now I must go to my husband; I think he groweth impatient.'

'He will forget all, when thou tellest him of the child in thy belly.'

'As to that,' Katherine smiled, 'I shall choose my occasion. My tidings merit a worthy delivery.'

Bella smiled with her, a woman's smile to another woman. 'And have no fear, Mistress of Orley. Thy son shall be born in safety and grow in peace.'

'Thou hast never told me aught but truth, Bella. So thy words comfort me . . . Nor shall I forget my Warrior Maiden, in the day when I am delivered of him. For I owe that safety and peace to her.'

'Thou art mistaken in one particular, none the less.'

'In what, Bella?'

'In believing that thou shalt not see her again. Her work for thee is done, indeed; yet shalt thou see her once more. And when that time cometh – which of you shall be the Helper?'

CHAPTER XX

My dear Bridget,

I don't know whether to say 'forgive me for writing to you like this' or 'forgive me for not writing to you sooner'. The fact is, if you and George can spare a day or two, I think your help is needed, and badly.

I say 'I think' because it's Jane who needs it, yet I doubt if she'd agree that she does, and in any case it's nothing I can put my finger on. I love the girl – you know that, of course – and she seems quite unaware of the fact; so most people would say my judgement's unreliable. But I'm dam' sure that something is seriously wrong, and that whatever it is, only someone like you and George would understand it.

Has she written to you at all? – I don't mean to ask for help, I mean just friendlily to tell you what she did after you left last summer? I don't even know that, so I'd better fill you in, in case she hasn't.

Two days after you went, she applied to the Council for Charley Unsworth's job. We were all delighted, of course, and very surprised; it must have meant a big drop in salary for her, and it was most unusual that she was able to leave her teaching post without notice. But apparently the schools in her borough were being reorganised, leaving hers overstaffed, so when she rang up her headmaster she was able to twist his arm and get herself made redundant right away.

And as for salary, she insisted she could manage – after all, the Curator's job includes a free flat in the Grange; and in any case she'd wanted more time to work on a book on the

Plantagenets which a publisher had commissioned. She had other books in mind, and the Curator's pay and flat would keep her fed, clothed and housed quite adequately till her book earnings increased.

Anyway, the Council gave her the job at once, and she moved in. I think that was my happiest day (and I hope I don't sound self-pityingly wistful) – when I drove her up to her old flat to collect her things in the Green Man's van. She was happy and energetic and entertaining and beautiful, and we worked hard and sweated and laughed and she told me all the silly personal stories which everyone has about his own belongings. We managed to pack, move, and unpack in one day – *and* have time for her to clean up, change into something eye-catching, and have dinner with me at the Green Man.

Next morning she started work like a beaver. She was ready for the first tour at ten o'clock, and she hasn't missed one since; whatever else is wrong now, it isn't her work. The Council were so pleased with her that she got away with murder – they were lending her workmen, reorganising lighting, and authorising little bits of restoration Charley had pleaded for in vain. She nosed around the Grange gardens, and very quickly (by what seemed to my lay mind a very elegant piece of deduction) located the eleventh-century well-head which had been abandoned when the Great Hall was built in the fourteenth; it had become covered with soil and forgotten. She dug the soil away, with Keith and me press-ganged into the heavy work, and now it's a feature of the place; she wrote an article on it (Keith's drawings, my photographs) for the county Archaeological Journal; apparently it's unique in some abstruse way.

Then she got it into her head that a hump of land between the house and the river might have been occupied in Saxon, Roman, and possibly Celtic times. So she sank a trial shaft (again with Keith's and my help, though she hovered over us as if we were apprentice surgeons trying a brain operation) and by God she was right. She found only a few clues, but from all three periods, and enough to justify a larger dig. The next thing we knew, she'd recruited and enthused a volunteer excavation party from the village; an unlikely mixture of people from the Withecombes to the postman, but she kept their interest and they're still at it, crowing over fragments of oyster-shell and the odd bronze pin. They now call themselves the Orley Archaeological Society, with Claire Withecombe as Hon. Sec.

So far, everything was fine. The Plantagenet book was going well, especially when the public tours stopped for the winter at the end of September and she had more time. The tours didn't stop altogether, because she was always ready to take people round by arrangement; she wrote to every school and college and appropriate society for miles, and she got quite a lot of response.

Don't get me wrong – everything still *is* going fine, as far as the job's concerned. Public tours start again next month, at Easter, and she's busy reorganising the Grange shop for them, among other things.

The trouble – which quite honestly frightens me – is in herself, as a person.

I'd better confess what happened to my own relationship with her, though you can probably guess it. In the first weeks, Keith and I both saw a lot of her, separately and together, and even though the competition for her was unspoken it must have been obvious. Jane isn't a tease, and she didn't behave like one; I think she genuinely liked us both, and as long as neither of us made the contest explicit and faced her with a choice, she was content with things as they were.

I know, don't tell me; feeling as I did (and do) I *should* have made it explicit. Faint heart, etc. etc. But I didn't. Probably, to be painfully honest, I was afraid of losing. She meant too much to me – and Keith was too alarmingly confident and attractive – for me to have the nerve to risk it. All right, I was a dam' fool.

The change in her came quite suddenly, just before

Christmas. The only way I can describe it is to say that she seemed to stop being a woman. It was as subtle, but as unmistakable, as that. I said she wasn't a tease, and it's true; but when she was herself, even without her provoking me, and without my ever making a pass at her, she couldn't so much as talk to me without being entirely and naturally a woman talking to a man. You knew her then; you know what I mean. About a week before Christmas, that stopped, like a switch being turned off.

At first, of course, I thought it meant she and Keith had become lovers, making her instinctively neutral towards me. But I'm pretty certain they hadn't – not then – because when the three of us were together, she was the same to him as she was to me.

The thing that really shook me (and it would sound trivial to anyone who hadn't known the old Jane) was when *she didn't dress up for Christmas*. Christmas is very much a village community occasion at Orley, and as Curator and a village personality she made no attempt to dodge it. She was in the Green Man on Christmas Eve, for the Christmas Day dinner, and for the Boxing Day kids' party; and for all of them she wore a dark blue skirt and sweater and no jewellery. Neat, smart, and utterly sexless – and this when every other woman in Orley, from schoolgirl to old bag, was flaunting herself like mad. She wasn't hostile; in a sense she wasn't even withdrawn; just neutral. She even kissed me under the mistletoe when a couple of other women did, and her mouth was about as alive as dry plastic.

She hasn't dressed up since.

In January and February, she *did* become withdrawn; she began to look tense and (I thought) ill. I plucked up my courage and mentioned to Keith, who is after all her doctor now. He looked at me blankly and said she was perfectly all right.

They became lovers about the end of January. Don't ask me how I know, but I'm certain of it. I'm also certain that there's no love or happiness in it, just a cold cynical hunger.

If there *were* love, I'd be sad and disappointed, of course, for myself, but I'd leave them to it and accept defeat – I'd have no choice, would I?

She does her job as well as ever. There's not a breath of criticism from the Council or anyone else. But she's cold and unhappy and sick and *she is not Jane*.

I could go on and on, but I'm sure I've said enough to tell you whether or not the trouble is something within your special area. I think it is. I hope to God you *can* come.

Sincerely,
Trevor Cox.

March 18.

Dear Trevor,

Why the hell didn't you call us before? Arriving tomorrow (Friday) about 5.30. Book us a room.

Love,
Bridget.

P.S. Yes, you *were* a dam' fool. She would have been yours for the asking.   B.

March 18.

Dear Jane,

Just a note to say George and I are overworked and feel like a break, so we're coming down to the Green Man for the weekend, and perhaps a day or two more if George can spare them. Hope you're having a ball being Curator; dying to hear all your news. Have dinner with us Friday night?

Love,
Bridget.

CHAPTER XXI

They called at Orley Cottage Hospital first, on their way to the Green Man, for a word with Keith. He received them politely, but from a certain distance, which puzzled them. It was Keith, after all, who had called them to Orley last summer in the first place. They had known him for some time – he had been at school with Bridget's brother – and although he had never been an intimate friend, there had always been an easy spontaneous warmth between them when they had met. There was none of that today.

He did not exactly snub them, nor did he actually say or do anything at which they could reasonably take offence. But he kept them, smilingly, at arm's length.

Bridget had intended to be partially frank with him, without revealing that Trevor had written to them; since they had, in fact, had a couple of letters from Jane in the autumn (though not since the change in her which had worried Trevor) they could have been vague about how recently she had written and pretend unease about her. Keith had had experience of Bridget's ability as a psychometrist, and she knew he respected it. But once she had met him and sniffed the air, she changed her mind.

She merely asked, casually: 'And how's Jane?'

'Oh, fine. She's made a big difference at the Grange. And she's writing a book.'

'Well, it's a healthy life out here, after being stuck in a town flat.'

'Yes.'

'Do you see much of her?'

'Quite a bit,' he replied non-committally, and went

straight on: 'You must come and look at our new intensive care unit. I'm rather proud of it.'

They duly admired the intensive care unit, and Jane was not mentioned again.

'Why is he shutting us out?' Bridget wondered when they were alone on the road again.

'I can't make up my mind,' George said. 'But I smell possessiveness . . . There's something wrong here, love.'

'Very wrong . . . Let's go and find Jane.'

'Softly, softly. Don't push her.'

'Daft,' Bridget smiled at him.

They went to the Green Man and settled in their room. Trevor, busy with other arrivals, was able to do little more than greet them; but the anxiety in his eyes, and his relief that they had answered his call so promptly, were obvious.

'Cheer up,' George told him, when they were briefly alone together. 'There'll be an answer. There always is, in these things, if you keep your nerve.'

Trevor smiled, not very convincingly. 'Just what do you mean by "these things"?'

'I mean the sort of thing people come running to Bridget and me for.'

'Do you always succeed?'

'I'd be a liar if I pretended that. But Bridget's pretty formidable, in her class.'

'And you?'

'I give her covering fire, from the flank.'

Trevor paused, then said: 'If you can help Jane . . . You know, I'd rather see her with Keith, but herself again, than the way she is now.'

'None of that,' George told him firmly. 'Keep your sights on what you *really* want. That's what I meant by keeping your nerve – among other things. Don't be so diffident. You want her, you go get her. You'd make her happier than Keith, that's for sure, so stop underestimating yourself.'

'I thought Keith was a friend of yours.'

'What's that got to do with it?'

Before Trevor could answer, a blue-rinsed American woman loudly required his attention, towing an affectionately silent husband behind her. The husband caught George's eye and unexpectedly winked. George winked back as Blue-Rinse swept Trevor away.

George went upstairs to join Bridget.

'Jesus!' he said when he saw her. 'You're giving no quarter, are you?'

Bridget looked splendid, in brown jersey silk with an unbuttoned shirt-neck, her hair high, wide and soft, with calculatedly escaping tendrils, in a somewhat Victorian style George had not seen before. Blue-Rinse won't like this, he thought maliciously.

'You approve?'

'Yes, I do. You can still surprise me.'

'I should hope so, darling.'

'What about Jane?'

'*This* is about Jane. If Trevor's right, I want a reaction from her.'

'If it doesn't alienate her – put distance between you.'

'Then we'll have to fall back on your charm,' she teased him, adding seriously: 'Trust me, love.'

George kissed her, carefully so as not to disturb the hair-do.

In the event, Jane surprised them; but there was something pitiful in the surprise.

They had gone into the bar lounge to wait for her, knowing she would look for them there. Blue-Rinse, as George had expected, couldn't keep her eyes off Bridget. (Nor, of course, could Blue-Rinse's husband.) George whispered a comment to Bridget, who smiled.

They ordered sherries and forgot about Blue-Rinse.

Twenty minutes later Jane appeared in the door, with Trevor at her elbow looking a little confused.

Jane had dressed. Long green, off-the-shoulder; an attractive dress, on the face of it; but the thing which saddened George was that she wore it without flair, without any of

208

her old female panache. She wore it with a mixture of apology and defiance, like a young spinster only used to dressing up for unavoidable garden-parties. Or maybe I'm exaggerating, George thought; but that's not Jane as we knew her.

She had not seen them yet. George said quietly: 'Trevor looks surprised.'

'He should look pleased,' Bridget said. 'That get-up, darling, is a cry for help. She's sicker than I thought, but she's trying to signal a welcome to us. She *wants* us here. And that gives us a flying start.'

They rose to greet her.

Jane smiled, quickly and eagerly, but the eagerness was immediately smothered, as though she were afraid of it. Trevor brought her over, and George rescued her from her shy and awkward greeting formulae by organising drinks.

If she were indeed crying for help, there was no evidence of it during dinner. Jane relaxed a little as Bridget deftly confined the conversation to Jane's job. She was more than ready to talk about that, and became quite loquacious; there was even life in her voice. So far, George told himself, so good. The crunch comes later – and I'd better not be in on it, to begin with. Bridget will break the ice more easily alone with her.

So when, after the coffee, Bridget asked Jane: 'Want to freshen up?' George stayed at the table and ordered another Drambuie.

Jane seemed to hesitate at the foot of the stairs, as though dreading the moment of truth. But Bridget stood behind her, friendlily inexorable, and she went on up.

Bridget closed the bedroom door behind them, and turned to face Jane.

'Well, Jane?'

Jane replied 'Well what?' in a dry throat.

Bridget went on looking at her, waiting.

Jane's voice had a panicky note in it. 'What do you want from me?'

'Oh, no, lass. It's you who want *us*.'

And then Jane burst into tears.

Bridget put her arms round her and led her to the dressing-table stool. 'Get it off your chest, love, then we'll mop you up and put your face back. If you've given up war-paint, I haven't, and I'll have something to suit you. At least we'll make you *look* like the old Jane.'

'That's cruel,' Jane spluttered through her tears.

'No it's not, because the old Jane's inside there somewhere, yelling to be let out . . . What happened, lass?'

It took Jane a minute or two to get her voice back. Then she said: 'Gadd didn't give up.'

'I didn't imagine he would. I tried to warn you, indirectly. Perhaps I should have been plainer. But I don't think you were in a mood to listen.'

'No, I suppose I wasn't.' Jane picked up a tissue and started dabbing. 'Everything was fine, for about three months. I was happy, and busy, and I thought Trevor wanted me . . .'

'Oh, God,' Bridget said under her breath.

'. . . and I was making friends with the village, and . . . oh, well. Then one night, Gadd was suddenly *there*. Oh, no, not in the chapel; I won *that* fight. Katherine and Hal are safe, and Gadd's physically dead . . . No, I was walking down by the river bank, I only saw him for a couple of seconds, but his eyes . . .' She started crying again. 'Bridget, I've never seen such hatred. And there was something else, too – as though he were *crowing* over me. As though I'd given him an opening he'd been waiting for – and I don't know *how* . . .'

Bridget put a hand on her arm, till she was calm again. 'Have you seen him since?'

'No, but I know when he's near.'

'He's not near now.'

'No. But he'll be back.'

'What happened afterwards?'

'I don't know. Nothing mattered except my work – he let

me get on with that. But everything else . . . You know, being *human*, being a *woman* – I wanted it to matter, but it stayed inside me, I couldn't bring it out . . . Do you know this is the first time I've dressed up for the evening, since before Christmas? And it's a pretty feeble effort, isn't it? This thing I'm wearing's all right – but I can't *do* it any more! *I can't be a woman!* And it's Gadd who won't let me . . . Bridget, I'm not deluding myself, am I? I mean, *I* know I'm not, but people "know" things which aren't true when they're mentally ill, don't they?'

'No, Jane. You're not deluding yourself.'

'I had to fight to make myself dress up tonight. But I was determined to do it.' She gave a little bark of a laugh. 'The Jane inside me yelling to get out. Well, I made it, more or less . . . But it's the same all the time, like a grey fog. Nothing *matters* any more.'

'Not even going to bed with Keith?' Bridget asked.

'Thank you for not saying "making love". That'd be a bad joke.'

'Why do you do it, then?'

'My body made me. Or Gadd made me – I don't know. Maybe *he* likes bad jokes.'

'And Keith? What does he feel about it?'

'He doesn't say. Perhaps Gadd won't let *him* be human, either.'

'Well, he's certainly not himself – and I've known him since he was a schoolboy.'

Jane shrugged. 'Anyway, going to bed with Keith isn't important. I told you, it just happens. And since Trevor doesn't care about me . . .'

'For Christ's sake,' Bridget burst out, 'why do you think George and I are here? Did you really imagine we just wanted a weekend in the country?'

Jane looked up, confused. 'But I thought . . .'

'We're here because Trevor's nearly out of his mind, worrying about you, and he sent for us. If you don't know Trevor loves you, you're sicker than I imagined . . . Now

211

don't start crying again, or we'll *never* get around to putting your face on.'

'I'm not fit to love, right now. Being Keith's whore is just about my level.'

'If you make one more remark like that,' Bridget told her, 'I shall slap your face. And when *I* slap, it takes more than powder to hide the result.'

Jane dropped her eyes and mumbled 'I'm sorry.'

'I should think so, too. Now listen to me. You licked Gadd once, Battle Maid, and you're going to lick him again. Once and for all. Will you let us help you?'

'If you think I'm worth . . .' Jane began, and stopped as Bridget raised a threatening palm, half-seriously.

Bridget lowered her hand again, without hurrying. 'I asked – will you let us help you?'

'D'you think I wouldn't do anything you tell me?' Jane said desperately. '*Anything!*'

George knew the signs well; the day had left Bridget a little unsure. Normally she came to bed with her hair in two long plaits. But tonight she climbed in beside him with her hair loose and free; as she held him close, it fell across their nakedness like Eve's in a modest painting of the Garden of Eden. That meant one of two things; an erotic whim (she knew how that drifting curtain fascinated him), or a little-girl uncertainty which occasionally affected her, and which no one but George was ever allowed to witness.

Tonight he could sense her vulnerability, and he stroked her head gently as she buried her cheek in his neck.

'I think Gadd is commuting,' she said at last.

He was used to that, too. The more worried she was, the more apparently flippant her phraseology tended to be. But the flippancy *was* only apparent, and the colloquialisms always expressed an exact meaning.

'Between Keith and Jane?'

He felt her nod.

212

'That,' he went on, 'could make exorcism both difficult and dangerous. Difficult for us, and dangerous for them.'

She nodded again, and they pondered in silence for a while.

'Look at them both today,' Bridget said at last. 'There's no doubt where Gadd was in residence. That cold poise, that arrogant command of the situation – Keith *was* Gadd. But Jane . . . Christ, darling, Gadd must have put her through the wringer. She's desperate but she's gutless. Whatever happened to the Battle Maid?'

'I'm afraid she was caught napping,' George said. 'She just wasn't expecting a counter-attack. She'd relaxed all her defences, and he just bided his time and then walked in. And he's done it so thoroughly that when he's not "in residence", as you put it, she's left like a limp rag . . . Arrogant is right. It's almost *safe* for him to commute . . . I wonder if he finds it equally safe to leave Keith?'

'I'd say yes – but I'm very much afraid it's for the opposite reason. With Jane, he can leave her to her own devices, probably for days at a time, because he's weakened her so much she can't pull herself together. With Keith, he can leave him alone because Keith *likes* being Gadd. Keith can be trusted to carry out Gadd's mandate unsupervised – again, probably for days at a time.'

'Oh, God . . . I hope you're wrong.'

'So do I, darling.'

'Because if you're right, we'll have to fight Keith as well as Gadd.'

'We've beaten worse than that.'

'I know we have,' George agreed. 'But if we win – and we can't afford not to – what happens to Keith?'

'If Jane wants to be rescued and Keith doesn't,' Bridget answered, 'then we go all out to rescue Jane. Right?'

'Well . . . Right.'

'Funny. Till a couple of years ago, you were a regular soldier. Sergeant-Major George Blake, R.E.M.E., no less. But I can be much more ruthless than you can.'

213

George sighed. 'Or more clear-sighted. If Keith's willingly enlisted himself with Gadd . . .'

'With Jane's body as his payment. Remember that.'

'Yes, that too . . . If he's a willing recruit, he's expendable from our point of view. But it's sad, all the same.'

'War is, soldier boy,' Bridget reminded him.

CHAPTER XXII

Bridget's uncertainty had disappeared by sunrise. She sat up in bed, suddenly, while the house was still silent; George opened his eyes and she looked down at him, smiling. Then she gave him a quick good-morning hug, which woke him thoroughly by its sheer vigour, and jumped out to pace the floor for a minute or two as though she were thinking hard. George watched the Viking body, admiring it anew as he always did, and waited.

After a while she sat down abruptly at the dressing-table, smiled at him again, and threw him her hairbrush without speaking.

George got out of bed and set to work, brushing and sorting and separating until the abundance of her hair lay smoothly down her bare back.

Her first words of the day were: 'Before we go any further – a little smokescreen, I think.'

'It might be a good idea,' he agreed.

They showered and towelled themselves vigorously, then without dressing, Bridget started to unpack a small attaché case. George checked with a compass that the dressing-table stood in the North, so he cleared it, and between them they laid out the copper pentacle, the candles, the wand, the scourge, the black- and white-handled knives, the coloured cords, the bowls of water and salt, the chalice, the incense-burner.

'*I exorcise thee, O thou creature of water . . .*'
'*Blessings be upon this creature of salt . . .*'
'*I conjure thee, O Circle of Power . . .*'
'*Ye Lords of the Watchtowers of the East . . .*'

Step by step the ritual unrolled, the Circle intensified; their bodies and minds moved within it, the scented smoke drifting across their skin, which began to glisten with the effort of their concentration . . .

A mile away in the Cottage Hospital, Keith was already on duty, examining a blood sample under a microscope while Nurse Monaghan stood at his shoulder. Suddenly, with no warning, the field of red and white corpuscles shifted and blurred before his eyes; he blinked and shook his head, and his vision cleared. But the being within him leaped on guard, and Keith stiffened.

Confusion . . . Interference . . . Resistance . . .

What is happening? Keith asked in his mind. He listened to the inner presence, but no clear answer came; only a sense of wariness, of prowling, of probing. Keith strove to ally himself with it, to add his own strength to it.

'Are you all right, doctor?' Nurse Monaghan asked, her voice concerned.

'Of course I am,' he snapped. Then the presence left him; but surely he could still help it, still put out his own feelers . . .

Nurse Monaghan watched him, frowning to herself and wondering. The doctor was acting very strangely, these days; ever since he'd started his affair with young Jane – and no good to either of them *that* was, to be sure . . .

In her bedroom in the Grange, Jane stirred uneasily in her sleep, and then began tossing from side to side, still unwaking.

Bridget and George banished the Circle and put away their working tools. They were both breathless, and needed another shower to wash away the sweat and reinvigorate themselves.

Then they dressed and went downstairs to breakfast.

Jane was their first concern; they had no doubts about that; but they would not simply abandon Keith till they had confirmed that Bridget was right about him. So that morning they split forces, George driving to the hospital, and Bridget walking through the Grange gardens to visit Jane.

George found Keith in his office; the doctor remained seated, and said 'Good morning, George' neither friendlily nor unfriendlily.

George said 'Morning, Keith,' and launched into surface talk. Keith leaned back in his chair and replied in kind, easily. Behind the talk, George kept all his psychic senses open, receptive, ready for any hint that the active essence of Jonathan Gadd lurked behind the calm eyes that faced him.

No sign; and George knew that if there had been any, by now he would have picked it up. Keith was on his own. Right, then; the bull by the horns.

'We're very worried about Jane,' George threw at him.

'You've no cause to be.'

'She's not herself, Keith, and you know it.'

'I know her a dam' sight better than you do, believe me.'

'Too close to see straight, perhaps?'

'I'm her friend and her doctor . . .'

'And her lover?'

'That, George, is our business.' Keith was still calm. 'In fact she is not registered with me as her doctor. But I *am* prepared to say there's nothing wrong with her – and there won't be, unless you and Bridget start meddling.'

'And that's your professional opinion – even though you're not her G.P., for obvious reasons?'

'Yes.'

'Then let me remind you that last summer, when you *were* involved, you called Bridget and me in on her case – as you might a couple of specialists. So it's hardly meddling. In fact, it'd be unethical for us to abdicate our specialist interest in her.'

Keith laughed. 'Don't lecture me on professional ethics, George. I know the small print better than you do.'

'All right. But let's be honest. You know quite a bit about our speciality yourself. And you know as well as we do

217

what's happened to Jane, and to you, since you wiped the blood off her sword in the chapel.'

Keith was still smiling, 'Do I?'

'And you also know that at this moment, you are capable of deciding – on on your own, individual judgement – whose side you are on.'

'You haven't lost your touch, George, I see.'

'No, I don't think I have.'

They stared at each other, unblinking.

'Are you challenging me?' Keith asked at last.

'I'm merely telling you what we intend to do. And inviting you to step out of our way. It's not you we're challenging.'

'And what *do* you intend to do, George?'

'The aim, you know. I've no reason to trust you with the details . . . Whose side are you on, Keith?'

Keith picked up his pen and a prescription pad. 'I'm sorry, George – it's been nice talking to you, but I've got a lot of work to do.'

'And so,' said George, 'have we.'

He turned and walked out.

'People believe a lot of things late at night, after a good dinner,' Jane said, 'that look pretty silly next morning.'

'So this morning,' Bridget replied almost conversationally, 'you don't believe that Jonathan Gadd is manipulating you – preventing you from being yourself?'

'It is a rather far-fetched explanation.'

'Explanation of what, Jane?'

'Of the fact that I haven't been quite myself. All right, I know I haven't; I've been through a bad patch. Haven't you, ever?'

'From time to time. One of those times was terrible – the Dark Night of the Soul indeed. But I've always known what was happening to me, and fought my way out.'

'I'll fight my way out, too.'

'Just "pull yourself together", eh?'

218

'If you like to put it that way, yes.'

Bridget leaned back in the library window-seat. 'It's interesting. I've now met three Janes. First, the human one. Yesterday, the terrified and almost defeated one. Today, the cold, self-possessed one. Except that I wouldn't call you *self*-possessed. I'm not talking to Jane. I'm talking to Jonathan Gadd. Jane Blair is gagged and bound in a corner of her own mind.' Her voice had become very quiet and intense. 'And listen to me, Jonathan Gadd. I and my High Priest are going to take away her gag, and cut her bonds, and drive you back to Hell where you belong. Do you hear me, Jonathan Gadd?'

Jane sat rigid, her forehead beading with perspiration.

'Jonathan Gadd is dead,' she said through clenched teeth. 'I killed him.'

'Jane Blair killed your body, Jonathan Gadd. But we still have to get rid of *you*. And when we've broken your hold on this world, you know what that means, don't you, Jonathan? You know what *your* Hell is, don't you? I doubt if the Lords of Karma will find *you* retrievable. Back to the elements from which you came. The cosmic scrap-heap, Jonathan!'

Jane was shuddering violently; only the whites of her eyes were visible under the half-closed lids. A deep and terrible voice that was not her own forced itself out of her lips. '*Damn thee, woman! My Master shall crush thee underfoot, as the vermin thou art . . .*'

Bridget had risen to her feet. She flung out her hands, pointing with both forefingers at the stricken girl, and cried out a Name.

Jane screamed, and slumped in her chair. As Bridget ran forward to make sure she did not fall, George threw open the door and hurried across to help her.

'Confrontation?' he asked.

'Yes. He's gone for a while, licking his wounds, but he'll be back. And soon. He's big, George. And he knows this is all or nothing.'

'Circle?'

'Right away, with her in it.'

'Here?'

'No . . .' She closed her eyes for a moment. 'The Great Bedchamber. Friendly territory.'

George picked up the unconscious Jane in his arms. He nodded his head towards the attaché case that stood on the window-seat. 'You came prepared. Good.'

'I had a hunch, darling.' She picked up the case, and followed George and his burden through the door. 'How was it with Keith?'

'Sold out. We have to forget him.'

'Too bad.'

'So apart from Trevor – he could have been helpful, but it's too late to get him – it's just the three of us.'

'Don't be too sure,' Bridget said. 'There might be one other. That's why I chose the Bedchamber.'

CHAPTER XXIII

A silver castle, foursquare, at the heart of the indigo immensity behind the North Wind. Jane could not be sure whether she was spiralling inwards, around and towards it, or drifting inexorably closer while the castle itself turned. The castle terrified her, yet she needed to approach it; it was inconceivably cold, beyond any coldness of air or flesh, and yet only by seeking it out could she rediscover warmth and life.

She was part of that infinite indigo space – indigo suffused with violet – yet all around her were shifting colours, shapes that came and went, swirling eddies within the great spiral, jostling her impalpably, some eager, some resentful, some curious, some indifferent. She resonated with each of them in a complex orchestration of pleasure and pain, which gradually became acceptable, self-compensating. For beyond them, circling against the spiral, around and around her like a satellite, lurked something else, something familiar and implacably hostile, a wounded black carnivore intent on destroying her, on revenging its own wounds, still unable to reach her, yet coming closer with each snarling orbit.

She must reach the castle before the thing closed with her . . . She willed the spiral to draw her in faster.

But from the castle, or from space itself, a voice that was not a voice seemed to whisper: *Not yet. Your time is not yet. Not all the way.*

She cried out from inside herself: *Who are you?*

Although she knew she was now spiralling outwards, as if at the voice's command, and although the fanged menace still ringed her, she was no longer quite so afraid.

221

I am the beauty of the green earth, and the white moon among the stars, and the mystery of the waters, and the desire of the heart of man . . .

The multicoloured forms were moving back, withdrawing from her; all around her a blue-violet wall – no, a sphere, with herself as its centre – was growing and strengthening, enfolding her, protecting her, softening the chill of space . . .

From me all things proceed, and unto me all things must return . . .

Within the blue-violet sphere, the magic circle of safety, the room was beginning to take shape, reassuring her. Reassuring, the cushions on which she lay. Reassuring, the carved pillars of the great four-poster a few yards away. Reassuring, the small bright candle-flames that flickered and glowed to North, South, East, and West. Doubly reassuring, the tall naked figures of Bridget and George, ritually flanking the heavy oak chest which served as an altar. Reassuring, too, the discovery that the voice had been Bridget's all the time . . . Or had it?

'*And thou who thinkest to seek for me, know thy seeking and yearning shall avail thee not, unless thou knowest the mystery: that if that which thou seekest thou findest not within thee, thou wilt never find it without thee. For behold, I have been with thee from the beginning; and I am that which is attained at the end of desire.*'

Jane sat up, in the middle of the Circle where they had lain her, and asked: 'Did you bring the Sword?'

They looked down at her, smiling a welcome. George said 'Of course', picked up the sword from the floor in front of the altar, and handed it to her.

Jane gripped it firmly, savouring the familiarity of the hilt.

'I think the Battle Maid's back with us,' Bridget said.

'In person,' Jane told her, 'I've got you to thank, haven't I? . . . It's strange – I've never been in a Magic Circle before.'

'You recognise it, then?'

'Oh, yes. I could see it forming around me, as I came back

222

along the spiral. I was very glad of it, because it kept *him* out. I'd been trying to reach the silver castle to escape him, and when the voice turned me back I thought I'd be afraid, but I wasn't once the Circle started growing and I found out the voice was yours.'

She was astonished at the matter-of-fact way the words came out, but Bridget and George seemed delighted. 'So you've glimpsed Caer Arianrhod and found your way back,' Bridget said. 'That *does* mean the old Jane's here again.'

Jane replied, wonderingly: 'It feels rather like a new Jane.'

'In a sense, it is – but really it's the old Jane reinvigorated.'

'I suppose that's it, yes . . . Forgive my asking – and don't think I mind, I'm just curious; why have you two got no clothes on?'

'We're normally skyclad in the Circle . . .'

'Nice word, that.'

'Isn't it? . . . Several reasons. We sum them up by saying "Skin is the livery of the Goddess". It's easier to raise psychic power this way – and easier to be well and truly *yourself*, which is the real secret of witchcraft.'

Jane thought about that for a moment, then nodded. 'That makes sense. Do you mind if I join you?'

'Not at all.'

Jane laid down the sword and took her clothes off, putting them neatly on a chair; leaving nothing on herself but the Moon Tree pendant. She picked up the sword again and spun around happily on her toes, making the blade whistle through the air. Then she stood astride, facing them, stroking the sword-point with her free hand. 'Gadd will be back, won't he?'

'Take it easy, Battle Maid,' Bridget warned her. 'You fell into the trap of over-confidence once before, remember? And maybe that was our fault, so I'm not letting it happen again. Yes, he'll be back, very soon – this Circle is the last battlefield, do you realise that?'

'I realise it.'

223

'Then realise that it won't be easy. He'll put all his strength into trying to break the Circle. We'll need all *our* strength to hold it.'

'And to hit back?'

'Holding the Circle *will* be hitting back. Either he breaks it, or he breaks himself against it.'

'Will it be *just* our strength, holding it?'

'No, of course not. We'll be working hard to make ourselves a channel for what *we* call the Goddess. But remember, he'll be calling on some formidable forces too. Dark ones.'

Jane looked a little more subdued. 'It all sounds a bit . . . well, cosmic.'

'It is,' George told her, 'believe you me. But don't be overawed. Hang on to your fighting spirit. You're going to need it.'

They sat down within the Circle, in a triangle facing each other; waiting, and listening.

Trevor, for some reason, was finding it very difficult to settle down to work this morning. Not that there was anything urgent that needed doing; his barman was supervising the unloading of a consignment of draught bitter from the brewer's, the receptionist-cum-barmaid could cope with any problems of the few guests, the chambermaid was busy doing out the rooms, and the chef was singing to himself in the kitchen. Trevor had some paperwork he should be attending to, but he could not bring his mind to bear on it. He knew well enough that there was one thing to make him restless – the fact that Bridget and George were taking Jane in hand, and that the outcome of their efforts might affect him fundamentally. But something told him his unease was not to be so simply explained.

He had no idea what Bridget and George were up to, or even if they were with Jane right now. Yet he knew that something critical was happening; he could feel it as a cat feels the imminence of thunder. He wanted to be there, to

224

join in, for good or ill. But whether this urge was to be trusted, or merely his own impatience prompting him to an unwise interference, he honestly could not tell.

One thing was certain; he could not work, could not stay in the Green Man.

He walked up the village street, greeting automatically the two or three people he passed.

The Long Walk was losing its winter look; there were more daffodils this year – Jane had managed to get a few pounds spent on new bulbs. There were young leaves everywhere, and birds calling and replying. But Trevor was not soothed.

He sat on the stone bench and tried to collect himself.

He thought of Jane.

Jane . . . She needed his help – needed his as well as Bridget's and George's – needed it *now* . . .

No, he must be deluding himself, letting his love inflame his imagination. He took a deep breath, clenching his fists on his knees.

A movement across the end of the Long Walk caught his eye. It was Keith, walking purposefully towards the Grange's front entrance.

Trevor rose and hurried after him, not really knowing why he did so. He rounded the corner of the house, and saw Keith rattling the door-handle angrily. Trevor almost ran, but Keith did not seem to hear him coming.

Keith stopped rattling the handle, and looked around on the ground. Then he stooped and picked up a brick that formed part of the border of a flower-bed. Trevor cried out, sensing his purpose, but Keith ignored him and stepped across the bed to a leaded window. With one violent jab of the brick, he smashed the glass next to the latch.

Trevor halted beside him and asked: 'What the hell do you think you're doing, man?'

Keith turned to face him, and Trevor caught his breath, because he could barely recognise the face, let alone the look in Keith's eyes. It *was* Keith – and yet . . .

225

'Keep away from me,' Keith growled, raising the brick that was still in his hand.

Trevor quick on his feet, lunged to grab at the threatening arm. But Keith's speed was superhuman. Trevor just managed to sway to the left as the brick came at his skull, and the blow glanced on his temple. He knew an instant of blinding pain, and then nothing more.

Within the Circle, Jane suddenly cried out: 'Trevor!' If George had not jumped to restrain her, she would have been out of the Circle.

'No, Jane! Whatever happens, you *must* stay inside!'

Jane subsided, already doubting her first impulse. 'I thought . . . I don't know . . . I thought I felt Trevor in trouble.' She screwed up her eyes, concentrating. 'I can't get it now. Oh, God, I hope he's all right.'

Bridget said 'Quiet a moment' and shut her eyes, her fingers to her temples. George kept his restraining arm round Jane's shoulders, but she made no more attempt to move; instead she watched Bridget anxiously.

After a while Bridget opened her eyes and told them: 'I'm sorry, I can get nothing of Trevor. I just don't know. But Gadd's closing in . . . If anything *has* happened to Trevor, Jane, it's Gadd's doing. Remember that. Let it feed your fires.'

Jane said nothing, but gripped the sword harder.

Bridget went to the altar, and picked up the two knives with the black handles. She handed one to George, and the three of them stood, instinctively facing towards the door that lay beyond the corner of the fourposter.

Jane was afraid, and knew that she was afraid. But it was a fear that she almost welcomed, because for the first time in months the threat came from outside her, instead of cancerously from within. And she had something positive to do; to add all her willpower to her companions', every last ounce of it, for the maintaining of the Circle.

She could almost see it, a faint violet wall shimmering beyond the great bed. Almost . . . No, she *could* see it. And beyond it, shifting and jostling, those same transient shapes she had been aware of as she rode the spiral, fluttering against it like moths outside a bright window. But she must ignore them, resist the temptation to worry about them, resist everything that could weaken her concentration . . .

She did not know what she expected; perhaps a gathering of darkness beyond the violet wall signalling Gadd's approach, a dazzle of clashing powers as Gadd attacked the Circle . . . The one thing she did not expect was the thing that happened: the door bursting open and Keith standing in it, bright-eyed with rage.

For that instant, she stood paralysed with astonishment, a breach in the trio of defence; she saw the Circle waver, then grow steady as Bridget and George took the shock of the assault.

Assault it was, she knew suddenly, and her own anger flared, giving her a rush of new strength. For Keith was Gadd; she saw them at last as the same, and her body – desecrated by Gadd as Katherine's, bought by Keith as her own – cried out its hatred of the betrayer.

Keith stamped towards them, to the very edge of the Circle, and stood there, his teeth bared.

Jane raised her sword, expecting action, movement, physical violence; but it did not come. She gasped as she realised the true nature of the battle. It was fought in silence, without movement; the four of them faced each other in a terrible tension, that grew and grew till it was an agony not to be borne – yet it must be borne, for it was irreversible, only to be released in total destruction – of the Circle, or of the thing which attacked it . . .

Jane heard herself scream as Trevor staggered in at the door, one side of his face stained with half-dried blood. The tension wavered and almost broke, and Keith would have been upon them if Trevor had not leaped at him, trying to drag him down. Keith threw him aside without turning, and Trevor fell back against the doorpost. The diversion had been enough to save her; the Circle held again, and

Trevor froze, transfixed by the massive equilibrium of power.

The only sounds Jane could hear were the thumping of her own heart and the rasping of her own breath. All she could see was the face of Keith who was Gadd.

She felt herself giving way, and in that moment she glimpsed the Abyss. She could not endure any longer . . .

Her free hand moved of its own accord to grasp at the Moon Tree, and her unpremeditated cry rang out: '*Goddess, Thy Helper!*'

Her enemy jerked his head round towards the great bed, snarling.

Then Jane saw her; Katherine, her sister from the womb of time, leaping from the bed as naked as she, chestnut hair streaming as she ran to her side. Her left hand grasped Jane's right, warm and real, and Jane, exulting, felt the strength flow between them. Felt, too, the tide of power turn, and knew that they would win.

Katherine laughed out loud. 'So, Master Gadd – the reckoning!'

Keith moaned and fell forward, arms outspread; it was as though the Circle were a solid wall, for he leaned against it as his strength waned, and then slid down it to the floor, where he lay still.

Jane and Katherine faced each other, smiling. Katherine opened her mouth, beginning to speak. But in that moment she became misty and insubstantial, and no sound came; only the smile.

Then she was gone, and the room was still.

Jane, not yet quite out of the spell, was aware that Bridget was banishing the Circle. Then, she ran to Trevor.

'I'm all right,' he told her, breathless. 'But watch *him*, for Christ's sake. He tried to kill me. I knew he was coming for you . . .'

'There's no need to watch him,' George said, kneeling beside the huddled figure that had been Keith and Gadd. 'He's dead.'

CHAPTER XXIV

It was George, of course, who took charge. Bridget, drained of all power, was pale with exhaustion. Jane sat against the wall cradling Trevor's wounded head against her bare breast and murmuring over him. Trevor, still dazed in body and mind, understandably surrendered to her cradling.

'Clothes on, everybody,' George said. 'Then we'll get moving. We've got time, but not too much – when we do call a doctor, Keith mustn't have been too long dead. Jane, you get Trevor back to his room as quickly as you can, but try not to be seen; then come straight back here. Trevor, you weren't here – you haven't been inside the Grange at all this morning, understand? You tripped over a tree-root and hit your face on a rock . . . You know the area, you can think of a convincing place. But get it attended to right away, or it could be nasty. Jane, we'll have all the working tools packed away before you get back. Then *you'll* ring for a doctor and say Keith's had a heart attack. We need you here because you're the Curator, and you're everyone's excuse for being in the place. There are no marks on Keith, no signs of injury – he's simply dead. I'll still be trying artificial respiration when the doctor arrives, for the look of the thing – not for any good it'll do, because believe me he was past it from the moment he reached the floor. The doc will be surprised but not incredulous, in the circumstances; heart attacks do happen, even at Keith's age, and there's no reason to think anything else. Any questions?'

'I suppose we do have to do it that way?' Jane said doubtfully.

'Can you see a coroner believing what really happened?'

229

'No.'

'Well then.'

'No, you're quite right . . . Can you make it, Trevor?'

'I can make it.'

Jane dressed quickly and tried to support Trevor downstairs, but he managed a smile at her and insisted that he could walk. When they were alone in the garden, and had made sure no one was in sight, Jane asked: 'Did *you* see her?'

'We all did, Jane. She saved the day, didn't she?'

'You knew that, too?'

'I haven't even begun to take it all in. I still don't know how I got to the bedchamber, or even how I knew that was where I had to go . . . But when I reached the door, and saw you three, and the altar, and the candles – and the Sword . . . and Keith standing there like a beast of prey . . . Somehow I knew what it was all about. I knew you were facing Gadd for the last time, and that it was touch and go. I probably did completely the wrong thing, but I *had* to go for him. Keith, or Gadd, or whoever it really was . . . Did I nearly wreck it all for you?'

'No, Trevor darling, you didn't. *I* haven't absorbed it either – but even if you broke my concentration for an instant, you broke his, too – and that gave me a chance to come back. And somehow, I think it triggered off my call to Katherine . . . Anyway, even in the middle of it all, I know a bit of me shouted for joy when you tackled him. God, you didn't realise what you were doing, the danger of it – but darling, I'm glad you did.'

Trevor said, carefully: 'You called me darling, twice.'

'Will three times convince you?' she asked.

On the Sunday afternoon, Jane walked with Bridget and George by the river. There had been heavy rain during the night, and now the sun shone in a clear sky, making everything sparkling and green.

They needed the brightness to ease their weariness.

The doctor himself, Keith's colleague at the hospital, had

230

not been difficult. He had not even been surprised; he told them he had been worried about Keith for some weeks, but Keith had rejected all suggestions that there was anything the matter with him, and had brusquely refused the friendly offer of an impartial examination. He was distressed about Keith's sudden death, obviously, but he had signed the death certificate in accordance with the clear evidence.

What *had* been burdensome was the way everyone had treated Jane. Her recent relationship with Keith was known by some, and suspected by others. But what emerged obliquely in their sympathy (for Jane was liked) was their disapproval of it. Not disapproval of Jane, but the implication that she had been in some way Keith's victim. Trevor, it was clear, had not been alone in his anxiety over Jane's strange state during the past few months; all Orley had been aware of it, and all Orley had blamed Keith for it. The village was fittingly subdued by Keith's death, remembering him as a good doctor and neighbour. But the ambivalence was there – sometimes subtly expressed, sometimes clumsily.

A few hours of this, and Jane was almost relieved to be called to the Grange by the police. Somebody had noticed, and reported, the smashed window, and Jane had to go through the big house room by room with the village sergeant to assure him that nothing had been stolen. It was late evening before the sergeant decided that the broken window was mere vandalism. Then, of course, Jane had to get help to board up the window till it could be expertly repaired.

She had hurried back in the growing dark to the Green Man, anxious about Trevor; the doctor had patched and cleaned his wound, and no stitches had been necessary, but it was very painful and he was under sedation. Jane had sat beside him till the small hours, watching his drugged sleep; Bridget had finally come in and ordered her to bed at 4 a.m.

She had slept till midday, and had been both relieved and annoyed to find Trevor back at work, wincing but cheerful.

231

She had told him off, and he had basked in her concern while he teased her about it, so that in the end she had had to laugh with him. But he had, at least, promised to rest for the afternoon; so now, escaping the pressures and the voices and the sympathetic faces, she was strolling at ease along the river bank with the Blakes.

She talked with them about Katherine, wondering if she would ever see her again; but that, no one could tell her. In the end, inevitably, she faced the question of Keith.

'Do you feel sorry he's dead?' Bridget asked, with no hint in her voice of how she believed Jane ought to feel.

'He tried to kill Trevor,' Jane said. 'And he let Gadd in, willingly. Welcomed him in, in exchange for power I suppose, and for . . . well, you know. I'm afraid that's all I can think of right now; so at the moment, yes, I *am* glad he's dead. I can't be hypocritical about it.' She smiled ruefully. 'I'm a woman again – I have been ever since you carried me into the Circle and put the Sword in my hand. But maybe I've become too primitive a woman. You know – death to anyone who hurts my man.'

'Don't deny that, either,' Bridget said. 'Take it out and look at it, so that you can control it – but never deny it . . . You know he *is* your man?'

'Oh yes. Oh, *yes*.' She walked on a few paces, her smile no longer rueful, and then said seriously: 'I suppose after a while I *will* get around to mourning the Keith we used to know, the friend, before the cracks in his soul widened, so to speak. One day – but not yet. Trevor will do it first, because he's more forgiving than I am . . . But I'll never feel *responsible* for Keith's death. He killed himself, really. That's what I'll get round to being sorry about. Sorry that he joined himself to Gadd's destruction.'

'I wouldn't say he shared it ultimately,' Bridget told her. 'I haven't any private line to the Lords of Karma; they keep their own counsel. But my guess is that Gadd no longer exists as an individual entity – he'd gone too far for salvaging – but that Keith has lives and lessons to come . . .

232

Sorry, I'm off again. You don't want a lecture on rein-carnation right now.'

'I don't think I could take it in, today. I'll just take your word about Keith. I hope you're right.'

'Look what the rain's done,' George interrupted, point-ing ahead.

A willow tree was leaning at an unnatural angle across the water, which was muddy with the wreckage of several yards of collapsed bank. Jane said, 'Oh dear – more work for the gardeners,' and ran forward to look.

They saw her halt, and there was something about the sudden rigidity of her back that made them hurry to join her.

She pointed, without speaking, at the skull which grinned up at them from the newly-ruptured earth.

The skeleton was already disintegrating. One arm was missing altogether, and the bones of one leg had tumbled to the water's edge, where the femur rocked and jerked, trap-ped between the current and a tree-root.

'Not only the gardeners,' Jane said at last, in a strained voice. 'More work for Sergeant Wilson, too . . . I'd better call him.'

George said 'Wait a minute', and climbed down for a closer look. Bridget, too, laid a restraining hand on Jane's arm, and Jane could feel it quivering.

'It'll be just routine for the sergeant,' George said. 'This is centuries old . . . But it's not routine for us. It wasn't just the rain that unearthed this. Call it a by-product of yesterday.'

Bridget said 'Yes'.

'You mean that's *Gadd*?' Jane cried, incredulous.

'I know it's Gadd,' Bridget told her. 'But apart from *my* certainty – is it so suprising? Katherine and Hal must have hidden the body somewhere. This'd be a very likely place.' She stepped down to join her husband, and Jane followed reluctantly.

'If you want convincing,' George said, 'look at this.'

He lifted in his palm, carefully, a white metal medallion

233

that lay on the rib-cage; snapped the corroded neck-chain, and stood up with his find. 'Don't touch it. One of us is enough.'

They examined it as he turned it over. On one side was an inverted pentagram; on the other, a strange design like three Maltese crosses growing out of an arrangement of lines and rings.

'You know your Goetia better than I do,' Bridget said. 'Can you recognise it?'

'It's the sigil of Sitri. Look – round the rim. S-I-T-R-I.'

'Isn't he the Lechery one?'

'He can be called upon to inflame it, yes. Enslave a man to a woman or a woman to a man . . . I wonder what Gadd was up to, in that last Black Mass? . . . I'll destroy this, with your permission, Jane. A blowlamp'll do it.'

Jane shuddered. 'Please do . . . I hope this really is the end. I've had enough.'

'It's the end,' Bridget said.

Trevor woke from his afternoon's sleep, feeling much better. The effect of last night's drugs had completely worn off, and the pain in his temple had almost gone. He stretched, lying on his back, his hands behind his head on the pillow.

Perhaps it was Jane's footstep that had wakened him, for she came in now, without knocking, and looked down at him, smiling.

'You're back,' he said.

'Yes. In more senses than one.'

'That's true. The woman Jane is back, victorious. Over me, in particular.'

'Not *over* you. *With* you.'

How radiant she is, Trevor thought; how glowing. Bridget talked to me about the Goddess, once, and about every real woman being a channel for Her. I enjoyed the discussion, but I looked on it as academic, at the time. How wrong I was!

'How do you feel?' the Goddess asked.

234

'As good as new.'

She nodded. 'That's fine. All the same, you're staying right there till dinner-time. Then you can come down and be a guest in your own dining-room for once.'

Trevor found that all his diffidence had evaporated. He told her: 'There's only one way of making sure I stay here till dinner-time.'

She smiled again; locked the door, and came to him.